THE HORN OF THE GODS

Vidar raised Gjallarhorn to his lips.

And he blew softly, at first, listening to the eerie timbre that sounded at once like horses dying and gateposts cracking and the world wrenching loose from its foundations. It got into his blood, set his heart pounding, stole the strength from his arms and legs—until he was the horn and the horn was he, one entity, blind and senseless, roaring one vast obscenity against the endless, dripping Silence.

The cry grew within him, and a part of him heard it reverberating from the walls of Skatalund to the distant hills, like a huge wave that broke upon the sky and the plain, shattering sanity beneath its impossible weight.

The figures of the thursar giants burst from their black tents, holding their heads with their hands, twisting in agony.

He remembered what it was like to be a god...

The Hammer and The Horn

by Michael
Jan Friedman

POPULAR LIBRARY

An Imprint of Warner Books, Inc.

A Warner Communications Company

Popular Library books are published by
Warner Books, Inc.
666 Fifth Avenue
New York, N.Y. 10103

 A Warner Communications Company

Printed in the United States of America

First Printing: June, 1985
10 9 8 7 6 5 4 3 2 1

For Joan—my wife, my inspiration, my heart's friend

"Man would rather will even nothingness than not will."

Nietzsche

I

Vidar had never felt more alone. He stood in the center of the little gallery, but he might have been standing in the center of the universe. He watched the local arts patrons—those with money and those without—run their fingers along the cold, sharp edges of his sculptures, laughing at their own recklessness. The iron gleamed dully in the glare of the overhead track lights.

It was his first show in over a year. He was nervous and he knew it, because for the last few minutes—since the first invited guests had arrived—he'd had a hard time figuring out something to do with his hands. If he put them in his pockets, he'd look too disinterested. If he folded his arms in front of him, he'd look unapproachable—and besides, his biceps were too large for his corduroy sport jacket. If he intertwined his fingers and let his hands dangle, he'd look like—well, like someone who didn't know what to do with his hands.

A tall woman with prematurely gray hair, worn long,

looked up from one of his sculptures and smiled at him.

He smiled back. His hands clasped one another in front of his chest, as if he were praying. His fingers writhed.

The woman's eyes fell to the sculpture again. Vidar wondered if she was a patron with money or without money.

A hand roosted on his shoulder. Vidar turned to find the person attached to it.

It was Frank Cerucci, the owner of the gallery.

"How's it going, my man?"

Vidar shrugged. "You tell me."

"Looks good," said Frank. "Good crowd. Hey, where's the old confidence? This isn't your first show, is it? You new at this?"

"Feels that way," said Vidar.

"Well, you should have toked up before you arrived, like I told you," said Frank, turning his palms up and grinning beneath his dark, handlebar mustache.

"I did," said Vidar. "It didn't help."

Frank shook his head, and as he did so his bald pate caught the light. "'Cause you're too damn big. A little guy like me, it takes me maybe two hits and I'm buzzing. Somebody your size needs something the size of a cigar to get off."

"When I can afford a joint that size," said Vidar, "I won't have any reason to be nervous."

"Right," said Frank. "Hey, I see a paying customer. Catch you later."

Vidar nodded, and Frank joined the pow-wow around a piece Vidar called *Elfcandle*. He watched as the gallery owner invoked the grace of the sculpture with an undulation of his hand. Yes—Vidar was proud of that one.

But as he looked around at the rest of his work, he was not quite so proud. Few of these pieces had any real life to them, any feeling. And abstract art was nothing without feeling.

He sighed—not too loudly, he hoped. How could he have imparted any life to his sculptures when he felt none himself? For the last six months, he had been dead inside.

At first, he'd thought that Alissa's departure had been the cause of it all. Little by little, however, he came to sense that there was something else. Something that imposed itself on him like a physical burden, separating him from life's warmth and its rhythms—something that kept him awake at night, staring out the kitchen window at the frozen reservoir.

Was it time for a change? He thought that he had finally found his place in life—after years of searching, more years than he cared to count. To him, sculpting had begun as a joy and grown into an adventure. Vidar liked working with his hands, and he liked the hardness of the materials that he shaped. It was a thing he could do—and enjoy the doing of.

In the time he'd had to reflect on his relationship with Alissa, he'd come to only one conclusion—that he liked her for the same reasons he liked metal and wood and stone. For its hardness, its intransigence.

Its strength.

She was a sculptor, too, though she worked only in wood. Alissa liked it, she'd said, because it had once been alive. In her hands, it lived again.

But Alissa wouldn't yield as the iron yielded, or the wood. And neither would he. Compromise was not in their natures. So they parted. She left for Greenwich Village in her little red Volkswagen, and he stayed in the old house near Woodstock, which he had bought before he'd been constrained by a sculptor's income.

Perhaps he needed a break, some time away from people and work. Maybe it would do him some good to lose himself in the mountains somewhere. They said that an artist could burn himself out, although he hadn't been one long enough to test the theory until now.

Then again, he suspected another thing, separate from his sculpting and Alissa and Woodstock. He wondered sometimes, when he couldn't sleep, if it were not this other thing that called to him, wrenching his soul from the foundation he had built here.

The last possibility was the one he would not think about. Not now, not ever. It was ancient history.

"Mr. Volund?"

Vidar emerged from his brooding at the sound of his surname. It was the gray-haired woman who had addressed him.

"Uh, yes?" he said.

"I was just admiring your *Elfcandle*. You're a very talented man."

"Why, thank you," said Vidar. "You can call me by my first name, though. Vidar."

"That's a very unusual name," she said. "Scandinavian, isn't it?"

"Yes," he said.

"Well, I'm Mrs. Dunstable. Rita. I live in the city, really, but I'm out here visiting with friends, and I'm delighted that Frank invited us all to your show. My husband's firm buys art as an investment and . . ."

Vidar didn't hear anything after that. For him, the world had suddenly narrowed to the width of the gallery's front door—and its only occupant was the woman that had left him six months ago.

It was Alissa. She was hard to miss, with that cascade of bright, copper hair that fell over one shoulder. Alissa was smiling, and he wondered for a moment which smile it was—the hopeful smile or the hurt smile.

As she came closer, he recognized it for the hopeful one. Be kind, he told himself. Not like the last time you saw her.

She came to a stop halfway across the room and just stood there with her hands tucked deep in the pockets of her jeans. Her tennis sneakers were sopping wet—she'd never known how to dress for the weather.

He closed the gap uneasily.

"What brings you here?" he said, and as soon as he'd spoken he heard the resentment in his voice. She frowned. "Wait," he said. "I didn't mean it that way."

"I know," she said. Then, "I made a couple of calls. Frank's wife said that you'd be here."

He nodded, his mind churning up emotions. "How've you been?" he ventured.

She shrugged. "Can we go outside?"

He laughed, but she didn't. "Are you serious? I'm in the middle of a show. And it's raining."

"No kidding," she said, brushing a wet strand of red-golden hair off her forehead. "Does that mean that I have to truck back down to the Village without even saying what I wanted to say?"

Vidar rolled his eyes. He swore softly.

Without another word, she turned and went out the door. For a moment, Vidar managed to restrain himself. He watched her go. Then he strode out after her.

Alissa was headed for her car—the same old, red Volkswagen, except that one of the fenders had been smashed in. He took hold of her arm, as gently as he could, before she could turn the door handle.

The rain was a fine mist, the sky an opalescent glow of clouds. Her face was wet when she turned toward him, but not with tears. She never cried.

"I'm glad you came," he said.

"Me too," she returned. "I think. I guess I had to see you again."

"Is something wrong, Alissa?"

She laughed. "You're such a protector," she said. "Does there have to be something wrong for me to want to see you?"

He said nothing, waiting for her to go on. He knew well enough that sometimes anything he said would be the wrong thing.

"I met someone," she said.

That hurt.

"Don't worry," she said. "It's over."

"Then why bring it up?"

"Because," she said, "I wanted to. Because he was a lot like you—except he wasn't you. I was tempted, though."

"Were you?" His words sounded empty, even to him.

"Sure," she said. She frowned. "No, not really."

For a few moments, there was silence. Her eyelashes glistened with collected mist.

"He wanted to have a family with me, Vidar." Alissa's throat muscles tightened, and she swallowed. "I'd forgotten that some men still want to do things like that."

Vidar nodded. "Some men," he echoed.

She glared at him. "That's it, right? No change of heart? No sudden desire to father a long line of big, brawny blonds?" Anger mixed with hurt in her voice.

He said nothing. What could he say? How could he tell her why he would never father a child again?

She looked away from him. "That's what I thought," she said. "Sorry to bother you. Good luck with your show." Shrugging him off, she flung open the door of the car and inserted herself into it.

"Alissa," he said helplessly. But if she had stopped to listen, there was nothing else he could have added. Of course, she didn't stop. He watched the car swing out of the narrow driveway onto the street, tires squealing, and speed away. It was only after she'd gone halfway down the block that he saw the headlights go on.

"Damn," he said. "Goddamn!" He pounded his fist against his thigh.

Vidar walked back inside the gallery, where Frank was speaking in concerned, apologetic tones to Mrs. Dunstable. He sounded like a head waiter explaining why the filet mignon was cold. When he caught sight of Vidar, he pulled him over to where the gray-haired woman stood. This time, when she looked up from *Elfcandle*, she was not smiling.

"I'm sorry," said Vidar a little lamely. "An emergency." He shrugged his shoulders. "I apologize for that. Now, weren't you going to say something about *Elfcandle*?"

She seemed to soften for a moment, then thought better of it. "No," she said, "I don't think so. I can't recall." Mrs. Dunstable smiled tightly and glided across the room.

Vidar looked down at his sculpture. He ran his palm along one of the iron flames that raged about the iron disc of the sun. He pondered the precision with which he had just screwed up his best chance at reviving his career. Anger threatened to choke him. Before he knew what was happening, his hand had closed about the metal, twisting a slender, graceful flame into a grotesque knot.

Quickly, he removed his hand, looking about to see if anyone had noticed how easily the metal bent in his grasp.

Apparently, no one had.

II

Vidar's fingers flexed about his sword hilt, stiff and curled like claws. It was cold on Vigrid, colder than he had ever imagined. The steel-gray clouds muttered like thunder, and snow fell in great sheets before the wind, muffling all other sounds. The icy crust of the ground crunched distantly beneath his horse's hooves.

Then the sun gained the horizon and a sea of blood washed over the mountains, bathing the hrimthursars' stronghold in its light. His joints creaked with the cold, and the rime of his frozen breath streaked his beard like age itself. His horse snorted, restless, shivering in the grip of the wind.

Suddenly, on his right, the armies of the hrimthursar appeared on the edge of the world, boiling over a ridge of earth like mounted pestilence. The sun rose, a shield covered with gore, too far away to give heat. From Odin's shoulder, a pair of ravens screeched insanely.

They spurred their steeds now, his kinsmen, and as they drew nearer they could see the wolves Loki had gathered about him like a coat. Vidar drew his sword, and its edge was already bloodied—with the light of this deadly dawn.

He turned to find Thor, and the Hurler was at his shoulder. Thor glowered at him in brotherly fashion, his beard bristling with morning's flames, his white wisps of breath clinging to the air. Then an expression of great pain came over the Thunderer.

"Forget the cold, brother," said Vidar. "Fight hard."

"But I have no weapon," said Thor. And his face became a mask of agony.

"No weapon?" Vidar repeated dumbly, his tongue suddenly dry and swollen in his mouth.

"I've lost the hammer," Thor said, though it was beyond reason. Then it was not Thor who rode beside him on Vigrid, but Modi. "Help me," he said, grimacing.

"How?" asked Vidar.

"Come help me, Jawbreaker. I'm hurt."

And Vidar saw that the blood had drained from Modi's face as if from a corpse.

Modi fell away from him, growing smaller and more distant, but Vidar could not help himself. He galloped numbly toward the rising sun and the hrimthursar and the wolves. And when he glanced about on either side, he saw that the ranks of his kinsmen had melted into the snow. Darkness descended and seized him like a gloved fist, and he was suddenly, terribly alone. He could smell the breath of the wolves now, hot breath on his throat. . . .

He thrashed awake, cold with sweat on his face and his chest. His room was dark but for the pale light of the crescent moon in a nest of clouds. He lay there, silent, listening to his own pulse. Rain tapped lightly on the window.

Vidar lifted himself on one elbow and peered at the clock. Almost four-thirty.

Then he heard the call again.

"Vidar! Answer me, damn you!"

It really was Modi. The voice was familiar, even after all this time. And he was here, in this world. Anger surfaced in Vidar. He bit it back, opening his mind slowly. "Where are you?"

"The gorge," Modi said. "Crete, I think you call it."

"What are you doing in Midgard?" There was a red tinge to his question that he could not conceal. Why should he?

"I'm hurt, Jawbreaker. I've lost the hammer. I'm . . . vulnerable, damn it."

"What do you want from me?" Vidar asked.

"I need your help—or I wouldn't have called to you. Have you changed that much? You were my father's brother."

"Half brother," said Vidar.

"Good," said Modi. "Let me die then. Maybe Vali was right about you, uncle."

Vidar bit his lip. He had no choice, really. "I'm coming. It'll take some time—maybe a day and a half. That's the best I can do."

"Hurry," said Modi. And that was it.

Vidar lay silent in bed. He knew now that there had been good reason for his uneasiness the past few weeks—and Modi was mixed up with it, somehow.

He reached for a joint on his night table, then thought better of it. Vidar sat up, swung his legs over the side of the mattress and dialed the phone.

The voice at the other end was barely awake and more than a little annoyed.

"Hello? Who is this?"

"It's me, Phil."

There was a pause. "Jeez, Vidar, it's almost five o'clock in the morning."

"I know, Phil. Sorry, but it's an emergency."

Silence for a moment. "Okay," said Phil. "What's up?"

"I need a big favor, Phil. Plane reservations for Athens. First flight out of Kennedy, if you can swing it."

"Athens? Are you kidding?"

"Nope. And one other thing."

"What's that?"

"About a thousand dollars' worth of drachma."

"Drachma? What's that?"

"Greek money."

"Oh yeah? That ain't gonna be easy."

"C'mon, Phil—I'm counting on you. You're the only one I know who's got the connections."

"Yeah, I know. Okay, I'll see what I can do."

"Good. I'm leaving in a few minutes. I'll call again when I get over the bridge."

"Gotcha."

"Thanks, Phil. I appreciate it."

"Don't worry about it," said Phil. "I owe you. I guess this grand is on me, huh?"

"Well . . ." said Vidar.

"That's what I thought," said Phil. "Okay, see you later."

"Bye."

Vidar placed the phone receiver in its cradle, got up and went over to his closet. The air was cold enough to raise goose-bumps on his arms. He slid aside the closet door, snapped on the light. Outside, a bird tittered. He took out a pair of jeans, a gray sweatshirt that zipped down the front, a pair of hiking boots, a canteen that had been dented pretty badly last summer and a navy blue windbreaker.

He laid them out on the bed. Then he showered quickly, coming awake as the hot water streamed through his closely cropped beard and down his chest. It warmed him and it felt good.

Afterward, the air was chill against his bare skin. He surveyed himself in the mirror as he toweled off. People had always said that he looked like an artist, even before he'd become one. There was the long, dirty-blond hair that reached almost to his shoulders, the gray eyes, the beard that turned from red to gold in shadow and in sunlight.

He shrugged, knowing that he'd once looked quite different. The beard had been longer and fuller, the hair bound in a single braid. The face had been somewhat younger, and even the eyes had had a different cast to them. But that was a long time ago.

Vidar dressed, then rummaged through the lower drawer in his dresser until he found a blue nylon backpack. It was old and worn, and he'd lost the frame to it years ago. He stuffed it into the pocket of his windbreaker, turned off the light and went down the stairs, past the ground floor and into the basement. Switching on the light, he crossed to the corner where the cement floor seemed to have cracked. A water beetle scurried away behind an old easy chair stained with age.

Vidar bent and worked his fingers into the crack. Then he straightened and lifted a slab of concrete, easing it to the floor a few feet away. There was nothing underneath but wet earth. The rain, having grown a bit in force, pattered on a basement window. He took the shovel that leaned against the wall nearby and plunged it into the moist soil. He lifted and tossed a shovelful onto the floor, to one side of the hole.

Vidar worked to the staccato rhythm of the rain until a piece of animal skin emerged, barely distinguishable in color from the earth around it. Bending again, he wrested the leather-wrapped package from its hiding place. It wasn't very big—about the size of a toaster-oven. He considered it, turning it over and over in his hands, brushing the loose dirt from it.

Then he unwrapped it and gazed at the contents. A ram's horn, just a ram's horn. But he couldn't just leave it here. It would be too dangerous. And there was more than that—

a bond of sorts had grown between him and the horn, the result of his boyhood training.

Wrapping it again, Vidar took out the nylon pack and shoved the horn inside. Then, looping a strap over one shoulder, he bent to replace the dirt he'd dug up. When that was finished, he put the slab of cement back in position, shut off the light and went back upstairs. Almost as an afterthought, he stopped by the closet next to the kitchen and took out some medical supplies—bandages and salve— and tucked them into the pack with the hide-bound horn.

There was only one lock on the house, that on the front door, and he often left that unlocked. This time he locked it and put the key in his jacket pocket. It was still drizzling in dreary October fashion when the screen door banged closed behind him. The rain stung his face, but it made him alert.

His car, a '78 Skylark, needed coaxing before the engine would turn over. When it did, he turned on his headlights and pulled out of the blacktop driveway onto the road that meandered down the hillside. At the white brick church, Vidar turned left onto Route 28. It was empty, of course, and traffic to and from Woodstock was sparse at this late hour.

The rain gave the road a melancholy glaze. When he reached the Thruway, he turned toward New York City. The highway was dark and all but deserted. Every few minutes, a car would pass him headed north, its headlights igniting beads of fire on his windshield. Only once did a truck overtake him. He was halfway to Westchester County before the rain slackened.

"Modi," he said out loud, and the sound came strangely out of his mouth. What business was he on here? Who had hurt him? Who, even among the Aesir, would dare to tangle with the son of Thor?

Unless—it was a trap. But why? Vidar had long ago

ceased to be a threat to those in power. He and Modi had
never been the best of friends, Modi having barely grown
to manhood when he'd left. But Thor had been a staunch
ally and as good a brother as one of Odin's sons could be.
Modi looked to be growing in that direction.

But what if the balance of power had shifted? What if
Vali had lost what he'd fought so hard for? Would a new
king in Asgard have considered Vidar a dangerous quantity?

All he'd asked when he parted ways with them was to
be left alone. Up until now, that request had been honored,
as far as he knew. They were glad to be rid of him, especially
Vali.

Assuming the worst—that Vali, or some other Aesir
chief was tying up a loose end—would they dare to ambush
him in the gorge—here, on his own world? He weighed
the possibility. It was not likely. For one thing, they could
have really caught him by surprise, and now he was on his
guard. For another, they could have picked more appealing
bait than a wounded Modi, and more likely bait as well.
Still, it wouldn't hurt to be careful.

Vidar shook his head, as a truck going in the opposite
direction topped a hill and speared the road with its headlights. So long since he'd had to think this way, suspecting
everything, inspecting motives from six different vantage
points and hunting every possibility down until he reached
its lair. In more than a thousand years, he'd become rusty.

The cloud cover broke, and the stars came out between
the tattered remnants of the gray sky. He reached the Bronx
a little before the sunrise, crossed the Whitestone Bridge
while morning's first rays rippled serpentine over Little Neck
Bay, and cracked the window open to get some fresh air
into his lungs. It was Sunday, and there was little traffic on
the roads.

Phil lived in Douglas Manor, one of the headlands pro-
jecting northward into the Long Island Sound. It was a well-
to-do area, but then, Phil owned a chain of hardware stores

he'd launched with some financial help from Vidar. It was too early for anyone to be out, but the sunrise was delightful. Vidar parked the car, locked it and started to ring the bell—but knocked softly instead.

Phil came to the door. He was a tall, lanky man in his forties, with a wisp of yellow hair dangling over his forehead. He held an index finger to his lips.

"The wife's sleeping," he whispered, stepping outside. The air was only slightly cold, and it smelled of salt breezes. "I thought you were going to call first, so I..."

"I know, Phil. I just didn't feel like stopping once I was in the car. Too antsy, I guess."

Phil nodded, his face as open as a child's. "First plane leaves at nine sharp. You're on it. There's a guy coming over in about"—he consulted his watch—"ten minutes, with a thousand dollars in drachma. Want some breakfast?"

Vidar smiled. "Sure."

They went inside. Phil's kitchen was small and warm. It faced the water, a narrow strip of which was visible between two neighbors' houses.

Phil put some coffee on. "How do you like your eggs?"

Vidar shook his head. "Just some toast and butter, thanks. I'm a little worked up."

Phil looked at him, nodded, put two slices of bread in the toaster and two eggs on the pan. There was a moment of silence and the scent of ground coffee beans.

"How are the kids?" Vidar asked.

"Oh, pretty good. Melissa's away at her grandmother's this weekend, so it's just Dinah and Bobby and me." Phil made a clucking sound with his tongue as he tried to keep the eggs from sticking. "Will you be gone long?"

Vidar shrugged. "Could be."

"Business?"

"Sort of. Family business."

"I didn't know you had relatives in Greece." Phil looked at him quizzically. "You don't look Greek, y'know."

"They've only been there a short time," said Vidar.

"In other words, it's none of my business. 'Nuff said."

"It's not that, Phil. Maybe I'll tell you all about it when I get back."

"Okay. Anything you want me to take care of while you're away?"

Vidar shrugged, thought for a while. He watched the sunlight play over that corridor of water. "No, I don't think so. I shut everything off at the house. And I just paid most of the bills, but . . . well, if I decide to hang around Greece for a while, maybe you'd better check up there from time to time. Here." Vidar took his keys out of his pocket and put them on the table. "You'll need these."

Phil poured the coffee, set a cup before Vidar. "Could be a while, then?"

Vidar sipped at the coffee, then shrugged. "Hard to say, Phil."

Phil shook his head. "I don't like it when you're so mysterious."

The doorbell rang. "Must be the man with the drachmas," said Phil, and rose to answer it. Vidar got up and took the bread out of the toaster. He flipped the eggs while Phil transacted at the front door. Vidar heard the door close. Phil was a very resourceful guy.

There was some talk about the World Series, and then about Phil's search for a college for Melissa. After breakfast, Phil went upstairs to get dressed while Vidar washed the dishes. By 7:30, they were on the road, headed for Kennedy Airport in the Skylark.

"She's still holding up, huh?" Phil asked, feeling a little uncomfortable, perhaps, in the early morning silence.

"Best damn car I ever had," said Vidar.

Phil dropped him off at the American Airlines terminal and shook his hand. "Be good, now," he said. "And if you need me, holler."

"I'll do that," Vidar said and watched him go. "Thanks

for breakfast." Then he entered the building with his pack slung over his shoulder.

His visits with Phil always went like that, it seemed. Mostly small talk. All the words—Vidar's at least—had to be between the lines.

He picked up his tickets at the appropriate counter and went on to his gate. The x-ray machine showed nothing in particular at the security check-through. Much to everyone's surprise, the plane took off on time.

It was a ten-hour flight, and Vidar took most of that time to sleep. He had laid his backpack underneath his seat but hooked his foot into one of the straps. Just in case.

He woke over Switzerland, as they passed among clouds piled as high as mountains against the heavens. Vidar scanned their ghostly terrain. It reminded him of places he'd been, long and long ago, on Odin's raids—Jotunheim, where the hrimthursar dwelt in their mammoth caves and their stone city.

The in-flight movie was *The Sting*. The landing was uneventful.

Greece's climate was hot and dry, just as he remembered it. And the sun wasn't even up yet. The sky that encircled Athens' airport terminal was blue-black and full of stars.

Once inside the terminal, he bought a one-way ticket on a domestic flight to Hania, on the western extremity of Crete. It was not quite six in the morning, and his flight would not leave until after seven, so he sprawled in a seat in the waiting area near a spattering of young backpackers.

Closing his eyes, he reached out. "Modi?"

There was a sluggishness in the quality of the reply.

"Damn you, Vidar, what takes so long?"

"I've come half a fair-sized world, that's what takes so long. I'm outside Athens now. It'll be midday before I can get there."

"Take your time. I'll probably have bled to death by then."

"Good news for the local carrion-feeders, then. Who attacked you, Modi?"

"Utgard-thursar. A pack of them."

Vidar paused for a moment. "Utgard-thursar? What were you doing in Utgard, if I might ask?"

Modi chuckled, then coughed terribly. His mental voice began to fade out.

"Let's talk later, Jawbreaker. I'm weary with hunting and fain would lie down."

"Talk, Modi. I'm not exactly pleased with your company here. And I'm the only one near enough to help, or you wouldn't have tried me. What's so interesting in Utgard?"

Modi grunted. "Uprising. The thursar nomads."

"And what's that to you?"

"The Utgard-thursar don't just rise up by themselves. They've been under human domination for generations now, and they've never lifted so much as a spear. Someone must be behind it, Vidar—or at least, that's Vali's thinking. One of us, perhaps."

Vidar pondered that. "I give up. Who?"

"Hod."

"Then he's still alive?"

Modi sighed. "Yes. Listen..." There was genuine fatigue in his mind now.

"Go ahead and rest," Vidar told him.

"Thanks, Jawbreaker. You're a prince."

Then Modi broke contact. Vidar opened his eyes and saw that all his fellow hikers were sleeping. The ticket desk had been deserted. Only a security guard stood awake just inside the glass doors.

Hod. Could it be? No one knew for sure what had become of him. Not even Vali, who would have liked to have put an end to Hod way back before the battle on Vigrid.

Vidar shook his head. Did he really want any part of this? If Hod wanted to make war with Vali, let him. Why should he interfere, as long as they left Earth alone. But—would they? Probably not. They'd devastate whatever stood in their way, those two, and that included Asgard itself. Just like the old days. Odin would no doubt have approved.

Vidar glanced at the pack in his lap. They were distant, but he could hear the sounds of Ragnarok. "Hoo boy. Getting a little melodramatic, aren't we?" Vidar breathed to himself.

"Hey mister." Vidar looked up. A boy stood there in blue jeans and a T-shirt that read "Fencers Make Great Lovers." "Have you got the time?"

Vidar shrugged. "Sorry, I don't have a watch."

"Don't be. It's cool." Then, "You headed for Crete?"

"Yes. Hania."

"Going to the gorge?" the boy asked.

"As a matter of fact, I am. How did you know?"

"What else is there in that part of the island? Nobody goes to Hania for the night life."

"True." Vidar laughed, recalling how much truer it had been the last time he'd been there—more than a thousand years ago. "I guess you've been there before?"

"You mean the gorge? Once. Loved it." The boy sat down across from Vidar, scratching the beginnings of a beard. "Great place. You feel like you're on the Ponderosa. And there's a spot, maybe three kilometers down, where the river pools up and the sun streaks down from the hills and you almost feel the presence of the gods."

"Really?" said Vidar.

The boy smiled. "I know it sounds ridiculous. I get a little carried away. But if there's any spot on earth where Poseidon and Apollo and Aphrodite still hang out, this has got to be it."

Vidar found that he was still smiling. "You sound like you're into mythology. Not many people are these days."

"Oh, I love that stuff." The boy's face brightened.

"Do you know anything about the Norse gods?"

"Yeah, sure." The boy leaned forward. "Odin, Thor and Loki. Baldur the Beautiful. Frey. Heimdall, the guardian of Bifrost. Asgard and Jotunheim."

Vidar nodded. "Do you know who Vidar was?"

The boy frowned. "Vidar? Is that with an *r* at the end?"

"Yes, with an *r*."

He thought for a moment. "No, I never heard of that one. Who was he?"

Vidar shrugged. "One of them. A bastard-son of Odin. He slew the Fenris wolves—or many of them, at least— at Ragnarok."

"No kidding." The boy shook his head. "I'll have to take another look at my books when I get home."

Then the dawn seeped in at the far end of the parking lot, and the rim of the world blazed with fire. A little while later, a clerk announced that the flight to Hania was ready for boarding. Vidar and the boy and the other backpackers climbed up the stairs into the plane.

"Wait a minute," said the boy, sitting down across the aisle from Vidar. "I remember him now—Vidar, I mean. Wasn't he the guy that chased Hod across the nine worlds to kill him for slaying Baldur?"

"No," said Vidar. "That was Vali."

III

A tale of the Aesir, my lords? Very well, then...

You know, it was not unusual for Baldur to range over Midgard with his brothers, Hod and Vali. They were all three Frigga's sons and all bound together—and though both Hod and Vali loved Baldur more than one another, it was only natural. For who did not love Baldur even more than himself?

It happened one chill and starless night that the sons of Frigga came to a white-frothed, rushing river. Vali, whose eyes were nearly as sharp as those of Heimdall, Asgard's watchman, spied a lone figure on the other side. Though he could make out no more than the man's silhouette in the fog that rose from the water, he could see that he stood by a flat-bottomed boat moored to a post on the bank.

"Ho!" cried Vali. "I see that you're a ferryman, and we three need a ride to the other side."

For a long while, there was no reply. Then the man

said, "It's true, I'm a ferryman. But I don't work for nothing. What have you got that I might want?"

The brothers looked at one another. They had been traveling so long on foot, they had nothing of value to offer. But Hod bristled at the man's arrogance, and it roused him to anger.

"Be careful how you grasp for payment," said Hod in his hollow, quiet voice. "We three are Aesir-born—and I myself could bring down a storm on your head that would wipe you from the face of these gray highlands forever."

"Go ahead," said the ferryman. "But then how will you cross this flood? Besides, what would the Aesir be doing here without their mighty steeds and all alone?"

"Vali," said Baldur then, turning to his brother, "can you turn this man's mind to our ends? I fear that Hod will sweep the ferryman away and strand us on this shore."

Vali nodded, but moments later, his brows beetled and he shook his head. "That is no weak-minded mortal hiding behind the fog," he said. "I cannot bend him to my will. Perhaps Hod's way is best—at least he'll know he's been paid for his insolence."

Baldur looked across the flood, through the mist, and called out himself to the stranger. "If we can prove that we are who we say, don't you think it would be wise to do our bidding?"

The ferryman paused, as if doubt had wormed its way into his mind. "If you can prove you are who you say," he echoed. "Let me ask you this—for, I think, only the Aesir would know this—what is the name for the earth that stretches far around us—in each and every world?"

"Men call it Earth," said Baldur. "The Aesir say Midgard and the Vanir Field, the thursar call it Most

Green and the light elves call it Clay. The dark elves call it Roof of the World."

"So far, so good," said the ferryman. "What is the name for the sky?"

"Men name it Heaven," said Baldur. "The Aesir say Home and the Vanir Windfarer. The thursar call it Unreachable, the light elves The Sea Above and the dark elves Too Bright."

"What, then," asked the ferryman, "is the name for the sun?"

"Men call it the Sun," said Baldur patiently. "The Aesir say Delight and the Vanir call it Wealth. The giants named it Thawtime long ago, the light elves Everglow and the dark ones Coin of Gold."

"And the moon," said the ferryman, "how is that known?"

"Men call it the Moon," Baldur answered. "But the Aesir call it Wraith and the Vanir Sunshadow. In Jotunheim, it's known as Nightmother. The *lyos* call it Pale One and the *dwarvin* Traveler."

"What about the wind, that sweeps through every world?"

"Men call it Wind," said Baldur. "The Aesir say Bringer and the Vanir Seedbearer. The thursar call it Knife's Edge and the light elves call it Whisper, while their dark cousins call it Snake's Breath."

"What then is the sea called?"

"Men call it Sea," said Baldur. "The Aesir say Waves and the Vanir say The Sky's Mirror. The giants call it Serpenthome, the light elves Thirstquencher and the dark elves The Deep."

"And the names for fire?"

"In Midgard, Fire is how it's known," said Baldur. "The Aesir say Hunger and the Vanir Woodgorger, while the *lyos* name it Deathflicker and the *dwarvin* call it Forger. But the giants name it Welcome."

"Well done," said the ferryman. "But anyone could have answered those questions, not only the Aesir. Now tell me this—"

"Wait," yelled Vali, tugging his cloak about him. He was not slow to wrath, and he had long ago lost his patience. "Is this going to go on forever?"

"I feel no need for haste," said the ferryman—and Baldur had to stay Hod's arm lest he raise a whirlwind on the spot.

"One more question," said Baldur. "That is all we will brook. And after that, I cannot be responsible for what Hod may do to you."

"I have no fear of the one you call Hod," said the stranger. "But if you can answer this question, then I will know you are Aesir, and perhaps I'll reconsider my improprieties. My question is this—what are the names of the halls in Asgard, one by one, and leaving none out?"

"The first," said Baldur, "is Thrudheim, where Thor the Thunderer lives with his wife, golden-haired Sif, and his two young sons, Modi and Magni. The second is Valaskjalff, Odin's seat, whence he rules Asaheim, and it's thatched with pure silver. The third is Sokkvabekk, lapped on all sides by cool water, where Odin drinks from golden goblets with his sons and brothers.

"The fourth is Gladsheim, where the Aesir hold their court. The sixth is Valhalla, vast and bright, where the men chosen from Midgard's fields arm themselves and practice their swordplay in the great courtyards, beside the river Thund. The seventh hall is Himinbjorg, where Heimdall sits when he's not watching the gate to Asgard. The eighth is Sessrumnir, where Freya holds sway over her handmaidens and Frey over his warriors.

"The ninth was built for Niord, the father of Frey and Freya, and the king of the Vanir. It raises its proud head over the harbor. And the tenth is Vidi, where Vidar lives, amid tall grass and strong, young saplings."

"Is that all?" asked the ferryman.

"Yes," said Baldur. "Now we would like to avail ourselves of your services."

"But you left out one hall," said the shadowy ferryman. "It was built only recently, while you were away. It's called Breidablik, and it occupies a broad place between rows of yew trees. It has pillars of red gold and a roof of silver, and it befits the son of Odin who will someday create worlds out of nothingness."

Then the ferryman was seen to move like smoke in the wind, and moments later, the ferry reached the bank where the Aesir stood. But it was empty. The ferryman was not in it.

Now, some say that that shadowy stranger on the far bank was Odin himself—and who am I, a poor skald, to dispute that?

> Sin Skolding
> Rogaland, 339 A.D.

IV

It was hot. This, Vidar knew, was above all the salient, inescapable fact of Greece. It had at the same time given birth to man's first great civilization and man's most volatile temperaments.

"Three thousand drachma," Vidar said, showing it to the keeper of the moped rental shop.

"It is not for sale. We rent, we do not sell," said the shopkeeper, a long, dark-skinned youth in black garb and sandals.

"Yes, of course," said Vidar. "Four thousand drachma."

"You do not understand. If I sell, I make the money once. If I rent, I make the money many times."

Vidar glared at him. "How much?"

"Ten thousand drachma."

"No," Vidar shook his head. "Five, with a full tank."

"Six. Why squabble?"

"Sold."

The Greek had gotten the best of the deal, Vidar observed

as he clanked out of town on a well-paved, southern-bound road between groves of orange trees and cypress.

"Hang in there, Modi," he said to himself.

Thirty miles later, he passed a truck that had overturned somehow and spilled crates of oranges all over the place. Vidar stopped to pick some up and stuff them into his pack. The driver of the truck was too busy cursing to mind.

From that point on, the road took to the hills, winding treacherously for another thirty miles or so along the heights, past tribes of goats and the ruins of ancient country altars. After he reached the town of Omalos, the mountains unfolded and the grass became greener. The air took on a crispness, and there was the scent of pine needles about him. Goatherds waved as he motored by, from great slopes that dwarfed both them and their charges.

Vidar left the moped in the care of the man that ran the lodge at the entrance to the gorge. There were signs all about—fifteen kilometers long and steep, rocky going in some spots, the gorge was not recommended for those with undependable internal organs.

He descended among the giant fir trees, among forested mountains and great, gray blocks of stone. The first clouds he'd seen since he'd landed in Greece hung wraithlike on the wind, and he felt small beneath the dome of azure blue sky. Cascades of pink flowers flooded the spaces between sun-bleached boulders.

The boy had been right—it was the path of the gods. He'd forgotten what this place was like.

After a couple of kilometers, the walls of stone closed in and the path leveled somewhat. A stream emerged from the rocks and ran quietly alongside. Water-smoothed trees leaned in from either bank, evidence of the spring floods that still ravaged the gorge. Cicadas whined. A bird cried out as if startled.

Vidar passed the pool the boy had spoken of, where the path turned sandy. The deep shadows of the trees shifted—

and the flat rock he'd been searching for came into view. How strange, he thought, that he should still recognize the thatch that had covered the cave like a roof before the birth of Charlemagne. Still untouched, unchanged? It must have been tended by someone, to remain as he remembered it. And well he remembered, for it was he who had placed the flat rock where it stood and covered the place with thatch.

Vidar clambered down from the path, picked his way across the field of bleached stones and stood before the cool breath of the cave. It was still disguised well. Unless one knew what to look for, it was indistinguishable from the melee of tumbled rocks and pink blossoms.

Hunkering down, he took a step into the darkness. It took a few moments for his eyes to adjust to the sudden relief from the light. He went in a step further, and—there— in a heap against the wall, it was red-bearded Modi, his body sprawled on the dirt floor. He had bundled a cloak up against his side, and his eyes were closed.

Something unfamiliar caught Vidar's eye, and he turned to face it, muscles tensing. A crucifix. Vidar straightened, reaching out to touch it. What was a crucifix doing here? It hung on the wall formed by the flat boulder, from an iron peg that had been driven into the stone. Below it hung a wooden shelf and a wood-framed picture of Jesus, halo and all, along with a pool of melted wax that had probably been a candle.

"It's about time," a voice croaked, and it was Modi's. Vidar turned to see that his eyes had opened warily. They were bloodshot and wolflike, and they betrayed his pain. Nonetheless, he was Thor's son, and he strove to prop himself up on an elbow.

Vidar knelt down by him and took the canteen out of his pack. He'd filled it in the airport at Hania. Up close, he could see Modi's face plainly, and it was painfully haggard. So much for a trap, Vidar mused, administering the water from the canteen in a slow trickle between Modi's lips.

"Where are you hurt?" he asked, and then Modi pulled away his cloak to reveal the caked blood on the side of his shredded tunic. "Is this the worst?" he asked.

Modi nodded. Vidar unzipped a pouch in the side of his pack, took out a tube of salve and some bandages. It was then that he noticed the other body in the cave—a thursar, apparently, judging by the size of him. And the side of his head was caved in. His sword hilt still lay in the palm of his open hand.

Vidar tore away the rest of Modi's tunic and applied the healing ointment to the wound. Modi winced and groaned. The blade did not appear to have cut too deeply—probably glanced off a rib. He bound the spot and sought out the less serious injuries.

Then he poked his head out into the bright sunlight again, made sure that there were no hikers around and went down to the stream. There he refilled the canteen, catching the water as it fell in a miniature cascade from a stone ledge. Negotiating the rocks, he brought it back to the cave.

"Here," he told his patient. "This will be a little colder."

Modi sipped at it gratefully, spilling some over his great, red waterfall of a beard.

"Thanks, Jawbreaker," he rasped. "I owe you one."

"Forget it," Vidar said. "Don't make a habit of it, though— I hate long plane rides."

Modi's eyes narrowed. "I lost the hammer, Jawbreaker. The thursar have it. Hod might have his hands on it already, and you know what he can do with it."

Vidar nodded. "You've got a nasty cut, big boy. You can't just go charging back into Utgard—he'll be ready for you. Besides, it'll take him time to attune to it, and he wasn't trained to do that as we were. It won't be easy for him. Get your strength back—and then we'll see about Hod."

Modi laughed, coughed and clutched at his wound. "We, Vidar? You mean that you're coming out of hiding?"

Vidar shrugged. "Briefly. Just long enough to see this thing through, because if I let the family destroy itself, it will destroy Earth—Midgard—along with it. And you know how I feel about that." Vidar rummaged in his pack and found the oranges he'd picked up on the road. "Here," he said, peeling back the skin. "Suck on that for a while."

Modi grimaced. "Tastes too sweet."

"It's good for you. Have another one."

Modi took the second orange hungrily, despite his protests, and dispatched it. "You just love this little ball of filth, don't you?" he asked, his voice a little stronger now.

Vidar nodded. "It's been a long time, nephew. You look a lot like your father."

"You haven't changed much, Jawbreaker—though you no doubt like to think you have. Your hair is shorter, and you dress like a human. Otherwise, you look about the same. How do you pass the time these days?"

"I'm a sculptor. Mostly metal, some wood, some stone."

Modi nodded his great, shaggy head, then winced again. "Your father sculpted an entire world, and you're piddling around with bits of metal and wood."

"My father was *gaut*, a Creator. But he was also a mean son-of-a-bitch, and he would just as soon send thousands to their deaths as pick off a hangnail. I'd like to avoid that particular part of the family legacy, Modi. Vali, of course, feels otherwise. I trust he has restored the Golden Age to Asgard by now?"

"You don't really care, do you?" Modi asked. He sounded a little better, although he was still white as a sheet. He must have lost a lot of blood, Vidar noted.

"Let's not be bitter, nephew. I confess I'm curious about the family."

"You're an interesting character, Jawbreaker," Modi said. "Well, anyway—Vali still rules, and there haven't been any complaints about it. Magni—my brother, in case you've forgotten—has taken over the reins in Alfheim. In a way,

he's like you, although his motives are more easily understood. He just wants to hunt and drink and make free with
elfin maidens. But we visit him from time to time, Vali and
I, when we feel like a good boar chase."

"What about Hoenir?"

Modi frowned. "Don't know. A few years ago, Asgard-
time, he disappeared. At first, we thought he was off whor-
ing. Now we're not so sure."

"Any guesses?"

Modi shook his head.

"And you say Hod has come back?"

Modi nodded. "Some water, if you don't mind." This
time Vidar handed him the canteen, and he finished the
contents.

"How do you know that it's Hod?"

Modi spat, coughed and cursed elaborately at his pain.
Then he settled down, the fire in his eyes abating.

"There was an uprising in the hills around Dundafrost,
and Vali got wind of it through one of his spies there—an
Aesirman living among the humans. Of course, not having
a handle on the overall scheme of things, he just reported
what was happening in his own district. Hordes of thursar
appeared out of nowhere and descended on the glens north
of Dundafrost, wiping out whole villages of men and elves.
By the time Vali heard about it, they had moved to lay siege
to the city itself. Then his other spies began reporting huge
migrations of thursar—a religious gathering of some kind—
and it became apparent that it wasn't to worship Vali. The
name 'Ygg' kept coming up."

"Doesn't make sense," said Vidar. "Those thursar are
nomads. Ever since Utgard was born in Odin's cauldron of
a brain, the thursar tribes have fought among themselves.
They've never prized anything beyond grazing land for their
herds, and no two of them could be counted on to agree on
anything."

Modi snorted. "Maybe Utgard has changed since you

knew it. All it took was a leader—someone who could not only organize them but motivate them to slaughter. Someone who had a grudge."

Vidar smiled grimly. "So, naturally, Vali thought of Hod—who, from his poisoned perspective, had been responsible for all the evil in the nine worlds. My half brother Vali has a one-track mind, doesn't he?"

"But he was right, uncle," said Modi. "I was in Utgard when all this took place, if a continent away. Vali contacted me through one of his other spies and sent me to investigate. I went alone, so as not to draw too much attention. If it was Hod behind the killing, he would have been more than ready for any force we could send against him on short notice. And in any case, I was loathe to let this marauder know that we were keeping track of him." Modi coughed again. "How about another—what do you call them?"

"Oranges," said Vidar, extracting one from his pack. Modi devoured it.

"Too bad all you've got is this stuff," he said, wiping his mouth with the back of his hand. "You didn't happen to bring a few horns full of mead, by any chance?"

Vidar half smiled.

"Thought not," said Modi. "Anyway, I arrived in the vicinity of Dundafrost perhaps three days after I'd gotten word, having ridden all day and night, switching horses every chance I got. No one would deny Odin's blood a horse—at least to his face. Even a couple of miles from the city, I knew that the thursar's work there was finished. There was no trail of cooking smoke in the air, not even the smoke of the invaders' fires.

"The gates were open. I walked in uncontested, and surveyed this Ygg's handiwork. No pretty sight, Vidar. It was a city of corpses. And then I had my first proof—a standard, set up in the center of the city. It had been stuck into the soft greensward of a little park before the thursar had left—but a youth, wounded or dead already, had been lying there, so they just drove the shaft right through him. And listen, Jawbreaker . . ." Modi said, but was gripped by a sudden fit of coughing before he could finish the sentence. ". . . before you accuse Vali of paranoia—it was a red eagle on a field of black that fluttered over the gentle corpses at Dundafrost."

Modi slumped back against the cave wall but held Vidar's gaze. "Hod's emblem," said Vidar. "I know." Outside the little cave, there was a whine of cicadas, which rose and abated.

"I plucked it forth," said Modi, his voice weaker now, "and threw it over the ramparts." His eyes narrowed. "Then I left Dundafrost, for my mission was not yet completed, and rode through the glens seeking a sign by which to follow them. It turned out that their trail was well-marked. They left plenty of hoofprints and footprints and every now and then, a broken, tortured carcass of a man, the blood-eagle carved into his back."

Modi closed his eyes. "After a couple of days, I got close to them. They had gone up into the foothills near Skatalund, which is the seat of power in the Barri region, a place of men risen since Ragnarok. It seemed that they were concealing themselves to prepare for the next attack in secret. All throughout the hills, black tents had grown up like a forest of death. Night fell, and they left their tents to gather in a huge and barren, bowl-shaped valley. There must have been thousands of them there, with their sentries standing all around the lip of the bowl, under a thick and purplish sky.

"I took the liberty of plucking one of those sentries and cracking his skull open with Mjollnir. The hammer, bless it, made no noise, and the other watchmen took no notice. I tucked Mjollnir into my belt, picked up the thursar's spear and took his place. I could then see that there was a great torture session in progress. Perhaps a dozen humans, male and female, had been tied to stakes and were being burned alive. The smoke rose in red streamers. The victims screamed, and the thursar chanted, beating their spears against the ground.

"In the center of the circle of suffering, Vidar"—and Modi opened his eyes again—"in the middle of the horde, with all eyes upon him, stood a single figure, manlike in form. He laughed, and it reminded me of Loki—there was that terrible horse-whinny in his voice, that madness. He wore a great, elaborate helm, which concealed his face. At first, I missed the connection—then it hit me. It was a replica of Odin's war mask. The one he called Ygg.

"Then, strangely, there was a kind of dampening, as if a blanket had been laid over the din, and he turned in my direction. Our eyes met and locked, though his eyes were just shadow slits. For a moment, there were only the two of us, and we knew one another. Then he pointed to me. The sentries saw me, and the chase was on."

Modi drew a deep, tremulous breath. "Baldur's Beach was the nearest refuge I could think of, and that was nearly a day's ride. I clambered down the rocks to my horse, the thursar's spears for company. I made my escape. They followed, and their mounts were rested, while mine was bone-tired.

"The rest is easily told. They hunted me across Barri, but I managed to stay ahead of them—at least until the cliffs above the beach. I made my way down and they descended behind me, hurling spears and rocks. A couple lost their footing and fell, in their haste to skewer a god. Most of them survived and cornered me on the beach. We fought, but there were many of them. I lost, though somehow I managed to crawl through into Midgard. When I woke, I was alone here, and they were still on the other side—afraid to follow, perhaps. Except for this gentleman." Modi gestured wearily toward the thursar corpse. "He had hung on to me, I suppose. I must have killed him before I passed out. But the hammer, Vidar—Mjollnir was gone."

Vidar frowned. Having said his peace, Modi closed his eyes again. There was a brief, silent space between them. The cicadas tittered.

Modi sighed. "Sleep," said Vidar.

"But they can still come through. Gathering their courage..." He raised a hand to point to the recesses of the cave, beyond the body of the thursar. It was veiled in a deeper darkness, and there was a lazy hum in the air as if bees ruled there. "Pick up his sword."

Vidar shook his head. "I don't use them anymore. I haven't picked one up since Ragnarok."

Modi stared at him, his eyes feverish. "Stubborn son-of-a-bitch," he whispered. Then, "I didn't think you would come, uncle. You surprised me."

Vidar shrugged. "I'm just a hell of a nice guy."

Modi muttered something and drifted off. After he had yielded to sleep, Vidar knelt by his side. He strained to make out Modi's features in the shadows—the proud cheekbones and gentle mouth that had been his mother's, the jutting brow and broad nose and lantern jaw that had been Thor's.

Vidar looked up and glanced at the Christian icons on the wall. How ironic—that Jesus should bear mild witness to the suffering of an older, a pagan, god. And that someone had sensed the special quality of this place and chosen it for a chapel, a place to commune with his god, when it was truly a passageway into Odin's hell.

He looked once more into Modi's upturned face. The salve was the first medicine Vidar had been taught to make, and it was strong, but it would take too long. So he placed all the fingers of his right hand on Modi's right temple, and all the others on his left.

Then he split the pain and the damage with his patient, absorbing half—or so they used to say, before Ragnarok—into his own body, where it would take its toll only in the long run. And there was pain, all right—waves of it that came down over Vidar like waves of fire. In return, he gave Modi life and strength. When he was done, he wondered at his own generosity. Only hours ago, he had been wary of treachery.

Vidar stood up slowly, careful not to hit his head on the low, thatched ceiling, and went to sit down by the dead thursar. He stared into the darkness and waited.

V

When Freya was very young, she was also very foolish. She had hardly arrived in Asgard along with her brother, Frey, when she was invited by Odin himself to spend a day sailing on the sea. Odin, the lord of all Asaheim—indeed, of all the worlds, if the truth be told. Freya knew what Odin had in mind, for she had known men before, but she was also frightened—not only of the All-father himself, but also of his wife Frigga. It was true that Odin took others beside Frigga to his bed. In fact, the mothers of Vidar and Thor had been the All-father's concubines.

But this was different. Freya knew that Frigga saw in the girl's youth and perfect beauty a rival for her position at Odin's side. It was one thing to have one's husband sleep with others—it was quite another to be replaced as queen of Asaheim.

Yet Odin was handsome in his way, and powerful.

Freya could not help but admit—at least to herself—
that she was attracted to him.

In the end, fear won out over lust, and Freya made
some excuse to put Odin off. But that alone was not
what marked her as foolish. Her true folly came in the
form of an elvish prince, tall and green-eyed and as
fair as the morning. His name was B'rising. He was a
visitor to Asgard. His people of Alfheim had created
an uneasy alliance with Odin and he was there to
cement that alliance. Just as Freya's presence was
meant to cement the alliance with the Vanir.

But it was a different alliance they enjoyed on the
afternoon when Odin would have sailed with Freya.
Afterward, when night had fallen and the elf returned
Freya to Sessrumnir, where she lived with her brother
Frey, B'rising lifted a necklace of beaten silver discs
from his neck and placed it over Freya's head. The
necklace gleamed on her breast in the moonlight. And
then he kissed her good night, but not before they
arranged to meet again the next day.

As she lay in bed that night, Freya inspected the
necklace. It was more beautiful than anything she had
ever seen in Vanaheim. In fact, she grew so enamored
of the necklace, B'rising himself became a shadow by
comparison.

The next morning, Freya was wakened by a pounding at the gates of Sessrumnir. Frey came to her and
said that Odin's guards, led by his sons Tyr and Hermod, were standing downstairs and would not leave
without her.

"What is this about?" Frey asked her, frantic and
confused.

Freya sighed and got out of bed. "It is nothing," she
said. "A mistake. But I'll go with them."

"Aesir or no Aesir," said Frey, "they will not take

my sister against her will if she has done nothing wrong."

A tear ran down Freya's nose, and she kissed Frey lightly on the cheek. "But I have done wrong," she said, and it wasn't until she spoke that the seriousness of her situation became tangible to her. "I have slept with an elf instead of Odin—and that is a crime in Asgard."

Frey watched open-mouthed as she dressed and went downstairs. Tyr and Hermod led her to Valask-jalff, where Odin and Frigga awaited her. As soon as she saw the queen of Asaheim, she knew who had betrayed her to Odin—and that she had been right to fear Frigga.

"I see that you are proud of your elf-tryst," said Odin, his face a mask of stone, his feelings unknow-able. "You still wear his necklace."

Freya let her head drop to her breast. She knew that if she could not evoke Odin's pity, she was lost.

"It is one thing for a warrior to bed an elf," said Odin. "But for a daughter of the Vanir—who are so like the Aesir—to do so is unthinkable. That necklace is not all that was recently parted from your lover's shoulders—his head rests now on a pike outside Glad-sheim. And yours will soon join it."

Freya raised her eyes again, and they were bright with tears. Never had Odin beheld eyes like those before, nor would he again. "My lord," she began, "what about your alliance with the Vanir?"

"Alliance!" Odin roared suddenly, half lifting out of his throne-seat. "No alliance will stop me from ruling Asgard as I please. Do you think the elves will stand against me because I've beheaded one of their princes? Or the Vanir because I've beheaded one of their whores?"

Freya would have said something then—for she was a princess of a proud people—but she bit her lip. Her position was precarious enough. "How can I make amends, my lord?" she asked. "Surely, there is some way I may pay you back for the wrong I've committed?"

Odin was well aware of what Freya was offering, but so was Frigga. And even the All-father could not insult his sons' mother by accepting that offer. Not at that point.

"A whore you've been," said Odin, "and a whore you'll be. If you've noticed, the hall named Valhalla lies all but empty. There are no warriors in it to fight my wars against the thursar. The elves that filled it are dead. The Vanir that filled it are dead. Now, I want mortals from Midgard to fill that hall to its rafters. You, Freya, will fill that hall."

"I, my lord?" she asked, sincerely puzzled, but thankful for her life.

"Yes," he said. "There is a king called Ottar, who rules a nation of warlike men. Now, we could recruit those warriors as we have recruited before—by appearing among them and promising them the highest of glories. But it is more expedient to sway one man and let him lead his entire host through the gate to Asaheim. One man," said Odin. "Surely, a whore like you can sway one man with her wiles."

Freya had all she could do to keep from flinging Odin's abuse back in his teeth. But her desire for life was greater than her pride in the end.

And it was not long before Ottar's armies filled Valhalla to its rafters. And each time the hall emptied, Freya filled it as a serving maid fills a drinking horn.

What's that, my lord? You say that it was too cruel a punishment for a girl so young? Perhaps. But would you change your mind if I said that after a while, Freya increased the frequency of her trips to Midgard—and without Odin's urging?

Ah, blessed is the work we do out of love.

Sin Skolding
Hlesey, 442 A.D.

VI

They came after nightfall in the gorge, when outside there was only starlight, and inside there was no light at all. There were two of them, and they rushed into the cave reckless of what they might find there. But their weapons were in their hands.

Vidar sprang to his feet, and that stopped them for an instant. He stood before two hulking shadows.

"Hold, and know you face the god Vidar," he said. "Go back and I give you your lives." He hoped that it sounded ominous enough. He was out of practice.

One of the two laughed—a rasping, guttural sound that Vidar remembered from long ago. Then a spearhead cut the air, jabbing savagely at his face. He stepped inside the thursar's reach and drove his fist into his ribs, but the giant's thick, leather armor absorbed much of the impact. Still, he staggered back, lost his footing and fell heavily against the floor of the cave.

Vidar braced for the other's attack, but instead of coming

straight at him, the thursar ran past—and leaped for the spattering of starlight that signaled an exit.

Vidar launched himself in that direction, grabbed and just missed as the thursar fled into the warmth of the Cretan night.

Then the first one bellowed and lunged at him again. Vidar managed to avoid the spearpoint and latch on to the thursar's spear arm at the wrist. He twisted, bringing the giant's arm up behind him into a hammerlock. Throwing his weight into the hold, he forced the thursar against the ground. With his left hand, the giant tried to claw at his tormentor—but Vidar had climbed atop his back and wedged the thursar's chin into the crook of his free arm. Slowly, he drew it back against the strength of the thursar's spine. Vidar strained and grunted. The intruder screamed horribly, but his cry was cut short by a sickening snap.

It was done. Vidar got to his feet, staring down at the dark hulk he had slain. The face, mercifully, was turned away from him. Vidar tried to recall the last time he had killed, and couldn't, though he knew it had been on Vigrid in Jotunheim. Then he looked up at the cave mouth and thought of the thursar that had escaped.

He couldn't go after him, whether he wanted to or not. There was still Modi to worry about.

Then, from the darkness behind him, as from the end of a long, stone corridor, there was the shuffle of approaching feet. Perhaps too many, thought Vidar, to handle without a weapon.

Reluctantly, he crouched and wrested the sword from the long-dead thursar's cold fingers, keeping his eye on the depths of the cavern. The footsteps were louder now. He moved to Modi's side, his fingers tightening on the hilt. They remembered quickly how to hold a sword.

I'm a warrior again, he thought, no matter what I do.

The hunched-over forms emerged from the ink-black

shadows, perhaps five or six that he could see, and more behind.

"Stand your ground," he snarled, "and know that you face the gods—not your craven, crawling god of the red eagle, but Vidar, son of Odin Valfather. Go back," he cried, "or you will die." Inside, Vidar cringed. He sounded like Basil Rathbone in *Robin Hood*.

The giants paused, as if sizing him up. Their eyes were like wet, black stones set beneath grotesquely jutting brows. Their cheekbones protruded like those of a naked skull and their mouths were cruel crevices full of jagged fangs. Odin had bred them from captives he'd taken in Jotunheim, from the hrimthursar. Vidar wished he had not been so intent on growing them large.

For a few moments, nothing happened, and Vidar became aware that the sight of Modi lying behind him might not be working wonders for his credibility. The wind blew softly outside the cave, and Vidar thought he could hear the gurgle of the stream that had quenched Modi's thirst.

Then the tallest among the thursar, crouching to avoid the low roof, stepped forward. Vidar braced for his attack, but the giant took his blade in both hands and presented its edge to him, palms up. He laid it on the ground and knelt. The others followed suit, one by one, even into the recesses beyond.

"In the name of Vali Who Rules, we place our swords at your feet," said the leader. "We pray that we are not too late to save the Lord Modi." The voice was deep, rumbling and raw, but there was a note of sincerity in it.

Vidar almost laughed. "Rise. By all means. What's your name?" he asked of the foremost. This was a new experience—a thursar laying his sword at the feet of an Aesirman!

"Stim," he said, expressionless. But there was something in his tone which told Vidar that walking between worlds was not something he looked forward to. For a thursar— even a friendly thursar—he sounded shaken.

"Look after Lord Modi, Stim. Guard him with your lives, and you will be rewarded. I must find one of your . . . race, who came through before you."

Stim looked at the cave mouth and nodded—warily, it seemed to Vidar. As the giant rose with his sword, Vidar wondered—could he trust this strange group of thursar with his nephew? All his training told him he could not. Thursar were thursar. But his instincts told him it was all right. If they had wanted to, they could have slain both him and Modi without such subterfuge.

His probe of the giant's mind only confirmed what he had known. They would watch over Modi come hell or high water.

Vaulting out of the cave and into the warm, dry night, he surveyed the terrain. The thursar must have headed downhill—uphill would have been too steep and have made for slower going. Sword in hand still, Vidar picked his way across the rocks to the sandy path and managed a brisk trot as it cut back and forth alongside the stream.

Moonlight and starlight swept aside the veil of darkness for him, where they were not obstructed by gnarled, water-honed trees and bushes full of the pink blossoms. Spiderwebs broke across his face. The cicadas sent up a chorus like tiny warriors beating swords on shields.

Gradually, Vidar had to slow his pace, lest he miss a bend in the increasingly difficult trail. Soon, he had to contain himself to a walk, laboriously picking his way between great boulders. To his left, the stream gurgled ever louder.

Moonlight and starlight, darkness and dim, sand and rock, thorn and flower, spiderweb and cicada song. Even here, so far from Asaheim, Odin's eternal battles endured.

The breeze was cool on his brow, where beads of sweat had gathered. In his hand, the dead thursar's brand grew heavy. The moon slipped behind a shoulder of rock.

Almost before he knew it, the thursar was upon him.

Vidar did not know what caused him to miss, but the other's sword whistled within a hand's-breadth of his face. Before he could bring his blade up to parry the next cut, he felt the dizzying force of the giant's foot in his stomach. Vidar barely managed to roll out of harm's way when the sword came slicing down.

He leaned against a moss-covered boulder and dragged himself to his feet. The thursar stood *en garde*, but made no move to press his advantage. Half in shadow and half in light, the creature of Utgard became a piece of the forest, hair and hide and stone, that had risen up in Vidar's way.

And it soon became apparent why the black-eyed one had paused in his attack. His breath was coming in huge, ragged gulps, his great chest heaving. No place in Utgard could have been blessed with this tropical weather, Vidar realized. The thursar was wearing a garment of thick animal skins, a heavy leather hauberk and furred, hide boots made for trekking in the snow.

His blood must be boiling after a run like that, Vidar mused. Even he, used to Earth's warmer climes, felt sweat run down the side of his face.

"Hear me," said Vidar, his voice no louder than necessary—almost intimate, for there might be backpackers camping nearby. "This is my world. I cannot leave you to walk this earth. You must go back the way you came."

The thursar stood gasping for breath, his weapon still raised. He said nothing.

There was something about the giant's hunched stance that evoked some pity in Vidar—despite the cruel, inhuman visage. He was alone on an alien world, cornered and hopeless. The stars above him were coldly unfamiliar. Yet he stood his ground. It was a quiet courage that Odin had not aimed for in his breeding of that Utgard race.

Vidar thought of the giants guarding Modi. The one called Stim had been obedient, even . . . gallant. Could they have changed that much since he'd known their ancestors?

Had they become more . . . human, for lack of a better word?

Once, he would not have thought twice about parting the thursar's head from his shoulders. He was no longer that warrior, or so he kept telling himself. And this was his world—Earth. He didn't have to abide by Odin's rules.

"Okay," said Vidar. "Let's forget that we're supposed to hack each other to pieces." He sat down on the boulder behind him and laid his sword across his knees.

The giant kept his silence, his swordpoint catching the moonlight. But he blinked once, twice, as if he could not believe what he was seeing.

"You're a problem, my friend. You're here on my world and I can't let you stay. I could slay you here and drag you back—but it's a hot night for such hard work, and I don't want to kill you. I really don't. Then, of course, there's the possibility that you might kill me, which doesn't exactly thrill me either." Vidar searched the giant's eyes. "And in that case, you would still be stuck here in Midgard—and your friend Stim would still be guarding the way back."

The mention of Stim seemed to have gotten a reaction—it was hard to tell on a thursar face.

"Here's an alternative," Vidar said. "Sheathe your sword and I'll guarantee you your life."

The giant swayed, his skin pallid and streaked with rivulets of sweat.

"How do I know you speak the truth?" he asked. It sounded like someone gargling with sandpaper.

"Good question," said Vidar. And with that, he tossed his blade into the sand at the other's feet. It was more a gesture than an act with practical significance, he knew. A full-blooded Aesirman did not need a sword to fight a single giant—though his chances would be better with a weapon in his hands than without one.

The thursar looked at the sword for a short time. He looked at Vidar, as if weighing the chance of a quick thrust. Then he sheathed his weapon.

"I will accept the word of a god," the giant said, with no little grace.

Vidar smiled, alighting. "Let's go, then." He paused as they turned back toward the cave to retrieve his blade. The giant watched him do this, still silent.

The walk back was the strangest part of the entire night. In his wildest dreams, Vidar had never pictured himself striding among pink blossoms beside a sapphire stream, with a thursar for company. His companion towered over him by a head and more.

"What is your name?" Vidar asked.

The thursar looked straight ahead, no doubt as uncomfortable as he. "Buri."

"Where are you from?"

"We are nomads. But my clan returns to the hills south of Lodur. I was born there."

"Is Lodur still a place of men?"

The giant turned to look at him, and nodded.

"Do men and thursar live so close together?" Vidar could not keep a note of surprise out of his voice.

"Of course," Buri rumbled. "In many places, we occupy the mountains while men live in their cities. Sometimes . . . thursar live in the cities, too." This last appeared to be a sore point with Buri, Vidar noticed.

"You know Stim?"

Buri nodded.

"Does he live with men?"

He nodded again.

"It has been a long time since I've seen Utgard," said Vidar. "Things must be very different from what I remember."

The giant turned forward again and shrugged. "The elders say that things have changed even within the span of their own lifetimes."

Vidar studied Buri's profile. "How have they changed?"

"The world has changed. Every year, the snow recedes

a little more, and the breadth of the land where life may survive widens by that much. But not enough for us."

"Why not?"

"Men grow more quickly than the belt of life. Before men ruled, we roamed the hills and the plains at will. Since my great-grandfather's time, men have built roads. They said the roads would be for everyone—men, thursar and elves. But now they do not let everyone pass over the roads— we must pay a tax to the overlord." Buri grunted. "It was better, they say, before there was a road to use. Men and elves have taken the fields we once gathered from, and they have made them crowded with grains and fruits. There is more to eat—but now we must pay for it." He grunted again. "It used to be ours for the taking. The same with the hunting and the fishing—men's treasures now. They used to be ours."

Vidar nodded. The balance of power had shifted, then, as Odin could never have foreseen.

"Is that why you fight now?" he asked.

Buri stayed silent so long that Vidar thought he would not answer. Then he said, "We fight for the god Ygg."

"Because he will change the world for you?"

The thursar's brow lowered and he glared at Vidar. "Because he is the god. The one we have awaited. The one who will lead us back to the old ways. Ygg the Destroyer."

A name Odin had once taken for himself, one of many. But who used it now? Vidar was not quite ready to believe that it was Hod. Not that Hod was not capable of raising Utgard against Vali—just that it was not his style to fight at the head of an army.

"What does Ygg ask of you?"

"That we destroy every man and elf that walks our world. Then," said Buri, and his features shifted so that Vidar thought he might have been smiling, "we will tear down Heaven itself."

A chill raced up Vidar's backbone. Whoever Ygg was,

he had designs on Asgard. Or was that just something to fire up the troops?

Then Vidar spotted the thatched roof and the flat rock, and he showed Buri the way across the rocks. The Aesirman went in first, and the giant waited outside.

Modi had awakened and propped himself up against the wall. Stim bent next to him. When Vidar entered, he could discern the shadowy movement of swords rising to the ready—but they fell again when he was recognized.

"Vidar, you bastard," said Modi. "You ought to be roasted over a slow fire for leaving me in a cave full of thursar." He laughed.

"I see you've met our friend Stim," said Vidar.

"Yes, we've become fast friends," Modi answered. "I trust you found the wild goose at the end of your chase."

"Yes, as a matter of fact, I did," said Vidar. "Buri," he called, and Buri's bulk suddenly shut off the starlight at the entrance to the cave. Stim rose to his feet, his sword extended.

"Wait," said Vidar. "I gave him his life." He stepped between Buri and Stim's swordpoint.

Modi glanced from Buri to Vidar and back again. "What do you intend to do with him? Send him on his merry way after he and his partners sliced me open and stole Mjollnir?"

"Killing him won't get the hammer back, Modi. He may be of some use to us."

"It's his kind that slaughtered women and children at Dundafrost. I don't care what you've told him, Jawbreaker—he's as good as dead."

Vidar shook his head. "I'm bound by my word, Modi. And I'm not going to let you or anyone else break it for me. You understand that, Stim?"

The giant froze, caught between two gods. He looked at Modi, who turned his head and spat. Then he turned back to Vidar. "I understand," he said.

Buri advanced another step into the cave. He kept a close

watch on Stim but left his own blade sheathed. Stim, for his part, glared at the intruder. Vidar saw the seeds of disaster.

"Buri," he said, "give me your sword." The nomad turned to look at him. For a long moment, he didn't move at all. Then he slowly lifted the sword from its place at his thigh and handed it to Vidar. He was totally defenseless now, at Vidar's mercy.

Both Stim and Modi relaxed a bit after that. Vidar handed the weapon to Modi. "A gift," he said, "for when you are fit enough to use it."

Modi took the hilt in one hand and laid the flat of the blade in the other, feeling its balance. "Elfin-made," he muttered. "Rest assured, nomad, that it will not get rusty in these hands. It will be the doom of your clan, I can tell you that." He eyed the giant. But Buri did not say a word.

"Stim has told me where Mjollnir might be found, Vidar," Modi continued—still watching Buri. His temples worked, as he chewed his words carefully. "Ygg, it seems, has begun to lay siege to Skatalund. Some of this one's play-fellows must have brought the hammer to him there, for he has been seen attempting to use it. Fortunately, he has not had time to attune to its forces." He gestured to Stim. "Tell him," he said.

"We spotted the hammer from the walls of Skatalund," said Stim. "Our prince did. He asked our priest, who is part Aesir, what it meant. And the priest told him we must send a war party to rescue the Lord Modi, though he has been trapped in another world. We broke through the siege lines where they had not been fully reinforced, rode down to Baldur's Beach—where we found the nomads camped. A couple got through to this place." He indicated Buri with an inclination of his great, shaggy head. "We pursued, and we found you, my lord, and the Lord Modi. But our instructions were these: to bring Thor's son back to Skatalund, so that he might save us from Mjollnir."

Modi barked. It was like a laugh, but with no humor in it. Then, before Vidar could offer a word of caution, he was on all fours. Vidar tried to take his arm, but Modi shook him off. Then he stood up with a great effort, grimacing and shaky, with the blood drained from his face—but he did not put out a hand to steady himself.

"I'm ready," he said, driving the sword into his belt up to the hilt. "I'm going after the hammer." Vidar marveled at his nephew's strength. He was not Thor's son for nothing.

"You know you're not healed yet," said Vidar.

"I can ride," Modi snarled. "Hod may already have attuned himself to the hammer. And if he has, Skatalund will be like Dundafrost by the time we get there. But we've got to get Mjollnir back, Vidar, while we still can. We can't wait."

Vidar nodded. "All right. Stim?"

"Yes, my lord."

"What are the chances that your people still hold the gate on the Utgard side?"

"Good, my lord. The enemy left but a skeleton guard outside the entrance." Stim's voice was as rough as Buri's, but he spoke at a more measured pace, the result of contact with men. "This one," he continued, gesturing toward Buri, "is the last of that guard."

"Good," said Vidar. "Perhaps you will be kind enough to ask one of your warriors to help Lord Modi support himself as he walks."

"That's not necessary," said Modi. "I'll walk on my own two feet, or I'll fall flat on my damned face."

"As you wish," said Vidar.

"What about your captive?" asked Modi. "Is he coming with us?"

Vidar did not turn to look at Buri. "Of course. He may come in handy."

Those of Stim's warriors that had hung back in the recesses of the cave turned now and hunkered off into the

darkness behind them. Modi followed, then a couple more
of the thursar, and Stim himself.

Vidar looked at Buri. "After you." And the giant walked
slowly into the pitch darkness. Vidar was the last to leave
the cave, but before he went, he took one last draught of
the clean island air, with its faint scent of pink blossoms.

Then there was a hum growing in his ears, until it drowned
out everything. Smells died. Sound was crowded out. Vidar
could not even feel the air around him. All was still and
utterly black as he placed one foot before the other, again
and again. Then, even the ground underfoot seemed to vanish. He felt himself drifting.

More than a thousand years ago, he had come through
such a gate, seeking the solace of isolation. Now he was
going back. Strange things came to mind, little things—
Phil's eggs, the Skylark, the Greek who had sold him the
moped, the overturned orange truck, the plaintive voice of
the cicadas . . .

Gradually, Vidar felt his senses returning. The ground
became solid again . . . a glimmer of light. The echoes of
conversation, guttural and distant. A not-unpleasant scent
of highland ferns, cold, and air that was like a draught in
the lungs . . .

Utgard.

VII

Look around you—these are mighty walls your lord has put up to protect you from your enemies. But they are as butterfly's wings compared to the walls that surround Asgard. The barriers around Odin's city rise two hundred feet straight up into the sky. They are made of shimmering black stones, so hard that an invader has yet to mar their smooth surfaces.

And who built those walls? The hrimthursar themselves, in the days before war broke out between the Aesir and the giants. For there was a time after Odin and his brothers had discovered Jotunheim, when the All-father and the giants were probing one another's strengths and weaknesses—still unsure of one another's intentions.

But Odin had seen enough of the giants' natures, and they were no less warlike than his own. He knew that it would be only a matter of time before they were at the throats of the Aesir. Nor was he reluctant to enter into such a war, for the blades of his sons were growing rusty with lack of use.

So Odin decided to make the first move. In seeming generosity, he offered any thursar who would help to build a wall around Asgard enough gold to cover him from head to foot. Gold, Odin knew, was as coveted by the hrimthursar as by the Aesir.

As for the wall—well, Odin himself could have laid stone upon stone with his magic. But what he sought was more than just a wall. He planned to take the cream of the giants' youth, use their strength, then hang them like ripe fruit from the walls they themselves had built. The other giants were not likely to forget such an act of cruelty. It would not only deprive Jotunheim of its most fearsome defenders—it would ensure hatred and fuel a hostility that would not wane until either the giants or the Aesir had been annihilated.

And so they came to Asgard, the young behemoths among the hrimthursar, and they were led by a hairy, big-boned lad named Loki. Odin saw at once that Loki was a craftier sort than his comrades. His eyes were brighter and he might not be so easy to dupe. More than that, he had commune with wolves and other wild creatures, and who-knew-what-other magics.

To blind this special one, it would take more than gold, though gold had drawn him through the gate to Asaheim. So Odin took Loki aside, as the leader of the giants, and promised him that if the wall were finished by the first day of fall, no less a light than Freya of the Vanir would be his bride. Loki had only to glimpse Freya's beauty from afar before he, like the other giants, was blinded by the promise of his reward.

The work went quickly. The giants had brought their strong, squat mountain ponies along to haul the sharp-edged, black boulders that they had split from the ribs

of Asaheim's hills. Where the slopes had been marked
by great, black outcroppings, the hrimthursar left them
smooth and even.

They began the work in midsummer, some ten dozen
towering giants. By the end of summer, they had already erected a wall no Aesirman could easily scale.
It was nearly a hundred feet tall and as strong as the
bones of Asaheim—for that was what it contained.

The sun grew colder and the leaves turned from
green to gold and copper—and the shadow cast by
the wall grew longer every day. Each morning saw the
strongest of the giants wresting great slabs of rock
from the earth. Each afternoon saw the giants' ponies
hauling huge mounds of shattered rock down the hillside to Asgard. And each evening saw the hrimthursar
piling stone on stone, as the sun spilled its blood on
the horizon.

Now, beside the path the giants took from quarry
to city stood the Aesir's apple orchards. They were
tended by Idunna, whose beauty was second only to
young Freya's. In fact, before Freya first visited in Asgard, Idunna had been considered the most comely
woman in all of Asaheim—and so she had been given
to Odin's eldest son, Bragi, as his wife.

Once, Loki had asked her for some fruit, for he and
his comrades were hungry, and the food supplied them
by the Aesir was not enough to fill the bellies of giants.
Though she was frightened by the hulking, black-eyed
thursar that shut out the sun with the breadth of his
shoulders, Idunna refused him the fruit.

"It is for the Aesir alone," she said, "for these apples
are what keep us young. Without them, we would shriv-
el and grow old. So, you see, we have none to spare."

Of course, it was not true that the Aesir depended
on mere fruit for their long lives. But it was all Idunna

could think of to save her well-tended orchards from the brutish wall-builders.

Loki grunted. He was not pleased with Idunna's refusal to share the apples, but he knew that he was not in his own land—and apples were not worth fighting over when the gold and Freya were almost close enough to touch.

No one knows how Loki and his band got wind of Odin's plan to betray them. Perhaps it was no more than a careless word here and there that enabled Loki—who was not stupid—to piece the puzzle together. Some say that it was Freya, who feared that Odin might actually give her—even for a short time—to the grisly giant, and wanted fighting to break out before that could even be considered.

What is known is this—when the wall stood almost two hundred feet tall and the bargain was nearly completed, Loki found out that Odin had played them all for fools. In the evening, after the hrimthursar had laid another layer of stone on top of the wall, they drew their swords from their sheathes. Then they made their way under cover of darkness into Asgard, and they slew whomever they met. Their blades ran wet and red with Aesir blood. All night long, they stalked the streets of the sleeping city. And when dawn looked about to break, they slipped out through the unfinished gate and found their ponies.

It was Idunna's bad luck to have risen early that day and taken her mare out to her beloved orchards. For Loki planned to set the trees on fire as his parting gesture to his former employer. When he spied copper-haired Idunna among the apple trees, he forgot about his torch and flung it aside. But the flame that was in his loins he quenched in Idunna.

The Aesir woke to corpses in their streets and the

smoke of burning apple trees on the air. When Bragi realized that his wife was gone and saw whence the smoke came, he gathered his brothers and took off in pursuit of the marauders.

They caught up with the giants—for their horses were bred for speed, not torturous mountain trails—near the gate that led to Jotunheim. The hrimthursar wheeled to face them.

"You would have hung thursar fruit from your walls," cried Loki. "But we have deprived you of that pleasure. And we've deprived you of that other fruit, the apples that keep you young. But the most precious fruit of all was denied to me, so I took Idunna instead. You hear me, Bragi? Tell your father that it was Loki who enjoyed his daughter-in-law!"

Then Bragi leaped forward on his stallion, ahead of even Thor, for he was eager to get at Loki's throat. The Aesir closed with the hrimthursar and much blood was spilled on both sides.

But Loki and a few others escaped, to bring the tale of Odin's treachery home to Jotunheim. It was too bad that he did—for Loki and his son would cause the Aesir much pain on Vigrid, the Iron Plain, when the sons of Odin brought Ragnarok to the giants.

Sin Skolding
Radsey, 481 A.D.

VIII

They emerged into a world that Odin had spun on the loom of a whim. It was twilight on a moonlit beach that jutted out into the sweep of an icy ocean—a black field where whitecaps were carved for a moment and then gone. Landward, there towered mighty cliffs, but wildflowers grew from crevices in the rock, in bright cascades of red, yellow and pale blue. The wind, harsh and full of salt, brought memories to Vidar out of a cold, endless sky. He had been here before many times, when his father was molding Utgard to suit his peculiar fancies.

But it had been Baldur's handiwork, this beach, where a barren shelf of rock would have sufficed. It was his greatest effort, this small stretch of beauty in a cruel world. But even Odin could not deny him that—Baldur, who was the best out of all of them.

Stim greeted his soldiers, perhaps a score of them, with a few clipped commands. They came together briskly in a martial formation, awaiting their gods' inspection.

Beyond them, however, there was another formation. There, where the beach narrowed to extend a slender finger of sandbar into the sea, huddled the ranks of the dead. Each warrior lay still, face up to the moon, his weapon on his chest and his helm—if he had one—by his side. Their blood stained the sand beneath them. Some had been dead longer than others, those who had been slain outright preceding the ones who had died from their wounds. Some were nomads, some obviously Stim's men—but in death they followed the same captain, the same god.

Last to be laid on the sandbar were the two thursar who had died in the cave—the one Modi had killed and the one whose neck Vidar had broken. At the far end of the corpse ranks, where the finger of beach ended, a long spear protruded from the sand. The waves rushed toward it, devoured themselves as they broke and gently embraced it. Then they withdrew, and rushed again.

Vidar had not forgotten the significance of the spear that is thrown over a mortal's head. At one time, it meant that the body, living or dead, had been consecrated to Odin. Now, it must be a dedication to Vali, who held Odin's place in Asgard.

"Stim," said Vidar, and the giant turned to him. "You have enough horses up there?" His hair whipping in his face, Vidar gestured to the cliffs above.

Stim nodded. "Yes. We have those we brought, as well as those whose riders no longer need them."

"Let's go, then," said Modi, shouting over the wind.

At a word from their leader, the thursar began to file up a narrow path cut into the rock. Again, Buri walked just ahead of Vidar.

It was a hard climb. But Vidar was dressed for it, as the others were not, and he might almost have enjoyed the dizzying view of the flower-falls and the lonely, white beach if it had not been for the dead that stared up at them. Eventually, the tide would take them. After a while, he looked down and saw that the spear had already been plucked from the sand. Those who worshiped Asgard would say that the sacrifice had been accepted. Vidar knew it was just the waves.

Modi made the ascent slowly but without complaint. Sometimes, his hand would clutch at his ribs, where he had been cut, but he made no sound.

At the top, they found more of Stim's company guarding the horses. The land beyond was one of green fields and large, snow-covered shoulders of bare rock. On the landward horizon, a massive bank of gray-blue storm clouds had locked into place. The wind was in their faces, and up here it was full of bluster. Overhead, it was still crystal-clear—but there was a chill in the world that made even the stars seem menacing.

October in Midgard, thought Vidar—Twelfthmonth in Utgard. Winter was just beginning here.

Vidar turned back to Buri, who was standing on the heights, staring down. His great bulk was silhouetted by the moon. Then he turned away, and Vidar searched for an emotion in that unguarded moment—sorrow, hatred, blood-lust, anything. But if something boiled up inside him, Vidar could not detect it.

"Well," said Modi, "what are we waiting for?" And he pulled himself onto the back of a steed the color of iron.

Vidar chose a roan stallion and mounted. He found a battle-axe suspended by a loop from the saddle, reached down and tossed it onto the frozen grass—then placed the sword he carried into a sheath on the other flank. One weapon was enough. He checked the straps on his backpack, not trusting himself to lash it to the saddle.

Modi came up beside him. "Can you smell that?" he asked. "It's the scent of lightning. I feel better already." In fact, there was a touch of ruddiness in his cheeks that had not been there before. His fiery beard tossed in the wind.

"Which way now, Stim?" Vidar called. The giant pointed.

"Into the storm, my lord. Skatalund lies that way."

Modi wheeled and spurred his horse into a fast trot with his hide-bound heels, falling into line with Stim and his troops. Vidar rode alongside Buri, and a couple of Stim's warriors brought up the rear.

For hours, they crossed the wild highlands, where the grass, though still green, was hard and cold beneath their horses' hooves. Great ribs of rock rose up before them, but Stim picked his way among them so as not to slow their pace.

The moon had climbed to its zenith when he led them down into a belt of fir woods. Deep among the trees, the howl of the wind was replaced by the nervous chittering of hardy winter birds and the snapping of branches underfoot. It grew darker as they went on. Then, there came a light patter, and drops of freezing rain began to fall on their faces. After the heat of the Mediterranean and the climb above Baldur's Beach, even that felt good to Vidar.

The forest seemed never to end. Day broke above them, but with little light, for the storm clouds blotted out the sun. At what they judged to be midday, they took a brief rest. The horses were fed and watered, and Vidar shared some questionable kind of meat with one of Stim's soldiers. Buri declined it when Vidar offered it to him, calling it "city food."

The afternoon was no less gloomy than the morning. If anything, the forest grew thicker, denser—and harder to pass through. The rain came and went, sometimes hard and sometimes a mere drizzle. Vidar had done some riding on Earth, but nothing nearly so prolonged as this. He felt his rump growing increasingly tender with each long hour.

Then they came to a point where the land fell off abruptly, and the trees grew at crazy angles out of the slope. The woods began to thin out, and Stim said that he thought they were almost free of them.

But night fell before they emerged onto a huge ridge of

earth and left the forest behind. The sky overhead was a deep, swollen purple, releasing a steady drizzle. It seemed that the worst of the storm was still ahead of them.

As they topped the ridge, though, they could see sprawled before them the valley that Skatalund commanded, a river running down from the gentler highlands off to their left and bending back sharply near the gates. The city itself was a fortress with walls of white stone and high, stately towers, in the manner of the Vanir before Ragnarok. But it was enclosed in a sea of black tents as thick as maggots on fresh carrion. On two sides, the nomad camp ran up into the very foothills.

Vidar pulled his horse up alongside Modi. "He has not yet unlocked Mjollnir's power," Modi said. "See the walls? Unscathed. But there are a lot more of those black tents than I saw before, Jawbreaker. A lot more."

"Well, there's less than two dozen of us here. That hardly constitutes the cavalry," said Vidar. "Any guesses as to where Ygg might be camped?"

Modi considered the sea of black tents, his blue eyes sparkling in the rain and the mist. "Yes," he said, "I think I can see his banner there." He raised his arm and pointed to a hollow between two small hills, perhaps a mile to their right. The tents seemed to be thickest there—and as Vidar searched more intently, he spotted the red eagle on a field of black. The pavilion beneath it was taller by half than the others around it.

Could it really be Hod at the head of this slaughter? What could have brought him back, after all this time? The throne of Asgard? It was unlike him. Hod was the one who dealt behind the scenes, the half brother that kept to himself. But where had he hidden all this time, and how might that have changed him?

Vidar felt an inexorable undertow snatching at his feet, carrying him out into a tumultuous sea he thought he had seen for the last time. Again, he stood at the center of the family's wars. Shivering against the cold, he clenched his teeth.

No. Not this time. Skatalund was as far as he would go.

"Vidar," said Modi. "I have a plan. Are you ready for such genius? You and I take down a couple of the thursar, put on their clothing and steal into Hod's encampment. We get as far as we can before we start cracking heads. Then we hope that there aren't too many heads between us and Hod."

Vidar had to smile. "Napoleon would turn over in his grave."

"Who?"

"Never mind."

The wind swept about them, sheeting them. A few scattered campfires labored to survive among the black tents. While they watched, one flickered and went out.

"Buri," said Vidar softly and glanced back at the giant. "Buri," he said, louder this time, so that the thursar could hear him, "how can we get through to Ygg?"

The captive stared at Vidar. "You are asking me to betray my comrades. And my god."

"Not true," said Vidar. "I gave you your life. I ask you now to preserve mine."

"What are you talking about?" asked Modi. "Do you want to dangle your life by the word of this killer? Don't forget, Vidar—he's our enemy. His brothers and cousins are sleeping in those tents down there."

The thursar's eyes narrowed. "I cannot do this. You may slay me, but I cannot."

Vidar brought his horse around, turning to face Buri. "Listen," he said. "If we have to blunder our way through, lives will be lost on both sides. If we can recover the thing that belongs to us, with no opposition, there will be no blood shed this night."

Buri's eyes glittered like stones in a shallow stream. "Lives were lost to obtain that thing."

Vidar met his thursar stare. "Perhaps you do not under-stand, Buri. We are gods. If we wish, we can sweep away every life in those tents as easily as you would crush a tic. But you know that that is not my way. If you do not get us through to Ygg, your entire army will be dead. In a matter of moments. Will you bear that responsiblity, Buri?" Vidar paused, knowing that with what he had in his backpack, he could fulfill that oath—and it frightened him to think so.

Buri's shaggy brows came together. The rain waxed in strength, pelting the turf on the ridge. "Swear that you will not use this power, and I will see you through safely."

"You will lead us through yourself?" asked Vidar.

"I will," said Buri.

"Suicide," said Modi. "Earth has softened your brains, Vidar."

"I swear," said Vidar, ignoring his kinsman. Lightning scored the tortured sky. Thunder roared in the distant hills.

"So large a group will never make it unseen," Buri said. "Perhaps three, including myself."

Vidar shook his head. "Make it five. Stim, you'll go, and one of your warriors. Feel up to it, Modi?"

Thor's son just glared at him.

"Guess so," said Vidar. "Ready, Buri?"

Without another word, the thursar spurred his steed forward past Vidar and, gently, over the lip of the ridge. Vidar followed, with the others behind them. Stim barked some orders to those who remained.

The descent directly before them was featureless and not too steep, but they would be easily spied against the pale, frozen grasses if they went that way. Instead, Buri led them across the slope, on a path parallel to and below the ridge, to a natural wall of black volcanic rock. Against this barrier, they would be hard to find.

Buri looked back over his shoulder. "Dismount," he said.

"No," said Vidar. "We've got no chance to get away on foot."

The giant shrugged and raised an arm toward the area just ahead. "The wounded," he whispered hoarsely.

Vidar saw his plan. Of course. The wounded would be the least likely to be up and about at this time of night. Lightning split the sky, revealing them and the sea of tents all at once. Vidar held his breath, but there were no sentries here to sound an alarm. Thunder rolled long and loud across the valley. The only sound after that was the sizzling of raindrops on rock, and the sucking of fresh mud on the horses' hooves.

In time, they entered among the tents. Vidar reached down and loosened the sword in its sheath. He imagined that those behind him were doing the same.

Like ghosts, they rode past the sleeping horde. Like wraiths out of nightmare, thought Vidar, picturing how they must look—bedraggled and armed with longswords. Did thursar have nightmares? he wondered. Would they know one if they did? Only Odin could have said, and he was truly a ghost now, living only in the memories of those who strove against one another in his wake. In Utgard, his lasting monument.

Buri was true to his word. He picked his way carefully, winding around the periphery of the camp, patient in his stealth. Then he turned and led them inward, around a hill and toward the heart of the matter. Past tents and more tents, silently, over a rise and across a shallow stream. Around another hill, past another cluster of sleeping thursar. The wind rose and fell, whistling, covering what little noise they made in their passage.

Suddenly, a sentry. Vidar drew his sword, striving to see the giant form clearly against the rain.

Buri slid off his horse, darting around a tent as the night-shrouded figure offered a challenge. Vidar croaked a curse when he saw Buri vanish—Modi had been right!

Stim or the other thursar with him answered, but the sentinel challenged them again—louder this time—and came closer, his spear held aloft. Lightning flashed overhead, and each was revealed to the other.

Vidar sprang from his horse, his point at the ready. But just as the sky groaned in agony, a huge shadow fell upon the watchman and bore him to the ground. Then there was a dull thud, and Vidar could see Buri kneeling over the other nomad, with a rock still clutched in his pawlike hand.

Buri was looking at something to Vidar's left. He turned and saw Modi holding a war-axe, his gaze full of death. "Have done," whispered Vidar, and Modi looked at him. "Don't blow it now, when we're so close." Modi lowered the weapon, slowly.

Buri let the rock drop and climbed back onto his horse's back.

The rain fell in blinding sheets suddenly, dousing what remained of the firelight, and improving their chances. They saw no other sentries—perhaps because Ygg did not expect to be attacked from behind. Vidar's clothes clung to him, drenched through, and his hands became numb with the cold.

When they finally came upon Ygg's pavilion, he could barely distinguish it from the general mud-slicked darkness. But Buri put up his hand, and Vidar gestured to the others. There were no guards around. It was almost too good to be true—they had ridden through the enemy's camp, right up to his doorstep.

Vidar signed for Stim to hold his horse's reins while he dismounted, and the giant did so. The other thursar did the same for Modi, who still held the axe in his right hand. Vidar let his sword remain in its saddle-sheath.

In the now-torrential rain, Modi's red mane ran like molten copper over his skull, but his eyes gleamed like tiny lanterns. He smiled, hefted the axe, the rain streaming down his face in rivulets and mingling in his beard.

Vidar stood between Thor's son and Ygg's tent. He shook his head, touching his forefinger to the center of his chest and hoping that Modi would see the sense in his going it alone. Stealth was their greatest weapon this night. Unless they could escape from this vast encampment, the hammer would avail them nothing.

And in close quarters, no one living could surpass Vidar's strength—not even a son of Thor. Modi's power was the sudden, fierce wrath of the storm, not the inexorable force of nature that could carve deep valleys into the reluctant earth with the patience of eternity. Odin's might expressed itself in each of his heirs differently.

Modi nodded, after a moment's deliberation. He wanted the hammer back. And when it came down to it, he was no fool. Vidar clasped his nephew's shoulder. Then he removed his windbreaker, lest the stiff fabric make a sound, and draped it over the bow of his saddle. The backpack came with it, and it too hung from the bow.

He could see no light coming from inside Ygg's pavilion. With a forefinger, Vidar nudged the heavy, black cloth aside—just a sliver. Darkness inside. In one fluid motion, he eased the oil-soaked cloth aside and crept forward, keeping low to the ground, and gentling the flap back into place.

Unmoving, on all fours, he gave his eyes time to adjust to the heavy layers of lightlessness. Patience. Patience. There—he could begin to make out a low bed of some kind. And the vague contours of a sleeper. Outside, thunder droned, but the tent cloth shut out most of the sound.

Patience, while his blood slowed in his veins. Vidar thought of roots working their way into the soil, deeper, inch by inch, seeking food and moisture. Wind carving rock on the heights. The wash of a spring flood that smoothed the bark off the trees on the bank. The subtle wrestling of granite against granite, as the world shifted its balance. Stalactites, forming over countless years. Silence accumulating in a subterranean chamber like an underground sea.

His eyes moved, only his eyes, searching for the hammer.

Its shaft was short—too short, it was said—but its head was too large for it to be easily concealed. Slowly, the contents of the tent revealed themselves to Vidar—spears gathered together in a corner, forming a tripod; bones on a wooden plate and a goblet on a small table; a chest, too small to contain Mjollnir, and a cloak of thick hide, huddled like a beast, next to the bed. Resting in the folds of the cloak was a mask—much, as Modi had said, like Odin's mask of destruction. The one he had donned when he led the Aesir and the Vanir at Ragnarok. The great brazen helm known as Ygg.

Ice water trickled down Vidar's spine. He knew the mask had been lost along with his father, that day on Vigrid—but this was a damn good copy. And no doubt it had the desired effect, judging by the number of nomads it had gathered under its banner.

The wearer, meanwhile, had his back turned to him. It would be so easy for Vidar to spring on him, snap his neckbone and end this battle. In the old days, he would not have hesitated. But if it was in fact Hod, there were so few of them left . . . and someone had to balance out against Vali. For Vali, in the end, could be just as much a threat to Midgard—Earth—as anyone. Vidar knew him well enough. No, the hammer would be quite sufficient, thank you.

And since it could not be anywhere else, it had to be under Ygg's bed. Vidar crept forward, froze. No reaction from the sleeper. He moved just a bit closer to the bed. Still no movement. He waited, breathing slowly, shallowly, his pulse slithering snake-soft. He was as still as one of the sculptures in his Woodstock studio.

Then, he decided, he was close enough, and he ventured to place his hand under the bed. There—bound in heavy leather, the hammer. His fingers closed around the shaft.

And other fingers closed around his wrist.

IX

Suddenly, his hand was wrenched back and twisted behind him. Ygg fell upon him, driving his face into the hard-packed earth. The power that flattened him then, knees and hips and shoulders crushed, was such as he had never felt before—not among the Aesir, in their long-ago wrestling tournaments, nor among the thursar in deadly, hand-to-hand skirmishes.

Vidar dug his left foot into the ground inside his attacker's calf. He pulled one hand back and wedged an elbow underneath his chest. Slowly, he propped himself up on that elbow, fighting desperately for leverage. The other wrenched his captive arm up toward his head, sending spasms of agony through his shoulder.

Then, Vidar brought his leg out wide and pushed—rolling forward and dislodging Ygg from his back. Scrambling to his feet, he failed to see the fist that slammed into his jaw, knocking him backward. He stumbled and grasped something—the table?—fell, and the other was upon him again.

This time, however, he knew what he was up against. As Ygg launched himself at Vidar's throat, he rolled backward, buried his hiking boot in Ygg's stomach and sent him flying into the side of the tent. A wooden support cracked and the pavilion began to cave in. Vidar dove for the hammer. Dragging it forth from its hiding place, he lurched out of the collapsing tent into a madhouse of rain and thunder.

As soon as he had torn free, he felt Modi grab him by the shoulders. He wrested the hammer from him, ripped away the leather binding and held it up against the glare of the lightning.

Then there were cries of surprise and warning, thursar cries that rumbled like the thunder, and Vidar pulled himself up into the saddle. Modi just stood there, turned toward Ygg's half-standing tent, as if ready to face him now. "Modi," Vidar yelled, his voice cutting through the clamor, "no time now! Modi!"

Without signing that he had heard, Modi drove the shaft of Mjollnir into his broad belt and vaulted onto his steed—his wound forgotten. Stim wheeled away, and Modi started after him. Vidar glanced at Buri. The giant's horse reared, and for a moment Vidar thought he might stay there. Then he galloped off, too, and Vidar was on his heels.

A spear shaft whistled past his head and was gone. Over a hill they rode, and through a cluster of black tents. On one side, a thursar warrior bulked up from behind a tent, planting himself in Modi's path. The hammer arced, and the giant slumped forward. The ruin that had been his skull was claimed quickly by the mud.

Behind Vidar, there was a cry, cut short. When he dared to dart a look over his shoulder, Vidar saw that Stim's comrade had been dragged off his horse. Another spear flew by him, and this time the shaft glanced off his shoulder, though the point missed. He pressed himself down against the roan, feeling its muscles rippling beneath the thick sheath of its flesh, and another line of tents rose before him. But beyond them, even in the lashing rain, he could see the ramparts of Skatalund rising like a mighty, sun-bleached skeleton into the gray, writhing storm clouds.

Vidar's steed pounded into one of the tents in its path, because they were so densely packed here that there was no room to go around it. For a sickening moment, he thought it would catch a tent pole and cripple itself. But they dragged free after a moment, and found nothing but empty fields between their headlong rush and the walls of the fortress.

Vidar looked back and saw mounted thursar emerge from the sea of tents, with others pursuing on foot, and close behind. But as he took that luxury, his horse leaped over something, and the jolt of landing tore him half out of the saddle.

He struggled not to fall, one leg hooked over the roan's back. Then he saw the backpack fly loose. Broken straps fluttering, it hit the ground to one side of him and bounced. Quickly, he hauled himself up into the saddle again and reined in, bringing the roan up short. It reared and pawed violently at the air, near choking.

Then he leaped and hit the ground with his shoulder, rolled and came to his feet. A web of lightning climbed into the sky and illuminated the wave of thursar behind him. He saw a spear fall towards him, and that was all the spectating he allowed himself. He bolted for the pack, tucked it under his arm like a football and ran for the city gates.

A great, gray horse came up on one side of him. It was Modi.

"Up you go, Jawbreaker," he bellowed, and leaned out of the saddle to help Vidar mount behind him. With the blue nylon pack in one arm and his nephew's middle in the other, Vidar struggled to keep his balance.

Another few moments, and they were out of range of

the nomad spear throwers. But a handful of thursar still rode after them, perhaps fifty yards behind, and galloping wildly. Stim and Buri had already reached the bone-white battlements.

As lightning seared the heavens and Skatalund gleamed like purest silver, Vidar saw the great gates swing open—a few feet and no more, but enough for them to pass through one at a time. Stim slipped out of sight, and Buri followed. One of their pursuers tried a spear-cast, but it fell far short. Then Modi guided his horse into the narrow opening, and the gates of Skatalund swung shut with a thunder of their own.

Behind the walls, the men and thursar of the city went about their separate tasks to secure the gates again. There was a faint clatter of spears outside, answered with the unmistakable twang of tightly strung bows. Vidar looked up and saw the archers. Then he heard the cries of the thursar, and the jeers of the bowmen. All around him, the humans raised their weapons and roared their approval, while their thursar comrades went about their business.

The humans wore helmets and body mail that Vidar marked as elves' work. He saw that beyond the outer wall, there was an inner wall just as tall. It would not be easy to take this city, for all Ygg's numbers, with these kinds of fortifications.

He slid off the rump of Modi's mount, and someone placed a warm, dry cloak about his shoulders. Vidar pulled it up over his head, for it was still raining hard—though, somehow, it seemed softer here in safe quarters.

"Welcome, Lord Vidar," said the one who had offered him the cloak, and kneeled. "We have been expecting you." All around them, the others kneeled, too, human and thursar alike. Only Buri remained standing, while Modi looked around approvingly.

Vidar looked into the face of the cloak-bearer. He was very young, sixteen or seventeen at the most. His hair was

fair where it stuck out from beneath his helm, and he had
only the faintest hint of a beard. He reminded Vidar of the
boy he'd met in the airport in Athens, although they did
not look alike. Rather, it was something in the eyes.

"Expecting me?"

"Yes, my lord, and the Lord Modi." His accent was a
little strange, different from what Vidar remembered. "Prince
Olof was sent word of your arrival."

"By whom?" asked Vidar.

The youth averted his eyes. "The Lord of Asgard. Vali
the Avenger."

"Through his priest," said Modi, trying to clarify things
for Vidar. A priest would have been one of Vali's Aesir
spies.

Vidar nodded, frowning. "Of course, the priest. Is Vali
here?"

The youth shook his head. "No, my lord, he is not."

"I'm not surprised. Why should he risk his skin when
he can risk ours?"

The youth did not answer. Underneath his light cloak,
Vidar thought he might have trembled a little.

"I forgot," said Vidar. "He's your god. What's your
name?"

"Eric, my lord."

"Eric, can we get out of the rain?"

He looked up and could not conceal a smile. "Yes, my
lord. I have been instructed to see to your comforts."

"Fine," said Vidar. "Please do so. And our friends, the
thursar, will come with us."

"Of course, my lord." But when Eric looked in the direction of Stim and Buri, he hesitated.

"What is it?" asked Vidar.

"My lord," said Eric, rising, "I recognize Stim, of
course—but I do not know the other. He wears the garb of
our enemies."

"Treat him as you would treat Stim," said Vidar. "He has sworn himself to me."

Eric was clearly troubled. But he said, "As you wish, my lord." Then he barked a command to the others, and they rose. Vidar realized that, young as he seemed, Eric was in charge here.

One of the others shouted a command to a man at the top of the inner wall, and a hand waved from the other side of the barrier. Then the second set of gates, somewhat smaller than the first, swung inward, and Skatalund was revealed to them.

Vidar had expected the inner city to be as ethereal as the walls that ringed it about. He was only half-disappointed. Here, there stood a graceful, slender tower of ivory hue; there, a rough-hewn, blockish building that seemed to fade into the steady, gray downpour. The two styles appeared to commingle, however, rather than strive against one another. The white towers rose against the indigo clouds, connected by great, sky-spanning bridges—whose architect had once seen Asgard, Vidar was certain. But in the dark, low-to-the-ground structures that shouldered among the graceful towers, there was a more sinister influence—unmistakably that of Jotunheim. Somehow, they complemented one another. Vidar would not have thought it possible—until he saw Skatalund.

A broad, cobbled road cut a wide path through the heart of the city. On either side, people who appeared to be farm-folk from the outlying countryside had constructed make-shift shelters for their families and what belongings they could carry. As Vidar emerged from the inner gates, he could see all eyes riveted on him. Here was their long-lost god, Vidar the Jawbreaker, and the son of Thor. Here were their saviors from Ygg the Destroyer. The Lord of Asgard had answered their prayers.

At the end of that road, however, reared a castle, not

unlike those that still stood on the banks of the Rhine, back in Midgard. The only difference was the stone of which it had been built—the same white stone that had been used to build Skatalund's walls and its towers. But the castle must have been the first and oldest structure, the rest of the city having grown up around it.

A horse-drawn chariot pulled up before them. Four of the giant thursar-bred horses, such as those that had carried them from Baldur's Beach, tossed their matched white heads and their silver manes before it. And the cart itself was made of a rich, brown wood, with stylized frescoes carved into it. Vidar did not look close at the carving-work, but he had a good idea that it would depict one battle or another between the Aesir and the hrimthursar. It was an ever-popular theme.

They stepped up into the chariot—Modi, Vidar, Stim, Buri and Eric—and turned up the road. Like a parade down Main Street, thought Vidar, as the driver clucked to the horses, and they picked up a little speed over the cobble-stones.

Vidar watched the faces of the people. Young and old, they peered at the cart from beneath homespun cowls and out of haggard faces. But many of them smiled, and there was chatter as the emissaries from Asgard went by. The humans got down on their knees. The thursar, who were fewer than the humans among the temporary shelters, merely inclined their heads with respect. Only those who belonged to Skatalund's garrison, marked by their armor, knelt when the chariot passed. Vidar wished he could decipher those craggy, expressionless faces. None of the thursar, he noticed, had remained with the human guards at the gates.

He asked Stim why this was so. The thursar said, "We are there when the need arises. Until then, our clans need us more at home."

The chariot brought them to the courtyard of the castle, where they passed two young sentinels, apparently stationed there for show more than anything else. They disembarked, trying to avoid the puddles that had collected among the uneven stones.

Eric guided them into a vestibule, where Vidar was able to hand his cloak over to an attendant. It was good to get out of the rain and close the door against the wind. Stim took his leave of them there, bowing his hulk of a body before the two Aesir as he departed for his clan's hearth.

Eric took off his helmet, smoothing back a shock of yellow hair, but left his byrnie on. Then he led them up a broad flight of stairs—darkwood steps, covered with woven carpet, and banisters chased with hunting motifs—to a high-ceilinged hall with long, narrow windows set into the stone. No one casually crossed their path; no one was startled by their appearance. The court had obviously been prepared for their arrival.

The floor of this hall was carpeted, too, and ancient tapestries graced the walls. Though there were braziers set between the windows, they were not lit, and the only light they could see by was that dismal quantity that filtered in through the southern exposure. There was a dank but homey smell to the place, and it reminded Vidar of the rainy, melancholy days of his youth—when he traced the rain-drops on a window with his finger, and knew he'd have to hone the healing art that day instead of his sword's edge.

They were a sorry echo of those days just then. Modi was still bandaged around his middle, and his late exertions, Vidar saw, had soaked the dressing with blood where he had sustained the wound. His tunic was drenched; his hair and great, red beard were matted; his boots sodden and his face streaked with mud. Mjollnir was stuck into his belt like an old broadaxe. His pallor was back, and he looked as if he might slump to the ground at any given moment.

For his own part—Vidar knew how he must appear. What would these people make of the Levi's brand on his rear end? What legends would come of that? He carried the bright blue backpack strung over one shoulder, hoping no one would take much notice of it.

Buri kept a pace behind them, another strange sight. A nomad in the castle of Skatalund, and one whose kinsmen were trying to burn down this very castle. But if Buri was a strange sight in this place, the place was a stranger sight for him. His black, bright eyes darted this way and that, as if warriors would spring at him out of the walls themselves and end his madness—he, who had trusted in an Aesirlord.

Truth be told, only Eric had the look of dignity about him. His back was straight and his step was lively, and his byrnie caught what there was of the light and threw it back in silver shadows upon the walls.

A great pair of wooden doors, carved with the sun and the moon and a field of stars, stood open at the hall's end. Once through these, Vidar found his party in a somewhat narrower hall, with more tapestries, but no windows. Eric indicated the first door on the left.

"Your room, my Lord Modi," he said and went down on his knee. Modi pushed the door open and peered inside.

"Not half bad," he said, managing a smile. Then, "I think I'll rest up a while, Vidar. See you later." And he went inside, shutting the door behind him.

Eric then showed Vidar his own room—opposite Modi's—and Buri was given the room beyond Vidar's. Eric did not flinch as he met Buri's gaze, but he did not go out of his way to be courteous, either. After the nomad had stalked wonderingly into what might have been his first knowledge of a roofed bedchamber, Eric opened Vidar's door for him. He knelt. "My lord, we hope that it will suit you," he said.

"Arise," said Vidar. "I wish you wouldn't kneel before me—it makes me nervous. And as for the room, I'm sure it will be fine, thanks."

Eric rose, inclined his head and returned down the hall by which they'd come. Vidar smiled, entering his chamber and closing the door. Even when he'd ridden at Odin's left hand, accepting worship had been the least of his pleasures. Now it gave him the feeling an audience feels when an actor flubs his lines. He was embarrassed by it.

He breathed a sigh of relief, leaned against the door and surveyed his quarters. The room was large, with high windows, a fireplace and big, woven rugs on the flagstone floor—but the Plaza, it wasn't. The furnishings were simple—a bed, ornately carved, a table and a chair. The table legs and the chair had also been worked into fantastic forms and ancient runes, but they were worn down with time's passage. Most important of all, there was a tub at the far end of the room, and steam rose from it in delicious billows.

There was also a change of clothing laid neatly on the bed, and Vidar was eager to remove his hiking boots. They had become waterlogged, and the mud was caked thick on them. He dragged them off with a groan, and wriggled his half-numb toes. He pulled his sweatshirt over his head and stripped off his jeans. Finally, he laid the backpack under his bed—for the time being. Then he sank into the wooden bathtub.

The water had been laced with aromatics. Vidar welcomed the heat and the heady scent. He felt the tension of his night ride and the lash of the storm recede from his muscles, and the musk of northern woodlands cleared his head.

His thoughts returned to that night—was it days ago, now?—in Woodstock, when he'd received Modi's call for help. The events that followed flowed through his memory like leaves on the wind. The flight to Athens, the cave, his encounter with Buri, Baldur's Beach. The recovery of the hammer.

Vidar paused in his reflections. It had been gnawing at him since he'd bolted from Ygg's tent. The grip he had finally broken—the strength of whoever wore that mask— was like no other he'd ever come across. Hod had never been that strong. He might have found a way to increase his power while in hiding. But he was apt to seek other ways than the physical to build his strength, ways that were more to his liking.

If not Hod, who else? No human or thursar could be so powerful, and Vidar doubted that even a half-blood Aesirman could have pinned him to the ground so quickly.

There was Magni. But he had neither the might nor the motivation. He was apparently just as adamant about being left alone to his own sphere as Vidar had been—although Magni had entertained Vali and Modi on various occasions. Or so Modi had said. Perhaps that was the price of autonomy.

Hoenir? He had the powers all right—but Vidar couldn't picture him at the head of a boy scout troop, much less a marauding army. Still, Hoenir was an unknown quantity until he turned up.

Vidar rose from the water, which was starting to lose its warmth, and toweled off with a piece of white fur left beside the tub for that purpose. The bath had done wonders for him. He had almost forgotten there was a siege going on outside.

He walked to the bed, shivering slightly, and pulled a cloak onto his shoulders, wrapping it about him. Had the room gotten colder? He saw that the fire in the hearth needed some more wood, so he padded across the flagstones on bare feet to replenish it. Then something on the mantle above the fire caught his eye. The flagstones were cold beneath his feet, but there was something colder inside his stomach as he recognized what had drawn him.

There, resting on the mantle, stood a large, stone icon. It was a not-so-crude representation of Vali—no doubt that it was Vali—and he held Gungnir, Odin's spear, at arm's length above his head.

Once, men had carved Odin in such a stance. It was the Val-father's battle position, as the mask had been his battle visage. Vidar picked it up, turned it slowly in his hands. The workmanship was good. Vali would be pleased with so fine a sculptor.

Vidar could not say why that figure chilled him as it did. Perhaps it was the way Vali had stepped into Odin's shoes, picking up where he had left off. Perhaps it was the shock of seeing Vali again—for it was an uncanny likeness—and remembering how cruel he could be. Perhaps it was both those things and more.

"No matter," Vidar whispered. He replaced the icon on the mantlepiece.

Ragnarok had not been enough to wipe out the evil in the universe. It had only pruned it.

Then he went back to the bed and stretched out next to the dry clothing, wrapped in the cloak. He dreamed of Heimdall, Asgard's sentinel, at Ragnarok. Once again, his half brother's ruined face turned up toward him, a horrible gash across his handsome cheek and temple. He spoke his last words, and then blood spilled over the verge of his lips like wine from a too-full goblet. But his eyes remained open, fixing him with their power. And they were Baldur's eyes. . . .

X

How many of you have heard of the giantess Skadi? No one had more right to revenge than she. Her father, Thiazi, had been taken captive in a raid on Asgard, and instead of being put to death quickly, he had been burned slowly at a stake.

Even the hrimthursar were not so cruel to their captives, thought Skadi, as she donned her father's iron helmet. For she was not as other maidens—Skadi was trained as a warrior, since Thiazi had had no sons, and she meant to avenge her father's ugly death by the strength of her own hands. She took Thiazi's spear and Thiazi's sword and one of Thiazi's horses and, by her courage and her spirit, gathered other giants to her cause.

She led her army up through the towering, black rocks and the shrieking winds and the bludgeoning hail of Jotunheim, through the broad gate that Heimdall guarded and into the pleasing sunshine of Asaheim. The watchman of the Aesir saw Skadi's host come through the gate like a riptide, and he knew that he was no match for so great a force. Nor could he endanger the unprepared Aesir by winding Gjallar-horn. But he fulfilled his charge and rode straight to Odin's seat to warn him of the invasion.

In the meantime, Skadi's army swept down from the hills where Loki had once quarried stone, and trampled all that was underfoot—the grass, the brush, small animals and crawling things. In fact, she almost trampled Odin's son, Baldur, who had been sleeping in the warmth of the sun before he was awakened by the tumult of crashing hooves.

"Aha!" yelled Skadi. "The first of the Aesir to feel my wrath!" And she brought her spear of hard ash up over her head, meaning to pin Baldur to the ground where he sat. But the Aesirman known as the Just One even in Jotunheim gazed at Skadi with his mild eyes—and she never threw that spear. Instead, without knowing why, she lowered it. It was as if she had encountered a friend and not an enemy.

"Who are you?" she asked.

"I'm called Baldur," he said simply. "Of the Aesir. And I think it's my city, Asgard, that you mean to raid."

"This is no raid," said Skadi. "I come on a mission of revenge. The Aesir cooked my father like a pig on a spit, and I mean to do the same to them."

Then Baldur's brows met, as he realized that there was something unusual about this giant. "You're a female," he said, astonished. "Yet you carry a spear as if you were a warrior."

"My father had no sons to avenge him," said Skadi.

Baldur shook his head. "The Aesir will not fight you. There is no honor in slaying a woman."

"They'll have no choice," she said. "Either they'll

fight me or I'll lay such a siege as Asgard has never known."

Baldur searched Skadi's small, black eyes, and saw that she meant what she said. "It was cruel, what the Aesir did to Thiazi. I'll grant you that," said Odin's son. "But you will not receive justice here. My father and brothers will slay all your men and leave you alone unscathed, to make your way back to Jotunheim defeated and dishonored. It will be said that your enemy thought so little of you, he did not even bother to throw his spear in your direction."

"He'll have no choice but to aim his spear at me," said Skadi, "when he feels my cold breath on his throat and sees my sword beneath his chin."

"But is there a way to avoid this?" asked Baldur, standing in the meadow alone and unarmed before the thursar host. "What if you were to turn about and return home with Baldur as your captive? I would allow this, if I had your promise that you would release me a year from today, and let me return to Asaheim. Then you would have repaid your father's memory, by taking Odin's son home bound to your horse's tether. You will escape the dishonor I foresee for you. And both sides will be spared unneeded bloodshed."

Skadi pondered his suggestion. She could not deny what a pleasure it would be to hold Baldur for a year in her father's hall, where the corridors had filled with a cold and lonely wind since Thiazi's death. And Baldur was nothing if not handsome—more handsome than anything or anyone Skadi had ever seen. With him in Jotunheim, the nights need not be so fearsome and desolate.

Then she thought of her father roasting at the stake, and her heart hardened once more. "No," she said. "My sword hungers and not for Baldur. I've seen your goodness. I cannot hold you responsible for what happened to Thiazi. But your father will know that my father did not lack children to avenge him."

And with that, she roared and spurred her pony. The ground-shaking host of giants followed her, splitting asunder to avoid trampling the son of Odin—as a river will flow on either side of a rock in its bed.

The Aesir repelled that invasion, and many on both sides were slaughtered before the surviving hrimthursar fled back to Jotunheim.

But Skadi was not among them. When she saw that there was no hope of victory, she flung herself on an Aesirman's spearpoint.

And thus proved Baldur wrong.

Sin Skolding
Algron, 361 A.D.

XI

When Vidar woke, it was already dusk. He went to the window and watched the sun scuttle across the blood-red terrain of the horizon. Snow was falling lightly. Cold, he wrapped the cloak more tightly about him.

There was a knock at the door. "Yes?" he asked.

"It's Eric, my lord. Prince Olof sent me to tell you that a feast will be held soon in your honor. Will you come, my lord?"

"Yes," said Vidar, realizing how very hungry he was. "Of course I'll come. When will dinner be ready?"

"When you are, my lord," said Eric. "The Lord Modi has already gone to the feast hall."

"Wait for me, then, Eric. I'll be ready in a minute."

"Yes, my lord."

Vidar went to the bed and considered his new garments. They looked comfortable, and his Earth-clothes couldn't be dry yet. He pulled on a yellow, woolen tunic; black, woolen breeches; and long, soft leather boots. Over the tunic he tied on a leather jerkin, and fastened a leather belt studded with discs of gold around his waist. Replacing the cloak on his shoulders, he brooched it at the neck. He left the broad-sword they had given him in its sheath, on the bed, though the hilt was finely wrought.

Why were people always offering him swords?

Vidar strode to the door and—as his hand reached for the latch—cursed himself under his breath. He had almost forgotten the backpack. Kneeling, he drew it forth from under the bed. Ygg had lost the hammer by being so care-less. Standing, he hefted the contents in his hands. It would take but a moment to prevent curious eyes from finding it.

The energy for the task came from the horn itself. The aura Vidar created, drawing on that energy—much as he would draw on himself to heal someone—would bend the light rays about it so that it would simply vanish. At least, that would be the effect on the human eye. Since his powers of perception were a little more acute, he could still make out the shadow of a light blue backpack.

Then he put it back underneath the bed.

When he finally opened the door, Eric was leaning on the wall outside. The youth straightened abruptly as Vidar filled the doorway. He had changed his clothes and now wore an outfit similar to Vidar's.

Vidar smiled. "I'm ready for that feast now. But tell me something, Eric. Do you know that piece of sculpture on my mantle?"

Eric's brows knit. "Yes, my lord."

"Who fashioned it?"

The youth gulped visibly. "I did, my lord."

"You did?" Vidar chuckled. "Well done. The features are good. And the spear must have been difficult." Eric fairly beamed. "Have you ever seen Vali?"

Eric nodded carefully. "Just once, my lord. Years ago, when things were peaceful."

"He's a bit leaner than that, I think," said Vidar. "But

then, you've seen him more recently than I have. So where's this dinner?"

Eric smiled, like any artist vindicated by his critics. He led Vidar to the end of this hall and up a broad set of stairs. Here, the steps were not carpeted. But the tapestries that adorned the wall were newer, larger and more vibrant in their colors than the ones he had seen earlier.

The largest of all depicted Ragnarok. Fenrir, shown here as a half wolf, half thursar with slavering jaws, brought Odin down. Loki stood ready to finish him with deadly fire. Surtur slew Frey and Jormungand felled Thor, but Modi wrested the hammer from his sire's fingers in order to shatter Jormungand's skull and avenge the Thunderer's death. At the center stood Heimdall, winding the horn and drawing the blade that would kill Loki from its sheath. The battlefield was strewn with the corpses of Aesir, Vanir and hrimthursar.

It was strange, thought Vidar, how Midgard-human mythology had transformed Surtur into a fire-demon, Jormungand into a world-spanning serpent and Fenrir into a huge wolf. Here, so much closer to the Aesir of their legends, the Utgard-humans had only erred to the extent that they had confused Fenrir with his father's wolf pack. Jormungand and Surtur were depicted as thursar warlords, which was no more or less than the truth.

At the top of the stairs, they continued on down a short corridor. The smell of roasted meat and mead accosted them there, and Vidar knew that the feast hall could not be too much farther. At the end of the corridor, the noise of men's oaths and knives and drinking horns reached them. They made a turn to the right, and the light blazing from the firepits flooded their path.

The feast hall spread before them, huge, high-ceilinged and spanned with great arches, filled to the wooden rafters with dense cooking smoke. All along the gray walls stood an armed honor guard of human soldiers. The hall was filled with long oak tables, at which were seated the pride of

Skatalund—nobles and high-ranking officers, from the look of them. Between each two men sat a noble lady, graced with a gown of soft fabric, dyed in a merry hue—green, gold, red or blue. There were no thursar among them, however.

At the rear of the hall stood a tremendous firepit with three large deer, skewered end to end, being roasted over leaping flames. Behind the firepit sprawled the largest board of all, evidently the prince's table, perpendicular to all the rest.

When Vidar entered, all heads turned his way, and there was a resounding shuffle as men freed themselves from their seats to bend their knees. From around the hearth came two figures—one, a tall and lanky man, with a silver-gray beard that still had streaks of gold in it, wore a long, flowing green cloak and tunic, but his head was bare of any ornament. The other wore a simple, black robe, but a circlet of yellow gold rested on his head, and his beard was cut close to his jawline. His expression was one of mild curiosity—almost mocking.

"My lord," said the man in the green cloak, "I am Prince Olof, your servant. And this is our high priest, Noggi." The black-robed one inclined his head slightly, then brought his eyes up again to fix them on Vidar's. He looked a bit like Bragi, and perhaps he was so descended, but there was no doubt in Vidar's mind. This was Vali's man, his half-Aesir spy in Skatalund.

"I hope you will honor me," Olof continued, "by eating at my table."

"Of course," said Vidar. "The pleasure will be mine." Then a bear of a man rose up from behind the red glow and shimmering heat waves of the pit. It was Modi.

"Jawbreaker! It's about time you got here," he bellowed. "I'm hungry enough to eat these fancy boots they gave me." Like Vidar, Modi had been given fresh garb. But he still wore the belt he had come in with, and Mjollnir tucked into it. In his right hand he held a long, ivory drinking horn. Though he might have refrained from eating until Vidar arrived—no doubt at his host's suggestion—there had been no such prohibition of mead.

"My lord?" said Olof and indicated the table. Vidar half smiled and followed the prince to his seat. Modi sat on Olof's right hand, the place of highest honor, befitting his status in Asgard. Vidar sat on his left and Noggi sat next to Vidar. Eric knelt before Olof's board, turned and took his place at one of the other tables.

"What do you think of my son, Lord Vidar?" asked Olof, watching Eric go.

"Your son? I did not know," said Vidar. "But I did notice his skill as a sculptor."

Olof smiled, as if surprised. "Yes, a sculptor. But a fine warrior, too, and my successor. Someday. His mother taught him to work with stone before she died, and when I see him chipping away I think of her, my lord. But sculpting is a boyish thing, not fit for man's hands. It's all right to play with such things when one is young—yet the world has not changed so much since my grandfather's days, when Barri was unified under one bloody prince—him. Eric is named after that warlike man. When I die, there will be vassals itching for my throne—and Eric will have to defend it, with Vali's blessing."

Vidar nodded politely, in no mood to argue the relative merits of slaughter and sculpture. But in glancing about the feast hall, he saw no sign of Buri.

"Where is my thursar companion?" he asked Olof. "Was he not invited to share your board?"

Before Olof could answer, Noggi interjected. "He was invited, my lord," said the high priest. "But he preferred to eat in his room. The thursar are not much for feasting— especially the nomads. Even our giant comrades here in Skatalund prefer their own hearths to this one. They are strange that way."

"Aye, my lord," said Olof, since Noggi had already spoken for him. Odin's son looked past the prince, however, and met the high priest's eyes.

"You would not deceive me, would you, Noggi?" Vidar asked.

"I, my lord?" said Noggi, without dismay.

Then the deer-laden spit was lifted from its place over the fire by four strapping men, stripped bare to the waist, and three butchers fell to carving the meat. "Ho, Gulda," roared the prince. "I can't wait for the venison—send in the rest of the food while we're waiting."

With a sign from Gulda, one of the butchers, a troop of serving men and maids filed in, carrying platters of pork, savory bird and smoked fish, with great jugs of mead and pitchers of tawny wine. Suddenly, the place seemed to fill with wonderful smells, and Vidar's stomach rumbled.

Wasn't there a siege going on outside?

"Have you so much food that we can feast like this, even with Ygg at your gates?" he asked Olof.

The prince turned to Vidar and his gray brows knit. "My lord, I hope that I have not offended you."

"What the prince means," said Noggi, leaning forward, "is that we do not wish to mock the souls of those whom Ygg has slain with our feasting. But we felt that so great an occasion as the coming of the gods to slay this demon, the arrival of the Aesir—warranted nothing less. As for our food stores, will they not be replenished when the sons of Odin bring Ygg to his knees?"

"Aye, Ygg," Olof spat. "We spend generations building roads, tilling the fields, spanning streams with bridges and setting aside land in which to hunt, where no man or thursar may put up a dwelling. And then Ygg appears out of nowhere, firing up the nomads to tear it all down. As if it were not a better life for them as well as us!" Olof pounded his fist on the table, making the boards shiver. "Where's that mead?"

A frightened serving maid filled Olof's horn almost instantly, and the horns of his guests about him. Modi drained his at a gulp, and wiped the dregs from his beard with the back of his hand.

"A song!" Modi howled, and the whole hall went dead-silent for a heartbeat. Then everyone was calling for a song, and the skald emerged from his shadowed corner, where he had been sitting all along. He stood before Olof, softly strumming his harp, and the flames that still danced in the firepit seemed to set his long hair and shoulders on fire. A brown-haired young man, recently bearded, he wore a blood-red tunic and black leggings, and his face was as thin and sharp as a crescent moon.

The skald began to sing, and Vidar saw that he was a man of no mean talent. He drained a horn of mead, the golden liquid pouring into him like mellow fire, and he listened closely to the words. It was a song of Hermod, Odin's son, who rode his father's steed down into Hel to plead for the release of Baldur. And even Hel herself—the bard's words rang, striking off stone—felt sadness in her heart. So much sadness, unaccustomed as she was to any emotion at all, that she agreed to release the god whom all loved—if indeed all loved him. When all of Creation wept for Baldur, he might return to the fields of Asaheim.

Hermod told this to Frigga, Baldur's mother—who also had given birth to his murderer, Hod, and his avenger, Vali—and she roamed the wide world over, her arms wrapped around Hermod's middle as his horse's hooves ate great distances. And at a word from Frigga, men wept for Baldur—strong men, who had never wept before nor would again. Trees wept, the sap running in sticky rivulets down their bark. The bear wept and the wolf, the deer and the rabbit, the serpent and the swine.

But then Frigga and Hermod came to the cave of an old, old woman—a woman so old even the stones did not remember her birthday. "Will you weep for my Baldur?" asked

Frigga. And the woman replied, "What does your Baldur mean to me? Let him stay in death's home, where the wind cuts like a knife. I will not weep."

And Hermod would have slain her then and ended her too-long life, but Frigga stayed his hand. "We have found the coldest heart of all here," she said. "And I know her. Whenever I did not feed a starving bird, I gave her strength. And whenever I sent a maiden crying out of spite, I gave her sustenance. She is me, my cruelty, and it is I who have doomed my son."

It was different from the Midgard version, thought Vidar—but strangely beautiful. And when it had ended, and all the food had been passed out and horns refilled, the skald knelt. Olof tossed him a coin, which he caught in midair, and he rose to go.

"Wait," said Noggi. "I would hear another song, and this one of Heimdall, my ancestor."

The skald smiled, tucked his coin away in a pouch at his belt, and set to strumming again. It was dawn, he sang, at the gate that led from Asaheim to Jotunheim, and Heimdall, the guardian of the Aesir, had watched the gate for two days and three nights. He was tired, but his relief had not yet arrived. The birds sang a tune for the morning. They sang so sweetly, in fact, that he became mesmerized by their song—and for the first and last time in the gods' long memory, Heimdall fell asleep at his post.

Nor was it a shallow nap, but a deep sleep, and he dreamed of things to come but far away, off in time's distance. For Heimdall had the eyes of an eagle, and he could see farther than any creature living. He dreamed of a great battlefield, and he recognized Vigrid—the field before the city of the hrimthursar—where no Aesirman or Vanirman had yet tread. Though he had never seen it, he knew it. It was full of warriors and swords leaping and wolves rending and men crying out. And he saw his brothers, Odin's blood, die on that field.

Then Heimdall saw himself, holding a pack of huge, gray wolves at bay with his mighty sword. He was winding Gjallarhorn, and the towers of the giants were falling as he blew with all his strength. Loki emerged from the wolves' midst, and they fought, Heimdall and the greatest warrior among the hrimthursar, until they had torn each other to pieces. And afterward, when he lay cold and bleeding his lifeblood out on the white snow, Vidar the Jawbreaker came to him, and he said, "Here is the horn, brother. I have no more use for it. Wind it against our enemies. It will not die with me, the voice of Asgard."

Vidar started out of his seat, but it was too late. Now he knew why Olof had been so confident, even though Modi could not have had time to attune to the hammer. Somehow the prince knew that Vidar carried the horn.

It seemed all eyes were on him now, as the last bits of melody began to fade. Vidar felt his face redden.

Noggi rose and lifted his drinking horn. "To Vidar the Horn-bearer!" he cried, and the men of Skatalund echoed his toast to the smoky rafters.

Modi began to laugh, long and loud, and his laughter drowned out all the others'. "Jawbreaker, my uncle, even I was fooled! What a jest! To think that you had the horn all the time, and I never knew it!" His eyes, red-webbed with too much mead, opened wide as he leaned forward to see Vidar. "Even when you dropped that silly pack, I never caught on!" He thumped on his head with his knuckles. "How could I have been so stupid?"

Modi was still laughing when a fully armed soldier burst into the hall and skidded to a halt before Olof. The man was plainly frightened.

"My lord," he said, forgetting to kneel even before the Aesir. "Ygg has brought down the heavens against us!"

"What are you saying?" asked Olof, his eyes narrowing.

"The stars have been blotted out, my lord, and lightning covers the ground in great strides." As if to emphasize the man's words, a low rumble of thunder was heard even through the thick, stone walls.

Olof, perhaps a little drunk, turned to Vidar and then to Modi. "Don't worry, Hammung," he said to the messenger. "The greatest weapons of Asgard are on our side." Then he rose, sweeping aside his cloak. "To the walls! Let's be rid of Ygg once and for all."

Modi dragged the hammer from his belt and raised it high in the air. "Follow me!" he cried and vaulted over the table. It was not a graceful motion, but he cleared the board and lurched forward. The court of Skatalund indeed followed right after him, emptying the hall.

Vidar poured out with the rest of them, trying to shake off the effects of the mead. Ygg had brought a storm from somewhere—and Hod was an elemental, a *stromrad*. It was within his power to do that, and to do it subtly, so that the force of the storm was upon them before they knew it.

Outside, the rain had stopped, but a strong scent of ozone permeated the wintry night air. One look at the heavens indicated why the garrison had become so frightened. Clouds roiled over one another like the coils of a monstrous, blue-gray serpent. Lightning whipped across the sky every which way. There was nothing natural about this display of elemental fury.

But the full strength of it had not yet been unleashed. Vidar had been around *stromrads* enough to know that until the wind blew and the rain fell, the sky-serpent was not ready to strike.

Vidar ran out of the courtyard, through the cobblestone streets, and the men of Skatalund made way for him. He reached the walls ahead of most. Then he clambered up a ladder to the ramparts of the inner barrier, where Modi and Olof already stood, gulping for air after their long run.

"It's almost upon us," said Modi. "We need the horn, Vidar, and quickly."

Vidar looked out on the plain, with its seething, dark

clouds above and its sea of black tents below. He shook his head. "Can't do it, Modi."

The son of Thor whirled on him, and Olof looked fearfully over Modi's shoulder. "What do you mean?" he roared. "I haven't had time to attune to the hammer yet. Even these people know that."

Vidar licked his lips. "Those are Buri's people out there. I gave my word I would not destroy them."

Modi took a step toward him, the hammer in his white-fisted hand. "You're joking, right? Don't tell me that you have pity after what they did in Dundafrost. Don't tell me that you'll not lift a finger to save these people here. Don't tell me that, Vidar."

"I didn't bring it here for that," said Vidar. "I brought it to keep it from being used that way. Look, Modi, we can get everybody inside the castle. The walls will hold. How long can Ygg keep this up?"

"Are you insane?" Modi bellowed, shaking the hammer. Only the ever-approaching thunder bawled louder.

"No, damn it," Vidar cried. "Those are not our enemies out there—they're pawns, children playing at war. There's just one enemy, and the horn will murder them all. Don't you remember what it can do, Modi?"

"Aye, I remember," said Modi. Lightning flashed, lighting up half his savage face. "I remember Heimdall's words—'Slay Asgard's enemies with it.'"

"Heimdall would not have done this," said Vidar. "He did not take the horn's power lightly. He wound it but once, and only when the world was coming to an end."

"Coward!" Modi spat. "You're just afraid to wind the horn, afraid to do what must be done."

"No," said Vidar, steeling with the accusation. "I'm afraid not to, just as you are. We're all afraid. But I'll take my chances before I'll kill thousands out of hand. Vali's got to be on his way, right? We can hold out until then."

Thunder crashed overhead. "Then if you won't," said Modi, "I will." Vidar saw that he meant it.

"Too late," said a voice in their brains.

"Who was that?" Modi muttered.

"I don't know," said Vidar.

"It is the one who holds Gjallarhorn in his hands—I, Noggi."

The mental voice was faint, as a full-blooded Aesirman's would have been clear. But it was strong enough for Noggi's purpose.

"Vali thought you might be reluctant to wind the horn," said the high priest. "So I took it upon myself."

"No!" cried Vidar out loud. Then he made contact with Noggi. "Where are you?"

"Somewhere you won't find me," said the half-breed.

"Listen," said Vidar. "You can't wind the horn."

"Why not? I'm more than half-Aesir. It's in my blood."

"Because you're not attuned to it. You're not a healer, and you haven't had the time even if you were."

"So?"

"The horn will not discriminate between friend and enemy," said Vidar. "It will kill us all, even you."

"And you think I'll believe you? You, the coward that stole it from Asgard in the first place?"

Vidar felt a breeze ruffle his hair. "Ask Modi."

There was silence for a moment, while Vidar stared at Thor's giant of a son.

"Answer, damn you," he whispered.

"It makes sense," Modi said to Noggi. "That's more or less how it would work with Mjollnir."

Noggi seemed to be pondering this new information. "An intriguing trade-off," said Noggi. "We die, but so does Ygg. And all those cursed nomads."

"Are you insane?" asked Vidar. Could he really mean to kill them all?

"Who are you to call me mad, Vidar? Can I do less for the love of Asaheim than my forebears did on Vigrid? What is my life against the security of Asgard?"

"What about our lives?" asked Vidar. "And those of Skatalund? Would you slay your own people to get at Ygg?"

"These? My people?" There was a pause. "The Aesir are my people. These are just . . . mortals."

"You are their priest," said Vidar.

"You know what I am," said Noggi. "I'm Vali's spy."

"But . . ."

"Enough! I must wind the horn now."

"Wait!" Vidar screamed in his mind. He clenched his fists in anticipation of Gjallarhorn's blast.

"Yes?"

"I'll do it," said Vidar. "It was charged to me."

"You're trying to trick me," said Noggi. "I'm not that much of a fool."

"I mean it. If I wind it, at least Skatalund will survive. At least, it should. If you wind it, we will all die."

"Swear," said Noggi. "Swear and I'll believe you."

"I swear," said Vidar.

"Not enough," said Modi, interrupting. "He swore not to wind the horn on another occasion. This must be a stronger oath than that one, Noggi."

"Whose side are you on?" Vidar asked out loud.

"My own," said Modi. "Of course."

"Well?" Noggi was getting impatient. "Are you backing down?"

"No," said Vidar, watching the sky-serpent undulate its bloated, purplish belly. "I swear. On my right to Midgard."

Modi nodded, satisfied. "He's not kidding, Noggi. He loves that wasteland more than you love Asgard."

"Done," said Noggi. "I'm in the prince's study, in the old watchtower. But I won't wait long."

XII

From his vantage point high up in the old watchtower, Vidar could turn to the west and still see stars where the sky-serpent had not yet strangled them with its coils. A light drizzle had started while he was climbing the stairs to reach Noggi and the horn, and the wind, more than a breeze now, was cold with mountain hoarfrost.

A numbness had grown in his brain, as the realization of what he had sworn himself to nudged closer and closer to his psyche and finally hunkered down like an unwelcome houseguest. There was no turning it out now. It would not leave until he had done what it demanded.

He looked at the ancient horn in his hands. It was the oldest thing he knew, created so long ago that even Odin had not been able to remember its making. Gjallarhorn belonged to the time before the Aesir, when there was nothing—just the colorless Void and the icy cold of eternity.

If the theft of the hammer had caused an uproar among Ygg's followers, it had subsided by now. Or he just could not hear it. The heavy, writhing cloud-cover absorbed nearly all the sound in the world, it seemed. Only infrequently did he catch a shout of warning in the streets of Skatalund below.

One blast and it would all be over. Hod—or whoever— would be dead. The threat to Asgard would be stifled. Ska- talund, relieved of the invaders at its gates. Modi, free to wander; Vali, happy on his throne. Was that not the way it should be? And if he were not a coward, would he not have done this sooner? His mind felt ice-locked. He could not think.

Soon, he could take Gjallarhorn and go home. This time, forever, and no threat or taunt would rouse him from Earth. He had forgotten what his family was like—but now that he'd had a refresher course, he knew he had been right to seek isolation. And Earth was as good a place as any.

Was there a flaw in that logic? Something in Vidar rose uneasily—but it was quickly stilled. No matter.

Vidar stared at the scattered campfires of the nomads, pinpoints of fire against the fabric of their black encampment. It was time. If only those campfires did not burn so brightly . . .

He raised Gjallarhorn to his lips.

And he blew softly, at first, listening to the eerie timbre that sounded at once like horses dying and gateposts crack- ing and the world wrenching loose from its foundations. It got into his blood, set his heart pounding, stole the strength from his arms and legs—until he was the horn and the horn was him, one entity, blind and senseless, roaring one vast obscenity against the endless, dripping Silence.

The cry grew within him, and a part of him heard it reverberating from the walls of Skatalund to the distant hills, like a huge wave that broke upon the sky and the plain, shattering sanity beneath its impossible weight.

The tiny figures of the thursar burst from their black tents, holding their heads with their hands, twisting in agony.

Then, the one, pure note, the exquisite, piercing bird cry

of death—the truth, against which all effort is blasphemy. The Ginnungagap, the pit, sundered to bring forth life, and its own end written in the blood of its afterbirth. The madness . . . the horror, unending sadness and torture. The shattering . . . the rapture . . .

He remembered what it was like to be a god. He was a mountain, as ancient as time and rooted in the heart of the world, shrugging clouds and shouldering winds. Somewhere at his feet, mortals—the dead, the dying, the yet-to-be-born—ran down his slopes, bleeding rivers.

It sickened him. His head swam with his immeasurable power, his infinity. He was Vidar, Jawbreaker, Leathershod, Wolfbane. He was Aesir, Odin's child, heir to power.

And in one, dark moment, he knew why he had brought the horn here in the first place. Hadn't he always intended to use it so?

After a time, it came away from his lips, that cornucopia of blood—slowly, yet its song still echoed from the sky to the hills and back again, let loose upon the world. His throat was torn, peeled raw by the blast. Suddenly he felt that all the strength had gone out of him. His knees threatened to buckle. Vidar put a hand out to steady himself against the wall.

There was a sound behind him. Wearily, as vertigo pulled at him, he turned and saw Buri. The giant's bulk blotted out the darkness of the stairway behind him. He held a sword, point glistening in the meager light, and unbloodied.

"You said that there would be no bloodshed," Buri growled. "You swore not to use the power." He took a step forward.

Vidar clung to consciousness. The room spun dizzily about him and beads of sweat ran down one side of his face.

"I betrayed everything," said Buri. "I was worse than a coward. Ygg was right . . ." He took another step forward and raised the sword. His eyes were black pits. And, madness of madnesses, he smelled of the blossoms in the gorge.

"...only the Aesir can lie without fear." Vidar fell to one knee. The horn slipped from his grasp and clattered against stone. Somewhere beyond this nightmare, he heard— or thought he heard—the faint call of distant trumpets.

Then Buri fell upon him. The final insanity was the warm softness of death.

XIII

Light. Vidar shut his eyes, turned away. Squinting, he looked about. It was the room he had been given by Prince Olof. He brought his legs over the side of the bed.

His head hurt. And his bones ached. He stood up a little shakily and saw that a small basin had been left for him on the mantle, next to the sculpture of Vali. His boots were still on his feet, he noticed.

Averting his face from the sunbeams that streamed in through his window, Vidar stumped over to the basin. Taking it into his hands, he lowered his whole face into the cold embrace of the water. It shook some of the cobwebs loose in his head, but his body still felt like wrack and ruin.

Buri . . . What happened? Had he been a hallucination born of weakness? He put the basin down again. Vali's sculpted face stared at him—haughty, penetrating, unapproachable, even as he lifted his spear. Cold as a mackerel, thought Vidar, although Eric had left that out of the likeness.

Somewhere in the back of his mind, a voice reminded

him that he had done something monstrous—but he ignored it. There was time enough to ponder that. Guilt had a patience all its own.

The door opened, and Vidar whirled at the unbidden entry. But when he saw who it was, the warmth drained from his face.

"Welcome, brother," said Vali the Avenger. He was tall and elegant in full battle gear, minus the helm. His hawkish features were in repose, and his golden-brown beard caught bright strands of morning light. But he had not changed—not really. He was still as lean-boned as a timber wolf, with a wolf's hooded eyes and hungry look. He surveyed Vidar quickly, casually. "I can't remember the last time I saw your face, Jawbreaker."

"Yes you can," said Vidar, striving to shrug off the weariness that clung to him like a sodden cloak. "It was when you assumed the throne of Asgard. You remember everything, Vali."

"So I do. May I come in, Vidar?"

"Why not?" said Vidar. "My home is your home."

Vali lowered his head slightly in acknowledgment and strode across the room to sit on the edge of Vidar's bed. "Won't you have a seat, too, Vidar? I left the chair for you."

Vidar shook his head. "I'm quite comfortable here," he said, "by this fine likeness of you."

Vali saw the statuette for the first time. He smiled, and his living countenance gave way to a host of subtle changes. He transformed his thin, angular face, putting on his mask of delight.

"Excellent. I agree—it is a fine likeness." Then his eyes fell on Vidar. "You, on the other hand, are a poor likeness of yourself. Winding the horn seems to have sapped your strength, brother."

Perhaps it was an intonation in Vali's voice, or a movement in the skin around his eyes. Perhaps it was the mere mention of the horn. But suddenly, the world clicked back into place. Vidar flushed angrily.

"You've played me for a fool, haven't you, Vali?"

His half brother shrugged. "Did you expect I wouldn't try? I owe the success of my gambit to your deprivation in Midgard—the old Vidar would have sniffed it out immediately."

Vidar knew he was right. "I dug up Gjallarhorn and brought it here like a dog fetching a bone." Vidar fashioned a half smile.

Vali said nothing.

"Then I wound it, like an obedient lackey. It was your subconscious suggestion all the time, wasn't it? And I never questioned why I had brought it along in the first place, much less why I would want to break my vow to the thursar and murder with it."

"You made a vow to Heimdall, too. At least, the old Vidar did." Vali's smile did not fade.

"So I did. But I wonder whom Heimdall would have called the enemy of Asgard in this instance—this son of Odin or that one."

Vali shrugged again. "As a loyal Aesirman, he would have wound the horn in the name of Asgard. And I, Vidar, in case you haven't noticed—I am Asgard."

"Hard not to notice that, Vali. You haven't changed much at all. Did you bring all of Asaheim with you to crush this wretched Ygg?"

"A portion, Vidar. The better part, the warriors that still bear more than a drop of Aesir or Vanir blood. And there are more of those than you might guess. Asgard is not quite what it was when we grew up in Odin's hall, Vidar—but it has come a long way since the shambles you saw last. I restored the old ideals before they could become lost—the ideals with which Odin built his empire."

Vidar nodded. "Cruelty, bloodshed and oppression."

Vali smiled. "Among others. You can't forge a sword without bathing it in fire, Vidar. For Asgard to exist, there must be war. Someone, something against which to strive. I realized that even before I assumed the throne. It had been Odin's best quality—the ability to turn our energies first this way and then that, so that we never fought among ourselves. As long as there were enemies, Asgard would stand."

"Isn't that a little cold-blooded, Vali? Wouldn't it be a challenge to rule without enemies, without wars, without scapegoats? Even Odin couldn't work that magic."

"Pretty words, Vidar. But that would be the end of Asgard as surely as Hod's armies. Without wars, can there really be an Asgard? What would become of us then? We would turn flaccid and spindly under the worst kind of plague—the ravages of peace."

"Kingship fits you like a glove, Vali. You're every inch Odin's son."

"I don't let petty moralities stand in my way, if that's what you mean," said Vali calmly. "Wasn't it a philosopher of Midgard that said, 'Every morality is a bit of tyranny against nature,' Vidar?"

"Nietzsche," said Vidar. "But he also said this: 'Whoever fights monsters should see to it that in the process he does not become a monster. And when you look long into an abyss, the abyss also looks into you.'"

"Stroke and counterstroke," said Vali. "I'm glad to see that your wits haven't abandoned you altogether."

"You've been to Midgard, then," said Vidar. "How else could you have known of Nietzsche?" The pieces of the puzzle—those he had not quite found until then—fit into place. "You were in Midgard when I went to help Modi, weren't you? Of course. You couldn't have entered my mind across the worldspan, so you had to be in the vicinity." Vidar laughed at his own naivete.

"True, brother. I was on your world. But I'll anticipate

your next question and tell you I cannot give you a reason for my presence there. I will say that Modi's wounding and his message to you came at a fortuitous time for me, since I was able to enter your mind at that point. I could not have planned such a thing, of course."

Vidar shook his head. "Of course. What about this Ygg character? Did he turn out to be Hod?"

Vali was silent for a moment. The mask of delight dropped, and he was once again expressionless, withdrawn behind stony battlements. "Hod," he said then, "seems to have escaped. I don't quite know how, but he was not among the tents we searched."

Vidar was stunned. How could Hod—or anyone—have escaped the music of Gjallarhorn? His surprise, however, was tempered with a sprinkling of satisfaction at Vali's consternation.

"But you've beaten him, haven't you?" said Vidar. "You've won anyway."

"Not necessarily," said Vali. "There are other thursar armies gathering elsewhere—we know that. If he can reach them, he'll be twice as dangerous as before, because he'll find a way to protect them as he protected himself." Vali paused for a moment again and fixed Vidar on the spit of his gaze.

"Will you help in the fight against him, Vidar? This time, of your own volition? Will you join us?"

"You and Modi?"

"Yes. And Hoenir."

"Hoenir? When did he turn up?"

"Days ago. In Utgard, when he heard about the trouble we were having here."

"Just like that?"

"I think you're evading the question, Vidar. Will you ride with us or not?"

"Not. I don't hold with your ideals, Vali. And I've no desire to help you in your sibling rivalry." He saw Vali's lips tighten across his teeth for just a second. "Is revenge so important now? Baldur has been dead so long, I can hardly remember what he looks like."

Vali smiled, unexpectedly. "Hod has become more to me than just an object of revenge. He has become the enemy I've been waiting for. A true threat to Asgard—one I didn't have to look for. If he hadn't shown up this way, I might have had to invent him. But he did. You've seen his handiwork. He's powerful, Vidar—more powerful than when he left. And you have a stake in his destruction, whether you like it or not. Or do you think Midgard will be spared when Hod marches across the worlds?"

Vidar remembered the sky-serpent and how quickly it had arisen. Then he shook his head. "No. Even with all his power and all his thursar, he can't stand up against you and Modi and Hoenir. Try talking to him. He must know he can't beat you. Or don't talk to him. Kill each other if you want. I'm going to take Gjallarhorn and go home."

For a moment, Vali said nothing, his aquiline eyes focusing on something beyond Vidar and this room that held them. "Wrong on both counts," he said finally.

"Meaning?" asked Vidar.

"Meaning you are either with us on the battlefield, or you stay here under guard—my guard. It really makes no difference to me, as long as you cannot tip the . . . odds . . . in Hod's favor."

"And Gjallarhorn?"

"Either way, it's mine now. I cannot trust anyone else with it, now that it's out in the open again. In fact, it should never have left."

"There's no middle ground, is there, Vali?"

The lord of Asgard shook his head. "Would it be any different if you were king, Vidar? I like all my enemies out in the open, where I can see them."

"In other words, I'm your enemy, too, now."

Vali shrugged. "Perhaps. Do you yourself know? Given

the opportunity, at some crucial moment..." His voice trailed off suggestively. "Temptation is a terrible thing."

Vidar shook his head. "Is this what Heimdall fought to preserve? Aesir against Aesir? Am I the best enemy you could find? Is Hod?"

"We've got enemies aplenty, Vidar. There's a world called Muspelheim that I came upon not too long ago, and it's not a lot different from Jotunheim, except for the climate. They're powerful there. They've raided Asgard more than once—after, of course, we raided them. And there are other enemies, perhaps more than we really need."

"All of which you sought out."

"How else to build an empire?"

"Then do you really need me? Do you think I abandoned Asgard because I wanted the throne? Would I be here now if you hadn't brought me?"

"I had hoped... you might join us, Vidar. Times have changed. For a while, I could allow you to wallow in your nasty little hovel of a world. Magni has done the same in Alfheim. But now even Magni has pledged me his allegiance, his sword, should it come to that. I can no longer accept any less."

Vali stood up. "Once you raised your voice for war, Vidar. You were the first to call for revenge in the councils after the hrimthursar ravaged Asgard. Now look at you—duped as easily as a calf, weak-hearted as a woman. Are *you* not the best proof of what I say? Only war makes us strong."

"What about the rest of the cosmos?" asked Vidar. "Utgard? Alfheim? Even this Muspelheim? Don't they have the right to practice a different philosophy?"

Vali put on the mask of good humor once more. "The right? They count the years, perhaps the decades, Vidar. We count the centuries, and even then we lose count. Only Asgard has the right to anything. All the other worlds are incidental."

"You sound like a man named Hitler, Vali. And you're making the same mistake he made. He didn't count on the possibility that even a Master Race might lose someday. Even Odin made that error, Vali, and now they're all gone— Heimdall, Frey, Thor, Hermod—they're all dead and forgotten. *They* were Asgard, not the towers you rebuilt or the halls you repopulated, or the swords you forged back together. And they're dead. You're just perpetuating a ghost— as Frigga did."

Vali stiffened visibly at that. For a heartbeat, Vidar thought he would draw his sword from its sheath. Then his half brother's face relaxed. "You've made your bed, Vidar," he said. "Now sleep in it." He turned toward the door.

"Irbor!" he snapped, and a tall, red-haired warrior appeared in the doorway. He carried a long spear and wore a broadsword at his hip. His broad nose and murky blue eyes spoke of his Vanir ancestry.

"This fellow is your charge now, Irbor," said Vali. "See to it that he does not escape and do himself harm. Oh, and Vidar," he added, addressing his half brother, "do not deceive yourself into thinking you can leave. Irbor and his brothers are descended from the blood of Frey and a woman of the Aesir, with very little dilution. They are not the weak mortals you are used to. Nor will the window be unguarded. Good day, brother."

Vali inclined his head slightly and left. After he had gone out of the room, Irbor stared at Vidar for a moment.

"Something wrong?" asked Vidar.

"I just wanted to see what a traitor looked like," said Irbor.

"Drop your spear and I'll show you what your intestines look like," said Vidar.

Irbor scowled. "Maybe some other time," he said. Then he exited and closed the door behind him.

Vidar looked about him. The sculpture of Vali seemed to be aiming its spear in his direction. He walked to the mantle, annoyed, and picked it up in one hand, raised it to dash it on the floor.

But no—it was Eric's work, and it wasn't fair to vent his frustration on another artist's creation. Eric . . .

He paused for a moment, his eyes narrowing. Then he realized that he still held the sculpture aloft, and he lowered it. Turning it about in the bright sunlight, he nodded to himself.

XIV

He finally found the one he sought in a cool, shadowed tavern in the depths of Skatalund, exchanging news with some of the other sentinels. It was not difficult to find purchase in the mind of another sculptor, though a true *baleyg* would have found it even easier.

"What are you saying, Eric?" asked a tall, narrow man with dark eyes.

"I say that I have my doubts," said Olof's son, and he kept his voice low.

"On what count?" asked another man, a blondbeard.

"On what is worse—Ygg's anger or Vali's generosity."

"That sounds too much like blasphemy, Eric," said a fourth man, older than the others.

"Don't worry," said Eric. "Priests don't drink in the taverns, last I looked."

The tall man nodded. "I know what you mean, Eric," he breathed. "Have you seen what happened to the thursar

114

out there? No? Well, I was one of the lucky ones sent out to search for Ygg. I have seen dead men before, but none such as these. Their mouths gaped open as if they still cried out their agony. And their eyes had rolled back into their heads." He paused. "Some still clasped their hands to their ears. Yrghhh!" He shivered visibly. "And the only blood about was a thin trickle from inside their brains—or where they had bitten through their lips."

"There are ways to die, but this is not one," said Eric. A silence descended on them. They sipped at their mead.

"But that was not Vali's doing," said the blondbeard. "It was that other one's."

Eric shrugged. "How do we know? They're gods. They do as they please and we clear out the bodies."

"I was glad to see them go," said the older man. "I breathed a lot easier when they were gone, and Gjallarhorn with them."

"But they are not all gone," said Eric.

"What do you mean?" asked the tall man.

"The Lord Vidar is still here—in the north corridor."

"He's the one that did it," said the blondbeard. "He frightens me most of all. Did you see how he was dressed when he came? Evil garb, I said to myself."

"But he does not stay of his own free will," rejoined Eric. "He is a . . . well, a prisoner, I think."

"Whose?" asked the older man, casting a surreptitious look about them.

"Lord Vali's," said Eric. "Who else's? There is a small army outside his door—nine guardsmen, I think—and at night three stand outside his window. Before he left, my father told me that all nine of them are descended from Frey."

"Frey died childless," said the older man, tracing a half-moon on his forehead.

The tall man clucked his tongue. "Superstitious, Orum,

aren't you? You need not fear even the gods once they are dead."

Orum glared at him. "Don't talk to me of fear, Tyrdall. If I were your age, I'd be ashamed not to have been chosen by Olof."

Tyrdall sipped at his mead. "Someone had to stay, in case more of the nomads showed up," said the tall man. "It's not my fault that I was picked to do the dirty work."

"That's true, Orum," said the blondbeard. "Do you think we're afraid to use our swords? It was the luck of the draw."

"Quiet down, all of you," said Eric. "It's bad enough that we have to stay here while our kinsmen soak up all the glory. Let's not bicker about it."

"You know," said the blondbeard, "we're no less imprisoned than the god in the castle. We can't leave any more than he can."

"Isn't that strange?" asked Orum. "I'm surprised that they can hold a son of Odin against his will—no matter how many of them there are. Has he tried to escape them?"

Eric shook his head. "Or I would have heard."

"Are you not surprised, Eric? That he has not tried to escape?" Again, the tall man had spoken.

"Or perhaps they are not his captors at all, but his bodyguards," said the blondbeard.

Eric shrugged. "He is unarmed and outnumbered, and his Frey's-brood companions have Asaheim's blood in them, too; so if they are his captors—but, damn, who knows the ways of the gods? Let's just hope that they all go away again—and take Ygg with them."

They all nodded and grunted their agreement. There was a pause in the conversation as they drained their vessels, and Vidar took advantage of it, having had time to study Eric's mind. He pulled a string, and though there was resistance, the youth did not seem to realize he was being manipulated.

"But he did save us from Ygg, the Lord Vidar did," said

Olof's son. "We would not be here drinking this pleasant brew if not for that."

The older man nodded. "That's just what I was thinking. Say what you want about the Aesir, they rescued us. And I'm grateful, no matter what the rest of you think."

Luck was with him, Vidar told himself. He had a willing accomplice in Orum.

"Perhaps," said Eric, "we can return the favor."

"What do you mean?" asked the blondbeard. "Would you have us free him?"

"Why not?" said Eric, a faint smile on his lips.

"Why not?" echoed Tyrdall. "I'll tell you why not— because men don't take sides when the gods themselves are at war."

"But Vidar is the one that struck our enemy down," said Eric. "Don't we owe him that much?"

"You forget," said the blondbeard, "that the Lord Vali rules this land, not Vidar. Would you draw sword against your god? The one that blessed your father's right to rule?"

"That's all right," said Eric, looking around him at his companions. "I'm not afraid to free our benefactor, even if the rest of you are. I thought you said that you wanted the Aesir out of here? Well, I'm going to help the Lord Vidar on his way, even if I have to try it alone."

"This is not like you," said the blondbeard. "You used to be more pious than any of us."

"Well, Harheil," said Olof's son, "I've seen things I never saw before. The sight of all those slain thursar, for instance. There comes a time to act." And he rose from the table, reaching into a pouch that hung from his belt and plinking down a gold coin.

"Hold, Eric," said Orum. "I am with you." He made the sign of Thor's hammer on his breast. "But now is not the time, is it? You said that at night they are but six outside his door."

"Six half-gods," said the tall man. "No pushovers."

"But still six, as opposed to nine," insisted Orum. "And there may be others among the gate-watchers that would stand with Eric."

Eric clapped him on the shoulder. "Exactly what I was thinking, Orum. Midnight, then, and bring your friends."

"I'm coming too," said Tyrdall. "I can't let you face those redbeards without me."

"Count me out," said Harheil, shaking his head. "I don't want to be known as one of his enemies when Vali next comes to Skatalund. Or when Olof returns."

"Then all I ask, Harheil, is this," said Eric. "Do not stop us, when the time comes."

Harheil looked into his comrade's eyes, and saw the fierce determination there. He nodded once, then got up and left.

Eric spoke in low tones to the others. "At midnight, then, we meet in my room. Wear your mail beneath your clothes and conceal your weapons. Come singly, if you can find others to help us. In the meantime, I will do my best to prepare Lord Vidar for our undertaking. Oh, and Tyrdall—he'll need a horse."

Vidar pulled another string.

"Make that two horses," said Eric.

"Two?" asked Tyrdall. "You would not think of—"

"But I would," said Eric, laughing suddenly, "I would."

Vidar had never entered the mind of a thursar, but he found Stim much easier to influence than he might have supposed. Unlike Irbor and his brothers—who had no doubt been alerted to the possibility by Vali—Stim had even fewer barriers of resistance than Eric. Perhaps it had something to do with his civilized state in Skatalund, but his psyche was like an open map to Vidar.

And he carried so much weight with his fellow thursar, it would have been child's play to recruit a couple dozen of them. But that, Vidar knew, would have aroused attention, possibly even led to strife in the city. Blasphemy and disobeying the prince's orders and all that, and Vidar had no wish to upset the delicate balance of human and thursar. As far as he knew, Noggi had been left in charge in Skatalund, and he did not know how the half-Aesir spy might seize on a given opportunity.

No, just Stim and two or three others would have to do. And when Stim visited Eric to propose the idea, Eric would not be adverse to it, of course. He would wonder a little at the coincidence but be glad at the company of their swords.

And at Stim's request, he would add a third horse to the two he'd planned to have in waiting.

At dusk, there was a knock on Vidar's door. "Come in," he said. It was Eric, who inclined his head slightly out of respect and brought in a tray of food. There was a pot of steaming liquid, with a cup next to it, a slab of meat, some moldy-looking cheese and a loaf of bread. Beneath all that, Vidar knew, was something else.

"Good evening, Lord Vidar," said Eric, placing the tray on the table by the window. He glanced furtively at the door ajar, then at Vidar himself.

"That's the longest dinner tray I ever saw," said Vidar, and Eric's eyes became big. Then, as Vidar's smile widened, the son of Olof tilted his head to one side, his brows meeting, and expelled a long breath. He seemed to realize some, if not all, of Vidar's hand in his own rescue.

"Stay for a moment, Eric," said the Aesirman, and the youth nodded. "What news do you have of Lord Vali?"

"He has gone, my lord, in pursuit of Ygg."

"Is Ygg alone?"

"I heard talk about other hordes he might have had up his sleeve, my lord. By now, he might have another army behind him."

Then Vali had spoken the truth, at least to the extent that Eric knew it. "Where is Vali headed?"

"North, my lord. That is where..."

"Enough," said a voice from outside, in the hallway. "The Lord Vidar must be hungry now." There was a muffled laugh from another of the sentinels.

Vidar winked at Eric, the youth bowed slightly—still wondering at Vidar's knowledge of their plan—and then left. One of Irbor's brothers slammed the door closed.

I wonder if he's baked a file into the bread, thought Vidar, smiling to himself. Lifting first the steaming pot and then the meat, cheese, bread and utensils, he last picked up the linen that underlay everything. Beneath it was a shortsword of elfin design—made for show and not efficiency, but all, no doubt, that Eric could sneak past his Frey's-brood captors.

Yet it would kill, if used properly. Vidar turned it about in his hands, the dying light sending a line of fire up along its edge. Once more, he thought, a sword is placed in my hands and I'm given a target for it. A target of Frey's blood, no less—half-Vanir, half-Aesir.

This time, however, it was different. He had *called* for the weapon. In a way, that fact shook him more than the grim mass slaughter he had brought down on Buri's people. This time, the sword was *his* idea.

Vidar pushed that thought from his mind. If he had to slay now to prevent some greater slaughter, then he would do it.

Outside, the light fled. He put the sword beneath his mattress.

Vidar knew the hour of midnight by Eric's approach. The others were just behind him as he ascended the steps that led to this hallway. There were ten of them—four thursar and six humans, including Eric.

Now was the time. Vidar drew the sword out from its hiding place and walked to the threshold. Holding the hilt in his left hand, he pounded on the door with the heel of his right.

There was muttering outside, and then footsteps. The door opened quickly, and Vidar slipped behind it. A redbeard strode in, his spear at the ready. As soon as he had cleared the threshold, Vidar should have brought the blade down on his neck. That had been his plan. But he hesitated, and the astonished guardian was able to ward off the blow with his shaft, when it finally came. He fell sideways into the room, cursing loudly.

Vidar shut the door behind him, his back to it. The redbeard regained his feet and assumed a defensive posture. Then he saw the size of Vidar's weapon—and he grinned. Vidar saw it was Irbor himself he confronted.

Then Vidar grinned too. "Come on, Vanirman. Show me that Hoenir was wrong, and that your ancestors were not a pack of pig-sodomists."

Irbor's eyes flashed beneath his helm, and he lunged. Vidar would have chopped the spear in two, had it been more than a feint.

"What do you have against pigs, Jawbreaker? That would be an improvement over the company you've kept in Midgard."

Another feint, but this time Vidar was poised to take advantage of it. Before Irbor could draw back, he reached out and lopped off the spearhead.

The redbeard was no longer grinning. Vidar dropped the sword behind him. "This is the way I prefer it, anyway," he said, advancing.

Irbor tried to poke him in the face, but he ducked and let the remnant of the spear splinter on the stone wall next to him. Then he lowered his shoulder and plowed into the half-breed, caught him by the waist and pinned him to the ground. Irbor kicked to get free, but he was no match for Asgard's former champion. Vidar's fingers closed around

Irbor's wrist, and before Vali's henchman had a chance to react, he applied pressure and flipped him over like a mackerel. A cry of pain wracked the redbeard.

Now Irbor was lying with his stomach against the stones, grunting, with Vidar on top of him. Odin's son still held Irbor's wrist, though by now it had probably been broken. With his other arm, Vidar tore his opponent's helm off. Irbor cursed and tried to shake him off his back, but Vidar clung to him. Then he worked his arm under Irbor's chin, until it was in the crook of his elbow. Vidar slowly drew the redbeard's head back until the neck bones creaked and his cries turned to croaking sounds.

"Swear to me, Irbor," he growled. "Swear that you'll never lift your hand against me. Ever."

Irbor struggled to dislodge him, and Vidar brought his head back just a bit more. One more slight jerk and he'd break his captor's neck.

"I swear," hissed Irbor.

"Good," said Vidar, withdrawing his arm and getting to his feet. "I hope your vows prove more honest than mine." Then he regained the sword, leaving Irbor where he lay, and made for the door. But when he flung it open, a body slumped against him. It was Orum, and Vidar saw in a moment that there was no help for him. Just beyond the threshold, a thursar lay face up, his throat torn open.

Irbor's brothers still stood, all intact, and they had managed to pin Eric's party against the far wall of the passage. One of the surviving humans held the fingers of his free hand over a shallow wound in his side. And the Asgardians were pressing.

"Pick on someone your own size," said Vidar, brandishing the shortsword. And with that, he hurled himself against the nearest spearman. The redbeard reacted by thrusting at his head—the wrong move, as Vidar deflected the point with the flat of his blade and buried his own weapon in the man's ribs. The Asgardian looked surprised as blood spilled from the corner of his mouth, and he began to shake horribly. Then he fell, and Vidar wrested his blade free.

For a moment, Irbor's remaining brothers stared at their slain sibling, seemingly unable to believe one of their number had been killed. Then they dropped back, blocking the hallway against Vidar's escape. There was a new, grimmer look on their faces.

"Come on," said Vidar to his rescuers. "Don't you want to bring home some trophies? Let's get this over with before their reinforcements arrive."

Stim was the first to come forward. One of Vidar's captors poked at him, drawing him up short, but then another thursar came up behind Stim and hacked at the brethren. Eric and a couple of human soldiers charged into the center of the line, bringing the redbeard's wrath down on them. Vidar launched himself at the guardian on the left.

Cut, jab, thrust, slice. Each side grunted, and suddenly there was blood on the floor. Stim slipped, but he managed to bring down a spearman with him. Vidar's blade found a redbeard's shoulder. His stomach tightened at the Vanirman's scream, but he smashed his hilt into the man's face before he could recover. When his knee came up to meet the spearman's groin, he doubled over. Vidar brought his hilt down again, this time on the back of the head, and his enemy slumped to the ground.

To his right, there was a long, piercing cry, and Vidar whirled in time to see the tall man fall, still clutching the spear that had ripped through leather jerkin and mail shirt. A moment later, another human fell dead beside him.

The three remaining spearmen fell back once more, still gallantly blocking the exit. Stim regained his feet, still apparently unhurt—and charged into them. But one of the redbeards warded off his downstroke and thrust for his belly. The giant rolled to one side, barely avoiding the point of the spear—but the Vanirman was upon him.

Suddenly, Eric slipped between them, before Vali's

henchman could finish off the thursar. The redbeard grinned and lunged for the son of Olof—but Eric flung his sword, desperately, at the spear, and deflected the blow. In the same instant, he fell forward and dug his sword into the warrior's stomach.

The Asgardian dropped his spear and fell to one knee, clutching at Eric's hilt, for the blade was still buried in his belly. He tried to draw it forth with one shuddering effort, but to no avail. Without so much as a whimper, he died.

Then another thursar's blade cut a high arc through the air and bit deep into a redbeard's neck, half-severing the head from the shoulders. Blood gouted forth, spattering the giant and Stim and Eric beside him.

Only one spearman still stood in their way. Sweat streamed down the side of his face as he pulled his point out of a dying thursar's breast. Then he set his feet squarely and looked straight at Vidar.

"Come, my lord," he said. "If I am to die this night, let me take a traitor with me."

The others began to advance on him, but Vidar held up his hand. "Wait," he said. "I'll handle this one alone."

He wasted no time, closing quickly and feinting for the man's knees, as if he meant to cut them out from under him. The redbeard was quicker than he thought. He fell for the decoy, but recovered in time to rake Vidar's chest with his point—before Odin's son turned the spear aside and drove his own point into the other's shoulder.

The last of his captors crumbled, and Vidar winced as he touched the place where his flesh had been ripped open. He looked at his fingers, warm with blood, and a rage filled him. Vidar raised his sword to put an end to the wounded Vanirman at his feet.

Then he checked himself. He glanced over his shoulder and saw Irbor, helmless now, staring aghast at the bodies of his brothers. Irbor cried out in anguish and in guilt, for he had sworn not to raise a hand against Odin's son.

Vidar heard the distant footfalls of his other three brothers—the instruments of his vengeance—even through the wail.

"This one's still alive," said Vidar. "My gift, Irbor." Then he signaled to Eric, and the three of them—including Stim—raced through the hall to the stairs, down the stairs to the antechamber, and out into the darkened courtyard. The starlight showed the promised horses waiting there.

Eric slipped into the saddle first, wheeling his mount. Vidar and Stim were a little slower, but they hoisted themselves up, too. Before they reached the inner wall, they were at full gallop, clattering hooves against cobblestones tearing the veil of silence away from the night.

As they approached, the inner gate opened just wide enough for a man on horseback to slip through. The outer gate, too, revealed a ribbon of blue-black sky. As the mighty ramparts of Skatalund loomed on either side of him and fell away, Vidar recognized a yellow-bearded man he had seen only through Eric's eyes waving to them from the wall.

Then he was free, having left Skatalund as he arrived—a desperate rider on horseback. But when Vidar turned from Skatalund to see the terrain ahead, he felt his gorge rise.

Ahead of them writhed a field of smoking pyres, where the black tents had stood. There was the smell of burnt flesh on the wind—thick and acrid, it rose from the places where the bodies had been piled. Black streamers and red-hot embers still filled the air, whipped by the northerly out of the hills.

Vidar reined his horse to a halt before the border of the thursars' encampment. Some of the tents, he saw, were still erect, black flaps fluttering. When Eric saw him stop, he brought his steed up short, turned around and joined him. Stim came up on his other flank.

"My lord," said Eric, "the smoke will provide cover for us, should Irbor's brothers and Noggi's men decide to give chase."

Vidar shook his head. "Vali burned them, but I murdered them. I can't go among them now. I can't bring myself to look at that—there must be another way."

"But, my lord," said Eric again, "the way is too long around. The tents go on and on, and they could be mounting up now in Skatalund to bring us back. Please, my lord..."

Vidar turned to face Eric and saw, suddenly, the face of another victim. A victim whose fate would be on his head, not Vali's, should harm befall him. He looked at Stim, who said nothing. He had gotten them into this, asked them to risk their lives. They had never even had a choice in the matter. If the safest way was through the field of death, he would force himself to go that way.

"Lead, Eric, and I'll follow you," said Vidar, but his voice was as lifeless as what awaited them. Eric nudged his horse into a canter and they negotiated a course through the pillars of smoke and ash, plumes that rose into the sky and gathered above them like an omen.

On their right, a pyre loomed from out of the ember-shot darkness. A thin, flat rivulet of blood glistened beneath their horses' hooves, running down the hillside between the rocks. Somewhere, a tent flap snapped in a sudden breeze, and Vidar buried his face in one hand, his eyes hot and burning. Even without a cloak, there was no hint of winter here.

He had played the tune of despair and they had danced to it, he mused. Here was applause for the bard—silence and the stare of death.

Eric rode ahead grimly, fighting to ignore the stench. On their left now, another pyre appeared, larger than the first. The horses whinnied, making shrill sounds against the soundlessness. Vidar caught a glimpse of a blackened jaw beneath a dark scalp, fingers like worms left in the sun wrapped around a dagger's hilt, legs twisted in impossible positions.

Gone to Valhalla, no doubt, where Ygg and not Odin would welcome them and feast them and let them fight in anticipation of the day of reckoning. Or so they had thought, all those who had fought for Asgard throughout the millenia.

Abruptly, the smoke turned to wisps and scattered, and they were past the tents of the siege-layers. Up ahead, Vidar could make out the foothills through which he had descended only three nights ago. Was it only three nights? It seemed like so much more time had gone by.

It was only two nights since he had betrayed his vow to Buri and slain his kinsmen. Two nights since someone had reached the prince's study in time to save Vidar and add Buri to the roles of the dead. But it was just a few minutes ago when he had sacrificed men and thursar to free himself from Irbor's brothers, and left the survivors to fend for themselves against the redbeards that still lived. Chalk up five humans and three thursar to a family squabble among the Aesir—the arithmetic of war. Clean and simple, unless you had just walked slowly among the corpses.

Eric signaled for a stop. The boy's face was black with soot, except where his sweat had traced a clear path down one cheek. "Where shall we go?" he asked, and Vidar realized with a start that he had not considered that question. A thought occurred to him—that he could find the passageway back to Midgard, leaving his kinsmen to thrash it out among themselves.

But it had gone a mite too far for him to slip away unnoticed now. Vali would not be content to ignore him again, as he had for so long—he had said so himself. And besides that, Vali had been in Midgard without his knowledge. No, like it or not, he would have to see this little drama through.

Where then? To join Vali and beg his forgiveness?

"Do either of you know where Vali was headed?" he asked.

Eric looked at Stim grimly. "Toward Indilthrar, my lord," he said.

"What is that?"

"The city of the thursar priests," said Stim. "It is supposed that Ygg fled there after..."

"After I slew his army?"

"Yes, my lord."

"How do we get to Indilthrar?"

The mask of soot could not conceal the look of fear on Eric's face. "It would mean death for us to go there, my lord," he said in a low voice. "Men shunned that place even before Ygg came. It has been said they worship the hrimthrusar there. Only the nomads may visit Indilthrar, and they—even they—are not allowed to sleep within its walls. City-thursar like Stim would be no more welcome than humans."

Stim nodded to confirm what Eric said. Vidar could not read his stony expression, but he sensed fear there, too.

The son of Odin looked back at the pure, white walls of Skatalund through the pillars of smoke. "Well, you won't be very welcome in Skatalund, either, boys. Fortunately or unfortunately, you're with me now. And let's forget the 'my lord' crap. I'm just Vidar from now on. All right?"

"Yes, my l—yes, Vidar," said Eric. Stim nodded.

"Good. Now, I may be crazy, but I think that I can nip this whole affair in the bud if I can just reach Ygg. Vali believes that Ygg is our brother Hod. If that's so, maybe I can drum some sense into him. Maybe not. But it's worth a try." Eric and Stim just stared at him. "Which way is Indilthrar?"

Eric pointed to the right, indicating a spot where the river that nurtured the city slipped through a break in the hills. "A road runs there," he said.

"Then let's go," said Vidar, guiding his steed in that direction. The pyres still spewed smoke on his right flank, but a fresh, cold breeze flowed down from the mountains on his left, pressing the smoke away from him. His companions followed suit, and they set off at a brisk trot, still mindful of those in Skatalund that might be tempted to give chase.

"Vidar?" said Eric. "I think I was in your hands before."

"Yes," said Vidar, feeling better with every hoofprint they put between themselves and the black tents. "Under my influence. Both of you."

"And now?" Eric asked.

"Now, you are your own man. Why?"

Eric shrugged, managing a half smile. "I never thought I would go to Indilthrar of my own free will."

XV

While they paced the gentle flow of the River Hil, Skatalund having long since disappeared behind a shoulder of snow-dusted hillside, Vidar pondered what Eric had told him—that it was a good five days' journey to the hold of the thursar priests. Vali had left with his army a full day-and-a-half before he had escaped, and there was little hope of overtaking him. After all, this road was the fastest route, and Vali had the same use of it they did. Even if the three of them kept on without sleep for the next three nights, they would still be forced to pass around or through his brother's forces, and he had no stomach for those odds. They would have to resign themselves to Vali's arrival there before them— and hope to reach Ygg through some less direct route once they got to the mountains, where they would have more cover to work with.

Vidar pulled his cloak about him against the cold. The gently sloping highlands they passed through had displayed more and more evidence of Twelfthmonth as they made their way north toward the mountains. Even the memory of Ygg's sky-serpent seemed absurd in the crystal-clear dome of might above them. There was snow on the ground, but the air was dry and feathery.

Once, they had to leave the road where it crossed over a tributary of the Hil. The bridge there had been burned by the invaders on their way to Skatalund, evidently. But their tough mountain horses did not complain when they were asked to wade through the hip-high, black, swirling current, and they were able to regain the road on the other side.

Was it truly Hod that had torn the countryside apart in his desire to conquer Utgard? If that was so, at least he would not be slain out of hand in Indilthrar. As much as Vali hated Baldur's murderer, Vidar had never raised a hand against him—either before the murder or after. He had not gone after him as Vali had done.

Until he wound the horn in Skatalund, that is. But there was a good chance Hod would understand Vali's influence in that. In fact, he and Hod had always had a mutual respect for one another, if not an excess of affection. Hod had never been a very warm person, not even as a child. If Vali was Odin's son, Hod had been Frigga's. Sometimes, the Valfather seemed not to know what to make of Hod.

But if Hod was Ygg, it could not be the Hod that Vidar had known ages ago. Time works its changes, Vidar thought. Where had Hod fled in order to escape his brother's avenger? How might he have changed in that far corner of the universe?

For one thing, he had grown stronger in exile. When Vidar had grappled with Ygg to recover Modi's hammer, he'd found power there that Hod had never possessed in Asgard.

Or was it Hod after all? What might Vidar be leading his allies into, if Ygg was someone else?

While Vidar pondered silently, the stars that had guided them for most of the night began to fade. There was a hint of rose on the horizon that was mirrored in the river and fragmented into rainbow shards by the current. A swarm of small, dark birds took flight suddenly, singing a shrill song of morning, while the wind carried them the scent of pine needles from the wooded slopes on either side.

There was a certain peacefulness about this world that Vidar had never felt here in the days before Ragnarok. Except for those few places where Odin had allowed Baldur to exert his influence on the Valfather's creation, Utgard had been a roiling cauldron. A brew of unfriendly ingredients that the Lord of Asgard had stirred together, although they were never meant to be in the same pot. It was like putting two Siamese fighting fish in the same bowl—or dropping an adder into a pit with a mongoose. It was a cruel curiosity that set things or people to warring and then found entertainment in the result.

Yet Utgard had transcended its origins in many ways. Men and thursar—at least, some thursar—lived together inside one set of walls. And places like this highland river valley had emerged, peaceful despite its Creator, its *gaut*.

When the sun's light chased the stars, turning the river to gold and the hills to silver, Vidar decided that the horses could use a rest—not to mention his companions. His legs were stiff as he dismounted and vaulted from the edge of the road onto the fertile greensward that framed the bright, murmuring Hil. He cupped his hands and took a drink of the ice-cold water, kneeling next to the current, and wiped the excess water on his face. It helped to stave off the fatigue he felt encroaching.

Eric and Stim joined him by the bank of the Hil, and after Stim had quenched his thirst, he filled a bladder with water and brought it back up to the road for the horses. Eric seemed uneasy about something, and Vidar asked him about it.

"I have a question," said Eric finally. "I used to think I knew what was right. Vali ruled in Heaven—and I believed that you and the rest of the Aesir ruled with him. Was this not so?"

Vidar laughed gently. "It was not so. Of the sons of Odin that survived Ragnarok, only Vali remained in Asgard. I was somewhere else. Have you ever heard of Midgard?"

Eric shook his head. "Was Midgard at war with Asgard?"

"No," said Vidar. "Midgard is not like this world. It could never hope to win such a war, even if it were so inclined. In fact, those who dwell in Midgard have never heard of Asgard, except for vague, dark legends that have been preserved."

The boy nodded, but still looked perplexed as Stim rejoined them. "I can guess your next question," said Vidar. "Why did Vali imprison me?" Eric nodded frankly, his breath freezing on the air. Vidar turned to Stim, and saw that he, too, was listening for an answer. The doubts that had floated to the surface in Eric still lay half submerged in the thursar's murky psyche—but they were there all the same.

"I guess," said Vidar, "Vali fears me. Or fears what I might do to his plans."

"What are his plans?" rumbled Stim suddenly, his eyes fixed on him like black pinpricks in eternity.

"His plans, Stim, are to make your world a battleground. And mine, too, eventually—if it suits him. Vali is a jealous ruler and one who never forgives. Cross him and he'll get even with you. Only once did anyone ever escape his wrath, and that was when his brother, Hod, slew Baldur the Beautiful and fled from Asgard.

"Maybe it was Vali's very thirst for revenge that kept him alive at Ragnarok. I don't know. But his ferocity has not died. Oh, his place on Asgard's throne has forced him to develop a thin layer of charm and a veneer, at least, of justness—but underneath, he burns with hatred for Hod."

"And the lord Vali believes that Hod is Ygg," said Eric. "I heard my father say as much. But why not let him have what he wants—Ygg's head?"

"Because even if he finally managed to work his revenge, the hunger that has shaped him all these years will not abate. It has become part of him. And if we let it, that hunger will destroy Utgard just as surely as the hordes that follow Ygg."

He seemed to have done little to put either Eric or Stim at ease. Perhaps he had given them too much to think about all at once. It was as if someone had told them that the earth beneath them was not the earth at all, but the sky—and the sky was not the sky, but the sea. Maybe, too, they felt that they had heard something blasphemous, something that no one would have dared to say in Skatalund, whether in temple or drinking hall. And the fact that a god had said it had not done much to ease the sting. After all, Vidar realized, these were still superstitious people, the Utgard-thursar and Utgard-human alike. The fact that their gods walked among them did not mitigate their awe—it fed it like dry firewood.

Soon, they got up and mounted again, lest Vali get too far ahead of them. The three of them rode in silence for a while. Now and then, a deserted farmhouse would come into view, its fields burned or stripped bare of stalks by the nomads. The sun rose slowly in the sky, and the air grew warmer, but Vidar's most effective measure of time was the growling of his stomach. Eric and Stim must have been hungry, too, but neither said a word.

The snow-powdered grass of the slopes gave way to forestland. Fir branches gleamed like emeralds against the bright blue day. Eventually, the festive sun and the faint, sweet smell of the wood pried Eric's lips apart.

"It's all too much for me, Vidar. I can't fathom the purposes of the gods. I don't know who or what to believe. But something in my heart tells me that I must follow you— although I can't imagine what kind of help I could muster that such as you would be in need of."

"Don't underestimate yourself," said Vidar. "Or over-estimate me. I couldn't have escaped Skatalund without you. Don't forget that."

Eric nodded and even managed a smile. "All right, then. I'm with you."

Vidar clapped him on the back. "Good." Then he turned to Stim. "And what about you?" he asked.

The graven-stone face did not change. But Stim rumbled something unintelligible deep inside his throat and nodded once. "I am also with you, Vidar," he said. "You can depend on me."

The remainder of the afternoon would have been pleasant if their purpose had not been so grim. At times, Vidar forgot that they were on their way to Indilthrar and just got lost in the magic of the Utgardian forest. The way the shadows and sunlight painted a pattern on the underbrush, the crackle of twigs beneath their horses' hooves, the glistening of glasslike frost on the upper branches—all these things struck a chord within him.

But night fell early. Surrounded by trees and east of a large hill, they lost the sun long before the sky turned dark, and the air grew chill all of a sudden. They traveled along the road in unnatural twilight—that will-o'-the-wisp time when the day thinned out and the world huddled close—and they talked in quiet tones of simple things, homey things.

"I have a cuckoo clock at home that sings 'Barnacle Bill the Sailor' and rings twelve bells at noon," said Vidar. Eric hooted, then knit his brows together.

"I've never heard 'Barnacle Bill the Sailor,'" he laughed.

"And you're not about to hear it now," said Vidar. "You're too young."

"But what is a cuckoo clock?" asked Stim.

"Yes," said Eric. "I was wondering that myself."

Vidar told them, and they chalked it up as just another of Asgard's wondrous artifacts. "But it was not made in Asaheim," he told them. "It was made in Midgard."

"Then Midgard, too, must be full of miracles," concluded Eric.

Vidar shrugged. "I never thought of it that way."

By the time true night fell, they were tired and hungry, and their mounts were beginning to get cranky. They had neither eaten nor slept since before Vidar's escape.

"I wish I had thought to have Tyrdall pack some food in these saddlebags," said Eric.

"Me too," said Vidar. Eric looked at him strangely and then laughed.

"I keep forgetting that you were in on the plan," he said.

Stim interrupted, placing a hand on Vidar's wrist. He pointed to a spot up the slope on their left.

"What is it?" asked Eric, his eyes not as effective as Stim's.

Vidar concentrated on the direction in which the giant gestured. There—a wooden dwelling of some kind. And a thin stream of black smoke rising from what must have been a hole in the roof.

"It appears that someone lives there," said Vidar.

"Yes," said Stim. "Perhaps there will be a bit of food in the cupboard set aside for travelers."

A grim thought fled through Vidar's mind. "If the owner was not slain by Ygg's hordes," he said. "That smoke may not indicate a cooking fire."

They looked at one another. "Let's see," said Eric. He led the way up the wooded slope, and the others followed.

Before they could reach the dwelling, however, a door opened and the figure of a man emerged into the newly kindled starlight. Eric brought his horse up a few yards short of the little house—just in case—though he could see after a moment that the man was not armed.

"Who is it?" asked the man.

"My name is Eric," said the boy. "My companions are called Vidar and Stim."

"Vidar, eh?" said the man, and there was an unmistakable note of amusement in his voice. "Like the god. And Stim— that's a thursar name. Is he a nomad?"

"No," said Eric. "He was raised in Skatalund, like myself."

The man paused a moment, seemingly lost in thought. "Well, off your horses, then, and come in. My traps have not been unkind to me, and there may be some extra meat on the spit."

The riders dismounted, tied their horses' reins around the lower branches of a broad, old elm that towered over the wooden house, and followed their host inside. It was not well lit, the only illumination coming from the cooking fire in a crudely built stone hearth.

"Be seated," said the man, his back toward them as he worked some meat off the spit. "We'll eat, and then you can stay the night—if you don't mind sleeping on the floor. There's a storm coming. I can feel it in my bones. At least you'll be dry here."

Then he turned around, smiling, and his face must have been handsome once. But now there were lines in it, the furrows plowed by a harsh life in the wilderness. His hair was long and pale yellow, leaning toward white. And his eye sockets were empty.

"Are you with the others that passed by here?" he asked.

"No," said Vidar. "What others?"

"Yesterday, a little before the day lost its warmth, an army filed through the valley. A large army, by the sound of it, and the length of time it took to pass by."

"Valland," said Eric. Their host seemed to freeze solid, for a moment. Then he resumed cutting up the meat he had placed before him.

"Valland," said the man. "It was long ago. You are Olof's son, then?"

"Yes," said the boy. "We thought you dead."

"No," said the man, bringing out a bladder full of liquid. "I'm sorry I have no mead to offer, poor host that I am. But sometimes the water in these hills can taste like mead." He poured a portion into each of four wooden cups. "You'll have to take your meat from the one plate—I have no others."

Vidar and his companions ate gladly, though no words were spoken. Eric watched Valland's every move, especially the subtle changes in his expression, and the other two watched Eric. When they were finished, Valland cut another chunk of meat from the spit—venison, it seemed, and as tasty as any Vidar could remember—and they ate that, too.

"I hope we are not cleaning out your winter food store," said Vidar.

"No," said their host. "This beast was just caught. My food store is ample, thank the gods."

Finally, they had satisfied both their hunger and their thirst. "Valland," said Eric. "I cannot believe it is you."

"Yes," said the man. "Older and wiser, but it is me." Their host paused. "Five winters ago, if you had crossed my threshold, I might have taken this carving knife to you." He turned the knife over in his hands. "I was bitter, and would have done anything to send your bones back to your father's city. Sweet revenge. But I have mellowed since. I no longer dream of revenge. I gambled, Eric, and I lost. I paid the price of darkness, and nearly paid more than that. But the thirst for power has left me. It's funny—I cannot even remember why I should want the throne of Skatalund. I have enough trouble getting around this little place."

Eric stared at the ruined face. "I'm sorry, Valland. You were my father's greatest chieftain. I always loved you when I was a baby."

The man nodded. "I ask but one thing in return for my hospitality," said Valland. "Do not tell your father of me. He thinks I am dead. Let him think so. Olof has not had the benefit of these years of darkness to cool off his hatred of me, and if he knew I was alive, he might not tolerate it. 'Don't turn your back on anyone,' he once told me. 'Even if you've cut off their arms and legs, beware of their teeth.'"

"I'll keep you secret," said Eric.

"We will too," said Vidar.

"Thank you, my friends. And now, I must sleep. I would offer you sleeping furs, if I had them. But the floor near the fire is not too cold." With that apology, he wrapped himself up in his cloak and turned toward the dying flames.

The others did likewise. But just as Vidar started to doze, he felt Eric's hand on his arm. The boy's eyes were red-rimmed. "Can we not help him?" he asked. "You are a god. You have the healing touch—you healed Modi. His eyes, my lord—is there anything you can do?"

Vidar sat up, and turned toward Eric. He glanced once at Valland's sleeping form. The man had rolled over, and his once-proud countenance was half-illuminated by the hearth fire.

"No," said Vidar. "It was too long ago. Even the Aesir cannot heal wounds so old. I could relieve him of his heartache, Eric, but Time has done that already."

The boy nodded, still fascinated by the sleeping figure. "There are tales of hospitality rewarded," he whispered. "Odin, in his travels, guested by a poor farmer, and the farmer given something precious as a reward. Isn't there something you can give him, Vidar?"

Vidar shook his head. "But there will come a time when you become prince in Skatalund. Perhaps you can think of something."

Eric looked at Vidar, and he seemed to gain a little more understanding of the relative powers of gods and men. He sighed and lay back against the floor, pulling his cloak about him.

Soon, Eric was asleep. Vidar lay awake a while longer, but sleep, after a while, laid its claim to him, too.

Vidar woke at the sound of a door closing. He looked up and saw Valland standing above them.

"Sorry to wake you," said the man, staring ahead. "I had to get up to survey the work my traps did last night. And while I was at it, I fed your horses. They sounded a mite hungry, though they didn't seem to mind the fresh blanket of snow. Mountain ponies?"

"Aye," said Stim. "Raised in the hills by my people."

Valland smiled. "You know," he said, "you never told me why you were traveling in this kind of weather."

"There is a war brewing," said Vidar. "It was Olof's side that passed through here before us."

Valland's brows raised. "Really?" He paused for a moment, perhaps remembering something of Skatalund. "I hope he wins."

The riders didn't stay for breakfast, turning down Valland's invitation. But they did accept the provisions he had prepared for them—meat, bread, water and honey-cakes.

Eric paused at the crest of a hill to look back at his father's former friend and enemy. The man was piling kindling against the side of his little house. After a moment, he clucked to his steed and turned around, leaving Valland to his simple life.

The snow, which had fallen throughout the night, made their going slower. Vidar wondered if Vali's forces had been caught in the same storm, or if they had been shielded on the other side of some mountain. In some places, the drifts rose as high as the horses' bellies, and Vidar feared that one of the beasts would catch a hoof in some concealed undergrowth and pull up lame.

But they kept on without incident, and the morning passed like frosty wine. The sky shrugged off its tattered clouds almost as soon as they started out, and the day turned blue and warm, despite the storm of the night before. The hills were blindingly white and silver.

By midday, the ground had leveled off somewhat, and they picked up their pace. They had reached some sort of plateau, where the snow hadn't piled quite as high, and in some places they could see the frozen road exposed by the wind.

They were almost upon it when they noticed something unusual in the landscape. Covered with snow like the rest of the terrain, it almost escaped their attention. Riding closer, they could see the outlines of a stone barricade and more stone structures behind it.

"G'walin," said Stim, turning to Eric.

Eric nodded.

"What's that?" asked Vidar.

"G'walin? It's the name of the place," said Eric.

"Sounds elvish," said Vidar.

"It is," said Stim. His eyes gleamed blackly in the strong sunlight.

"I don't hear anything," said Eric.

"I don't either," said Vidar. And then a thought came to him—ambush? Had Vali laid a trap for him, just in case he managed to escape and came after him on the road?

G'walin gave him no clue. It stood as silent as the snow.

XVI

Vali loved Baldur more than any of the gods. He saw in him the grace, the tranquility that he might never have—except in Baldur's company. But Baldur was not like the rest of the Aesir, it seemed. Though he was blood of their blood, he did not have the vitality the other gods were endowed with. Instead, he was like a star that flares for a time with a beauty far surpassing all the other stars—and then grows cold.

He was dying inside, being eaten from within by his own holy fire. He grew more pale and haggard with each new dawn. It was only a matter of time before Baldur would die.

His mother, Frigga, could not allow this. She split the burden of mortality with him, as only the Aesir may do, drawing death out of him like a leech. But she could not leave anything in its place, and after a time, his inner fire shriveled and went cold.

Then he was like a zombie, preserved by his mother's magic, denied his doom. He was torn between the fields of life and the funeral pyre.

And still, it was only a matter of time before he died. But Frigga's ministrations staved off that time and Baldur lingered. He wandered the streets of Asgard like a scarecrow, a ghost searching for his tomb. His eyes, of which Bragi sang, died long before he could.

Perhaps, in his way, Hod was the bravest of them all. He seemed to love Baldur as much as Vali did— they were sons of the same mother, though they were seldom all three seen together. Vali was quick to anger, relentless in combat. Hod was quiet, turned inward as Baldur was turned outward, but fearless for all that. And Baldur was . . . indescribable. He drew love to him like a lodestone draws iron, and he left a trail of compassion like a comet trails light.

Until he grew sick. Then he was a walking corpse, mocking his former self with each halting step. But Frigga would not let him go.

Hod did what he had to—or so they say. He took Baldur off with him to his brother's favorite spot in all of Asgard—where a waterfall pooled at the foot of a mighty oak tree. No one knows what was said between them—but Baldur was found in that pool the next morning, dead, floating—an arrow protruding from his body.

Hod's arrow.

But it had been shot into his breast, not his back. And there are those who wondered if Baldur had not invited the arrow himself. Hod could not tell anyone because he had disappeared.

Frigga cursed her son, Hod, with all her might. Odin's fury was terrible. Thor was not in Asgard at the time, but he later reviled himself in public, tearing at

his beard and his hair, for not having slain Hod long
before he could think of killing Baldur. There was sorrow such as Asgard had never seen.

Vali vowed to find Hod and murder him as he'd
murdered Baldur. He took off alone, before a larger
party could be brought together. Vali left by the gate
to Utgard and stalked his brother across the worlds,
traveling by day and by night. From Utgard to Midgard, from Midgard to Alfheim, from Alfheim into the
utter cold of Jotunheim—the land of the hrimthursar.
One god hunted another in the land of their enemies,
where the hunter, too, was hunted.

Once, Vali had to slay a thursar female who would
have given him away. Another time, he had to evade
the pursuit of twelve brothers, who wanted an Aesirman's head to hang over the hearth in their mead
hall. Then, Vali reached the gate that led from Jotunheim to Niflheim, and knew by his hunter's instincts
that Hod had gone that way—where none of the Aesir
but Odin, Hoenir and Lodur had ever walked.

What happened then, no one knows. Did Vali enter
Niflheim? There is no answer. But this is sure—Hod
had eluded him. And Vali returned from his journey
leaner than before—hungrier and perhaps emptier—
and he vowed that if he ever saw Hod again, his brother
would not escape.

For he believed that if he waited long enough, Hod
would return to Asgard....

More? But I grow thirsty, my lords, and tomorrow
is another day....

                                    Sin Skolding
                                    Rogaland, 352 A.D.

XVII

"Vidar," said Eric. "Look." The boy dismounted and walked a few feet in the snow. So intent had Vidar been on trying to discern movement in the elvish village that he had not noticed the thing near their horses' hooves.

Eric picked it up and some of the snow fell away. It was a corpse, armorless and bareheaded. An elvish corpse, its pale skin made paler by death. The face had been lean-boned and beardless, the staring eyes emerald green and almond-shaped—no different than the elves Vidar had known in Alfheim long ago. A thick clot of blood had frozen in its long, golden hair.

The boy eased the body to the ground and walked another few steps. "Here's another one," he called back. "A female, Vidar." He plodded on in the snow and found a third body.

Vidar winced at their wounds, at their stiff, grotesque postures. Not one was armed.

"Not Ygg," said Stim. "He was alone."

"Vali," said Vidar, and he knew that his brother had done this. But why? The elves were not his enemies—or were they?

Suddenly, Vidar had a premonition of disaster. "Eric," he called, "come back. Let's get out of here."

Then there was the creak of a gate and an opening gaped in the snow-covered walls of G'walin. A troop of horse-borne elves poured forth, and Vidar saw that some were armed with crossbows before he dug cruelly into his mount's sides with his heels.

The beast leaped forward and Vidar leaned out of the saddle. Eric loomed before him for an instant, and then the boy was securely behind him, hanging on to Vidar's middle.

They were past the village before the elves could cut them off. But they had those bows, and Vidar had not forgotten the skills of the *lyos*—the fair mountain-elves—with such weapons.

He glanced back and saw perhaps a score of them on their small, fleet ponies, which in the short run could weave circles around their heavier steeds. Stim was just behind him, and gaining, but his horse was frothing at the mouth.

After their arduous haul through the hills, neither steed could keep up this pace for long. Vidar's had a double burden, and though it was used to carrying the giant weight of the thursar warriors, his weight and Eric's combined would break the horse's heart before long.

He looked ahead and saw no cover. The forest on either side was too dense to go charging into, and the road itself was wide open, rising only slightly, without a hill or a bend in sight.

Perhaps the elves would be satisfied to run them off their land. Somehow, he doubted it. Not after seeing those corpses.

Then he heard a sharp *ping,* and an arrow skittered off the road just to one side of his horse's pounding hooves. Vidar leaned closer to the animal's neck, hoping to make as small a target as possible. The forest rushed by on either side, and the wind seemed to keen ever louder.

Another shaft bit into the road ahead, and another. Finally, there was a sickening *thwap,* and Vidar heard Stim cry out. He turned in time to see the giant catapulted over his horse's head into a dense clump of bushes. He reined his own steed in suddenly and wheeled the beast around, dropping off its back to see to Stim. At the same time, Eric clambered forward and placed the horse between his companions and the elves. He drew his sword and steeled himself.

"No!" cried Vidar, stopping in his tracks. "Drop your sword!" But before the boy could comply, the elves had already dropped their bows from their shoulders.

Eric's blade clattered against the road as their pursuers drew up before him. A couple still aimed their crossbows at Vidar. Stim was sprawled perhaps ten feet from the road, face up. Moving slowly, lest the elves mistake his intent, Vidar waded through the snow to where the giant lay. Blood trickled from Stim's temple, and nothing moved.

"Stim?" said Odin's son, touching his shoulder. He was grateful when he saw the giant wince. The black eyes opened beneath the snow-encrusted ridge of his brow, and they had the glitter of life in them. "Are you all right?"

The thursar nodded, dazed. He sat up painfully, propping his huge arms behind him. Then he turned his head and saw the elves amassed on the road. "You should have left me," he said in his gravel voice, low enough so that the elves could not hear him. "You had a chance."

Vidar shook his head. "Not one in a million. Come on. Let's find out what they have in mind." He offered Stim his hand. As the giant took it, he leaned back and pulled him to his feet. The thursar brushed off the snow he had accumulated in his fall, staring in his race's expressionless way at their captors.

"You know me," said Eric to the foremost elf, but loudly enough so that Vidar could hear. "I am Eric, Olof's son, of Skatalund. Why have we been run down like enemies? We have always been friends."

The elves sat their horses like lords. They were tall, men and women alike, armored in silver byrnies and silver helms. All that covered their legs were embroidered leggings. Their skin was pale, their faces finely sculpted, and their eyes were the wide, deep-set green orbs of which Frey had loved to sing. The males were beardless, but their hair fell like thread-of-gold to their shoulders. Even now, bent on violence, they reminded Vidar of children. The sun played so gently on their visages. . . .

"We know you, Eric," said the elf, "and we have no quarrel with you. But you ride with the Aesir, and that is a different matter these days. Did you not see the bodies along the road? There are many more that have been covered by the snow, where the lord Vali and his Aesir army ran them down."

"We are not on Vali's side," said Eric. "My lord Vidar would stop his armies before they can destroy anything else."

The elf shrugged. "Does it matter, this Aesirman or that one? They all kill elves, sooner or later, ey?" Then he gestured to his comrades, and they rode over to Vidar and Stim, still training their shafts on them. For a moment, Vidar thought that they would just shoot them on the spot. Then, when it became apparent that they would not, he walked over to where Eric sat. Stim came after him, glaring at the elves.

The leader of the elves pointed to Vidar's sword, sheathed at his saddle by Eric's side. The boy understood and dropped it like his own on the road. "Now the thursar," said the elf. Reluctantly, Stim disarmed himself.

"You do not understand," said Eric. "We cannot be detained. Vidar is our only hope of putting an end to the killing."

"No," said the elf. "*You* do not understand. There is no end—there is only vengeance." And with that, he spun his horse around, and the elvish ranks parted to let him pass.

"Move, Aesirman," said an elf behind Vidar. "You too, thursar." He gestured with his bow toward the village. They began to walk. Eric came up alongside.

"Their leader's name is Or'in," said the boy. "I met him once on a trading expedition to Dundafrost. His mother lived there with her entourage, overseeing commerce with Skatalund and some of the other big cities. Men had traded with the *lyos* in Dundafrost for centuries, until Ygg laid siege to it. When the city fell, Or'in's mother was slain with the others." Eric paused. "She was a queen. As her son, he has become a chieftain in their councils. He is bitter, I'm afraid."

"I'm not surprised," said Vidar. "Ygg killed his mother and Vali killed his friends. I hope that they don't all think the way he does about the Aesir."

Eric looked down at him hopefully. "Vidar, can you . . . do what you did to me? Do it to them, I mean?"

Vidar shook his head. "It doesn't work with everyone. With humans, yes, depending on their temperaments. Thursar as well. Even the Aesir and the Vanir, sometimes." He smarted as he recalled how Vali had duped him. "But I can tell you from long experience that elves cannot be influenced that way."

Eric shook his head. "So much for that idea," he said. Then he dismounted and walked beside his horse. "If you've got to walk, I guess I can, too."

On their way to G'walin, they passed another corpse. Another victim of the Aesir—perhaps Or'in hadn't been so wrong in his appraisal of them. Led by the elfqueen's son, they turned off the road, toward the gates of the village. A crowd had already gathered inside the walls. It grew louder as they approached, until they had come up to the snow-mantled walls themselves. Then the mass yielded to their passage. As Vidar entered the village, every face seemed to know him, and their expressions were far from kindly.

G'walin's people were a rippling wave of rainbows. Their cloaks were dyed blue and red and gold, their tunics deftly embroidered with delicate, twisting green vines or flowers or sheaves of grain. They wore wide, leather belts with buckles of silver or gold, boots of deerhide, and—if their legs were not bare, as was most often the case, it seemed—they wore brightly colored leggings. A few of them had headbands of braided leather, or wristbands and armbands of silver, or necklaces of semiprecious stones, perhaps depending on their station in society.

And they seemed to seethe with hatred for the Aesirman, the human and the thursar. It was more than strange to see such gentle faces twisted with violent emotion.

Vidar took note of the buildings as they were ushered past the crowd into the center of the village. The elves' dwellings were simple, stone structures rising against a carnelian sky. Each building had a heavy, wooden door, daubed with bright pigments to represent the same vines, flowers and grain-sheaves the elves wore on their clothing. It was not an uncheerful place, if one discounted the intentions of its inhabitants, thought Vidar.

The intruders were led by Or'in toward the only edifice in G'walin that boasted a second floor. The elves followed them all along their route, and while they did not press, there was no doubt what they would have liked to do with Vidar and his companions.

Two great, wooden doors, adorned with the sun and the moon and grapevines that bore fruit of every hue, opened before them. It was dark beyond those doors. Or'in dismounted, and someone took charge of his horse. Then the rest of the armed elves dismounted also. Or'in gestured for the prisoners to follow him inside.

When they did, the doors shut behind them, and Vidar had to stop in his tracks, until his eyes could adjust to the darkness. Gradually, a room took shape around him, where the windows had been draped over and the braziers left unlit. This room took up the entire space between the four walls. At the opposite end from the doors by which he had entered, he could barely make out a slight, huddled figure on an unimposing seat of pale stone.

"Come closer," said the one who sat there, wrapped in a worn, colorless cloak, and his voice was parched and brittle with age. Or'in approached, and Vidar followed, with Eric and Stim on either side of him. As he came closer, the son of Odin could now discern a small, armed entourage in the shadows behind the stone seat.

"My eyes—I cannot see very well, and the light gives them pain," said the one who beckoned them. "You must come closer." Or'in walked up to a spot beside the seated figure and indicated to Vidar that he should walk right up to it. He did so, until he could see the glittering, emerald eyes that peered up at him through long wisps of white hair. A necklace of golden beads fell from the slender, furrowed neck, almost into the lap that was lost in the folds of a gray robe.

"I am F'lar," said the ancient face, where only the eyes seemed alive. Overhead in the high-roofed chamber, as if at a signal, a bird took wing, circled, and came back to roost.

"I am Vidar. These are Eric and Stim of Skatalund, my companions."

"Aye," said the elf. "A strange company, as strange as any I have ever seen. It has been a long time since any of the Aesir came this way—and woe betide us that they chose to return. What I wish to know," he said, and his voice took on a certain resonance, "is why the Lord of Asgard needs so vast an army, and so much food to feed that army, and needs it so desperately that his soldiers would kill to get it."

"Is that what happened out there?" asked Vidar. "We saw the corpses, F'lar. Was it for food that they were killed?"

"Aye," spat the elf. "For food. We do not grow more than we need, and there was none to share with them. Vali seemed to acknowledge this, and rode away at the head of his armies. But before the length of his great, armed serpent could pass, it had lashed out at G'walin. Of course, Vali was safely gone. Yet he had made his displeasure known, killing first our unarmed emissaries, who only sought news from the soldiers that went by, and then seeking to scale the walls of G'walin itself.

"But we learned a lesson at Dundafrost," said F'lar. He sighed. "We had our crossbows ready, just in case. In case Ygg came this way. But it appears that Vali is no different from his brother Hod. I had forgotten," said the wizened old elf, "what the Aesir were like. I have been reminded."

"F'lar," said Vidar, "I can't explain what happened here, or make excuses for it. Vali is my half brother, but we have not been on the same side for a long time. He marches to Indilthrar now, to destroy Ygg—Hod. To mete out justice, he says. But you have seen how destructive Vali can be, as much a menace to Utgard as Ygg, perhaps. I'm on my way to Indilthrar to try to stop both of them."

"Certainly," said F'lar. "As they try to stop each other."

Vidar shook his head slowly. "What do you know of me, F'lar? I was never one to make war without provocation, even in the days before Utgard was created."

The elf lowered his head. When he raised it again, his ancient eyes were accusing. "You are Aesir," said F'lar. "War is in your blood."

"No," said Vidar. "We are all different. I was on my way to Indilthrar to talk sense to Ygg, to try to end this war before it goes any further. I want what you want—peace. But you must allow me to reach Ygg."

"Why do you call him Ygg?" asked F'lar. "Even the soldiers we spoke to before the killing started knew enough to call him by his true name, Hod." His voice was a rustling in the darkness.

"Even Vali does not know for sure that the one who wears the mask is his brother," said Vidar. "I do not know either."

Again, the elf lowered his head, as if pondering, and his guards muttered among themselves. His eyes still downcast, F'lar asked, "And if Ygg is not the Lord Hod? Then what?"

"Then, I suppose I would have to slay him," said Vidar.

"For his crimes?" asked F'lar. "For the death and destruction he brought down upon Dundafrost?"

"For what he might yet do," said Vidar. "To prevent another Dundafrost."

"But not if he is Hod?" asked F'lar, raising his eyes, and meeting Vidar's gaze with frightening intensity. "If he is your brother, he has committed no crimes? He presents no danger? Because he is Aesir, and the Aesir can slay as they please?" There was silence for a moment, as F'lar's fragile voice echoed and touched the recesses of the chamber with its irony.

"I would hear him, first," said Vidar. "I would try to talk him out of it."

"But you would not be able to," said the elf, and he laughed, a hideous, rasping laugh that sounded like twigs snapping underfoot in a midnight wood. "I think I like Vali's motives better. He will just take a sword to Hod's neck. Did you not love Baldur, Aesirman?" The elf's tone was rank with mockery.

"I did," said Vidar. "But it was a long time ago. People change. I did. I used to go lopping off heads and asking why later. Now I ask questions first."

"Too bad," hissed F'lar. "I would have wished you your

old self, then. I would see you all go up in flames at In-dilthrar. I do not *want* you to stop them, my lord. Oh, no. That would spoil our revenge."

A chill played up and down Vidar's spine. He had for-gotten—these were not the *lyos* of Alfheim, the gentlest race in all the nine worlds. These were the elves of Utgard, and even Odin could not have known what they would become—colder, more calculating than their counterparts whom Vidar had hunted with. This was the gift Utgard had given to the *lyos*—the concept of revenge.

"Don't you fear Vali?" asked Vidar. "Have you thought what he might do when he comes back from Indilthrar and finds that you have detained me—his brother?"

F'lar stared at him. "What can they do to us? Slay us? They did some of that here, and some at Dundafrost. Still we do not fear them. The last gods we worshiped were Odin and Frey, and they died in the Battle. Who should we have worshiped then—you?" And the elves behind him laughed—all save Or'in, whose grim countenance did not change.

Vidar felt his ears grow hot with anger, his heart pumping like a bellows. He leaned over toward F'lar, whose face was only half-visible in the shadows.

"Have a care, elf," he said. "Before this war is over, you may wish you had worshiped me." One of the guards mus-cled between the Aesirman and the wizened elf then and thrust crosswise at Vidar with the shaft of his spear. Vidar stumbled backward a step and latched onto the spear. Then he tore it from the guard's hands and broke it over his knee.

Another elf came at him, this time with the point, and Vidar ducked, so that the spearhead missed him and he could drive his fist into the guard's midsection. The elf doubled over and fell. Instinctively, he looked for the next spearman, but there wasn't any. What he faced was a picket of three crossbow bolts. Or'in had not moved from his place beside F'lar, but he, too, had trained his weapon at the Aesirman's heart.

"Don't, Vidar," said Eric, just behind him. Stim rumbled his assent.

"I won't," said Vidar, straightening, and suddenly sorry for what he had done—prove to F'lar that he was right, that the Aesir could not keep from violence.

F'lar spoke. "You are too dangerous to set free, Aesir-man. But we will not work our revenge by killing you—unless, of course, you again give us cause. No, my lord, I think you will spend some time with us." And he lowered his head, as if too tired to say any more.

Or'in flicked his hand in the direction of the doorway, and, still the target of F'lar's guardians, the three prisoners walked back the way they had come. The doors opened just before they reached them, and white glare assaulted their eyes. Vidar tried to shield them with his hands.

Just behind him, he heard Or'in's voice. "Move," he said. "We must close the doors for F'lar." Nearly as blind now as when he had entered the darkness of F'lar's house, Vidar shuffled forward. He could hear the crowd. It had not left. In fact, it seemed louder and higher-pitched than before. Between blinks, Vidar could still make out the cold, haughty faces of the elves—his accusers.

Someone took his arm and guided him through what he recognized as low-slung houses, along a winding path, where more of the elves stared at him from their windows. As they trundled through G'walin, the crowd seemed to grow. Vidar felt something glance off his shoulder—a rock.

Then, just when his eyes had finally adjusted to the bright sunlight, they came to a clearing, where the elvish dwellings stood well away. In the center of the space was a barrow, which rose out of the flat, trampled ground, as if to mark the grave of a great lord. Unlike the clearing itself, it was covered with snow.

But the *lyos* did not bury their dead. At least the elves of Alfheim did not.

The sun hung like a copper disk against the deep, blue

sky. Squinting, Vidar saw that there was an opening in the barrow large enough for a man to pass through. And next to the hole, there was a slab of rock, perhaps used to cover the opening, but now pushed aside.

One of the elves that had accompanied them put down his spear and picked up a bundle that lay on the ground. Another elf, a youth, brought a stone tray of red-hot coals. Vidar knew then what the bundle was for—a torch. And since there was no need for a torch in this cold, clear dome of day, he began to understand that the barrow was but an entrance to something else.

Soon, the torch was lit. The bearer descended into the entrance, revealing the moist, root-infested maw of a tunnel.

"Follow," said Or'in, and Vidar did, feeling the hard reality of a spearpoint in the small of his back. But just as he was about to enter the barrow, an elvish woman broke from the crowd and slapped him hard across the face. Her delicate features were twisted with fury, her mouth an ugly hole from which obscenities poured forth. Around her neck, silver plates jangled.

"Murderer!" she screamed. "You killed my brothers at Dundafrost, and now you would kill us all! Murderer!" Another elf took her by the shoulders and, with some difficulty, pulled her away.

That was the last thing Vidar saw under G'walin's blue sky. He descended into the barrow behind the torchbearer, and Eric and Stim and Or'in behind him, and the world narrowed to earthen walls and a flag of flame up ahead.

The elves led them into the earth.

XVIII

You say, what is in a name? It is by our names that we know ourselves, my lords, and that is how we plumb the true depths of our courage and our strength.

Learn as the Aesir did, at a wrestling match. Oh, such tournaments were something for the gods to look forward to, for they gave the young Aesirmen a taste of combat, before they gorged themselves on it in Jotunheim. But there was a glory attached to the mock combats themselves, aside from any raids to come, and Odin always gave a prize to the winner.

For Ragnarok was never far away, and Asgard must be ready.

In the joust, sturdy Hermod was always foremost. He knew horses better than any of his brothers. And when it came to wrestling, Thor was good—but Vidar was the best.

There was a hrimthursar named Brissung who had heard of Asgard's tournaments, and who could outgrapple any of his clansmen. He had never lost a wrestling match because he had a trick that never failed him.

Eager to pit himself against Odin's wrestlers, he made his way down from the cold, barren reaches where he lived, and found the gate to Asaheim. When he came out on the other side, Heimdall was waiting for him.

"Hold in peace," said Brissung. "I mean no harm to you or your kin. But I hear that no one can match Asgard's wrestlers, and I think that's a lie. They have never wrestled with me, and until they do that, no one can call himself a champion."

Heimdall laughed. "Go past, Brissung, but leave your spear here with me, and your knife. I think you've spent too much time in dark caves wrestling with rodents. What hrimthursar could ever outgrapple a son of Odin?"

So Brissung went down into Asgard. And when he appeared at the tournament, all eyes were upon him. Seldom had a giant set foot on the hallowed ground.

"I've come to challenge the best wrestler among you," he told Odin. The lord of Asgard laughed as Heimdall had.

"No one starts off here by wrestling the champion," Odin told him. "Let's see, first, if you can beat Tyr, my youngest son."

And Tyr stepped out of the crowd to face the giant. In those days, he still had the use of both his arms, before he lost one in a raid on Jotunheim. "Teach him a lesson, Stalker," cried one of his brothers in the crowd. It was a name Tyr had gotten as a small child, when he hunted down a ferret that had sneaked into the kitchen of Odin's hall.

Brissung shrugged off his cloak and removed his fur tunic, and Tyr stripped away his woolen shirt. Then they clashed, arms flailing, fingers gripping and slipping and clawing.

"I know you, Stalker," whispered Brissung, who had all to do to keep Tyr from throwing him. And as he uttered Tyr's nickname, the Aesirman felt the blood freeze in his veins, and the strength drained from his limbs. Brissung threw him easily.

As Tyr rose from the ground, a murmur rippled through the assemblage. "Is that the best you can do?" asked Brissung. "I thought I would find a better contest than that."

"Have no fear, giant," said Odin. "You'll face Thor next." And Thor stepped out from his place in the front of the crowd, already bare-chested. He had been hoping for a match with the insolent hrimthursar. He hated the entire race of them, and he made no bones about it.

"Set the record straight now, Thunderer," cried one of his brothers. For Thor had been called Thunderer since he acquired the hammer Mjollnir. And Thor charged into Brissung so hard that he almost knocked him down immediately. They shuffled and danced, each trying to gain the advantage. Then Brissung whispered, "You are no stranger to me, Thunderer," and Thor felt his strength drain from his arms and legs. With a mighty heave, Brissung threw him to the ground.

"Well," said the giant, "at least I'll go home without having gotten my breeches dirty."

Then Vidar stepped forward, even before he could be called. When Brissung saw him, it was his turn to laugh. "Is this your champion, Odin? He is neither as tall as my first opponent or as broad as my second. This will be the quickest work of all."

"Make him eat his taunts, Jawbreaker," shouted one of Vidar's brothers. For Vidar had been known as

Jawbreaker since he broke another Aesirman's jaw in a wrestling match.

"Wait," said Baldur, who had been observing the first two bouts. He took his brother Vidar aside. "You know that my ears are almost as good as Heimdall's, Vidar. I've been listening to this hrimthursar, and before each throw he has spoken his opponent's nickname. He knows yours now, too."

Vidar glared at the giant over his shoulder. "But what can I do?"

"The dark elf," said Baldur, "has a nickname, also—but only one other living being knows it. They believe that to know one's nickname is to have power over him. Remember the name I've called you since you won those boots at the last tournament?"

"Yes," said Vidar, eyeing the hrimthursar. "Leathershod."

"Let that be your true name, now. Hold that to you, because Brissung does not know it. Only you and I will know that name."

"Thanks, Baldur," said Vidar, pulling his tunic off.

"Now that you've taken counsel, perhaps you'll show me some spirit," said Brissung. "More than your brothers did, anyway."

"Yes," said Vidar. "I'll show you some spirit." They came together violently, and Brissung saw that Vidar was more cunning than the other two had been.

"You can't escape me, Jawbreaker," he said, and Vidar felt his muscles go limp. Brissung almost toppled him then, but he remembered what Baldur had whispered to him, and a portion of his strength returned.

"I can see right through you, Jawbreaker," said Brissung, wondering why his opponent had not fallen. "You're just a bag of tricks." Again he tried to throw Odin's son, and again he failed.

Then, with all the energy left to him, Vidar heaved and tossed Brissung on his back.

"Ho!" cried Odin. "Our champion has shown you a trick of his own, braggart. And for your insolence, we'll show you to the slave quarters, where you can brag to the other giants between hauling the road-stones and feeding the horses."

Then Odin turned to Vidar and asked, "What was it that Baldur told you, my son?"

But Vidar shrugged and told Odin it was nothing. For it was wiser, he thought, to trust one single being with something so precious than to trust even the Lord of Asgard with it.

What, my lord? Yes, I, too, have a secret name. Even I.

Sin Skolding
Rogaland, 386 A.D.

XIX

There was the smell of earthworms and loose dirt underfoot. The flickering torch flame that danced up ahead threw long, hard shadows against the earthen walls with every twist of the passage. From time to time, there was the prick of a spearpoint at Vidar's back. And the cold of a sunless place. But for those things, he knew nothing—not even where they were going. The earth swallowed all sound.

They walked for long hours until Vidar sensed that they were descending. The air grew mustier, thick with the sweet smell of roots and vines, but it was still air, and they could still breathe. Then the roots thinned out and disappeared altogether, and Vidar knew that they had gone down even deeper.

It came to him suddenly, and he wondered why he had not fit that piece to the puzzle before. The under-elves, the *dwarvin*. The master smiths and tunnel builders of Svartheim. But Odin had set only a few of them down here in

Utgard—and he had slain them all himself, hadn't he? Yet these tunnels—who else could have dug them? Not the elves of G'walin, surely.

The darkness began to weigh on him as if he held up all the earth above him on his shoulders. His eyes were dry, his throat likewise, and he had not eaten or quenched his thirst since they left Valland. Like an idiot wrath, a fast-food jingle came to him: "You deserve a break today..." He chuckled, but it was muffled by the walls of the passageway.

The tunnel twisted so that the torch disappeared, throwing them into shadow. They rounded the shoulder of earth and it reclaimed them. Onward, monotonously, Vidar followed the flame, his steps falling into a cadence, his feet moving of their own accord. He thought of Woodstock, of the half-finished sculpture in his studio—with its single window overlooking the reservoir—and longed for that sight.

He looked at the smooth texture of the tunnel walls and saw that the *dwarvin*— if it was the *dwarvin* who had cut these passages—had been sculptors of the earth no less than Odin and Baldur. They had taken Odin's work and made their own modifications as it suited them, but with uncanny skill.

And hadn't they been the ones who wrought the hammer, Mjollnir, and forged Frey's sword, and repaired the horn when it was cracked? The horn ... which Vali now carried, attuning it to his own being, so that he could wind it against Ygg. Slowly, Vidar's thoughts drifted toward the confrontation at Indilthrar.

Vali seemed to have the advantage. Modi rode by his side, and he was a factor in any battle. Not to mention Hoenir—ancient lecher and his father's brother. Hoenir carried no weapon such as Mjollnir, but the lore of the ages was at his right hand. Like Odin, he was *gaut,* a Creator.

But Ygg would not be taken without much bloodshed,

and perhaps not at all. Even Vali did not seem to know how many nomads Ygg could draw out of the hills to fight for him, and if Indilthrar was as well fortified as Skatalund, the siege could go either way. Then there was the sky-serpent. And who knew what other powers Hod might have discovered in his long hiding.

More windings, more darkness intertwined with deeper darkness, and still the redolence of dank, living earth. The chill ate into Vidar's bones and stiffened his knees.

But nothing mattered nearly so much as the horn. If Vali could bind it to him, the nomads at Indilthrar would have no more chance than their kinsmen at Skatalund. Yet Vali was no *lifling*, and untrained in such matters. . . .

So intent was Vidar on the impending war that he almost failed to notice a difference in the air—a movement, a breeze. Was the tunnel widening? Yes. It grew broader and taller as they walked. The light of the torch, which had waned slightly, flared with new vigor. But the darkness was also lessening, giving way like the night before the morning. Finally, the torch became unnecessary, and its bearer dashed it against one of the outcroppings of rock. It had burned to almost nothing anyway.

Still the tunnel wound through the earth, but now a ruby-red radiance was in sight. It did not lead them up, but straight ahead. Sudden warmth hit Vidar like a huge hand, stifling his breath and making his eyes sting. Cinders rode that wave of hot wind, and the acid smell of . . . molten metal?

As he approached the radiance, he heard a clanging and a wheezing, as if giants were choking in the earth. The tunnel ended in smoke and ruddy light. Vidar squinted and passed through into what seemed like a huge, vaulted chamber. The clanging stopped and two silhouettes appeared out of the hellish vapors—tall, limned by the light and half-concealed by the billowing smoke. Each of them held something weaponlike in his hand. The elf who had carried the torch signed for Vidar to stop. He stopped, and Stim and Eric and the others spilled out into the open space.

Or'in left the group and approached the sentinels. They must have known him, for their stances remained casual and their voices low. One of them left, wading through the smoke, and seemed to vanish. The other continued to talk with Or'in. At one point, the elf gestured toward Vidar, and both their heads turned his way. For a moment, they regarded him, twins in stance and stature—one bright in his pale hair and burnished armor, the other bare-breasted and dark with soot; one cloaked and adorned like a lord, the other with his black locks gathered tightly behind his head like a servant. What he held in his hands, Vidar realized, as the smoke began to subside, was a pair of blackened tongs.

So he had always remembered the under-elves, their green eyes gleaming from within faces as black as coal, hammers and tongs hanging from their belts, their feet bound in thick, leather sandals. Like the over-elves, their features were finely wrought and their skin smooth beneath the soot. Their beardlessness made them all look like youths. But unlike their cousins of Alfheim, the *dwarvin* had never been innocent—not on this world or any other. On Svartheim, even the Aesir did not seek them out, for they were as powerful as any race, in their own fashion. They had skills that not even the Aesir—save perhaps Odin—could comprehend.

Before long, other dark figures joined Or'in, and these were armed with true weapons—the swords they themselves had forged, enhanced with whatever runic fevers they had worked into the molten blood of the metal. The smoke had filtered away enough, by this time, to reveal part of the cavern—including the great, natural chimney that sundered the ceiling and let the distant light of day slip through.

There was more conversation—negotiation, it seemed—and Or'in kept gesturing at the captives. Finally, he seemed satisfied, and then a couple of *dwarvin* brought from the recesses of the cavern a sheaf of swords bound together at the hilt. Vidar almost laughed when he realized what they had been about—he, Eric and Stim had been bartered for a stack of blades.

Two of Or'in's elves came forward to accept the price of the slaves. Or'in spoke a few more words to his *dwarvin* counterparts, clasped their hands, and then returned to his party. He looked at Vidar and he smiled—a savage expression, for all the gentleness of his features.

"You will like it here, Aesirman," said the elf. "Our comrades will see to it that your great energies do not go to waste. It is only a pity that you will probably survive, but they suppose it bad luck to kill you. They are not as enlightened as the *lyos*."

Vidar shrugged. "Maybe when G'walin is overrun, you'll realize what a mistake you made."

Then Or'in turned to Eric. "I am sorry, but we cannot let you go free to let Vidar's whereabouts be known. Perhaps, at some later time, we will buy you back . . . but for now, your masters are the *dwarvin*."

Eric said nothing. He just looked at Vidar. Stim, strangely, was the one who spoke. "We will meet again, elfprince," he said, baring his fangs, and his voice echoed against the walls.

Or'in looked at Stim and smiled again. Then he raised his hand and went back into the tunnel. His elves followed, until the last of them had vanished.

The *dwarvin* gathered around them, grim in their dark tunics and their soot-streaked faces. Their swords glinted savagely in the glow from what Vidar could now see was a bellows fire.

"Come with us," said one of them, and Vidar moved to follow. They were only armed with swords, and not crossbows or spears, and he was tempted to try to escape. But where would he go? If there was another way out than the one by which they had entered, it would take some time to find it.

They crossed the chamber, passing by the great cauldron where red-hot iron still roiled, and left by an opening on the other side. Vidar found himself in another tunnel, but a short one, and this opened into an even larger cavern than the one they had first entered. There must have been a couple of dozen of the *dwarvin* there, working the bellows, bringing more loads of wood for the fire, pouring into stone molds or striking at the cooling metal with hammers. They sent up a clamor that filled the cavern to its smoke-filled heights, and no one stopped even to glance at the captives as they passed.

Vidar traversed another cavern, and then another, each one larger than the one before it, and busier with fire and sweat-slicked bodies. The heat had started out a welcome thing after the chill of the tunnel, but Vidar had now started to sweat freely in his woolen garb.

Before they entered the fifth cavern, Vidar knew that they had reached their destination. No smoke billowed forth from this place, and the stone-and-packed-earth floors gave way even at the entranceway to square-hewn pieces of blue-veined marble. The chamber was illuminated with great, gilded braziers on either side, and at the far end, and huge tapestries hung suspended between them on the walls. Overhead, there was no crack in the earth, but rather a frozen, golden rainfall of stalactites—created by the seeping of water through the mineral deposits above them.

With armed *dwarvin* on either side of them, Vidar, Eric and Stim walked into the chamber and trod the marble floor, the braziers' flames leaping up and striking light from floor and ceiling alike. Fire above and ice below, hot Nature and cold artifice, the warring of opposite forces here in the bowels of Utgard.

Even before he had gone very far, Vidar saw that this *dwarvin* society was a matriarchy. Enveloped within a true throne, which rose golden and shimmering and dragon-winged about her, with rubies and sapphires encrusted in its arms and the canopy that curled scroll-like over her head, the queen of the *dwarvin* was a sinuous, slender shadow. But Vidar could see her grace outlined in her posture, in the way the light and shadows dressed her face, and with a sense that sight had nothing to do with, he knew that she was beautiful. As he approached her, that beauty seemed to fill the cavern.

Yet, Vidar could see only half her face—a little more now and then a little less, as the braziers' flames danced with each movement in the air. She was dark and mysterious in the lizardlike embrace of her throne.

They stopped before her, and Vidar heard his own breathing—distinctly, as if it were the only sound in the chamber. He listened for the clamor of the smithies, but it had been overlaid with an intimate, immediate silence.

"You are the lord Vidar of the Aesir?" she asked simply. Her voice was low and melodic, like a deep-channeled river, but there was a tinge of irony in it.

"I am," he said, unable to see her eyes for the shadows of her canopy. "And whom do I have the pleasure of addressing?"

She tilted her head slightly. "I am known as B'rannit. I rule here in under-G'walin. And I have been charged with your keeping."

"What would you do with them?" he asked, indicating Eric and Stim. "They should be freed, my lady. This is no business of theirs—they are only my retainers."

"Three came in together, and three they shall stay," said B'rannit. She paused. "I have word from F'lar, the prince of G'walin, that you purposed to join Ygg in his city."

"I wanted to speak with him," Vidar said. "I wanted the

chance to come between him and Vali, for no one will win that battle."

B'rannit nodded, her face moving in and out of the firelight. "You believe that you can persuade Ygg to drop his sword and make peace?"

She made it sound absurd—and maybe it was. But he had to try it, if he ever escaped this place.

"I believe," he said, "that there is a chance. Some talking here, some talking there, and I can drive a wedge of time between Vali's headlong rush and Ygg's thirst for power. If you know of the hatred Vali has for Hod, you know it is not new—but I think I can cool his fire."

"We know more of the Aesir than you might imagine," said B'rannit. "We know of Vali's hatred, yes—of Baldur, as well. We know of the rivalries in Asgard, and we know that you have not been a part of them. Not since the Battle, at least. Where have you been, my lord?"

My lord? The words were ironic, given his present position, but there was something in B'rannit's voice that gave Vidar pause. Was she asking *where* he had been or why he had been *away*? He searched her face, unsure. Could there be hope here?

"I've been in Midgard," he told her. "But now I'm in Utgard, and I am your captive, while my kinsmen prepare to devastate your world."

B'rannit laughed, and it was like the jangling of silver bells. "A captive?" she said. "Do you think, my lord, that just because a fool like F'lar asks us to jail you—that we are also foolish? No, my friend. We of under-G'walin agree with you. When the Aesir war, only the Aesir can stop it."

Eric whooped and clapped Stim on the shoulder. The giant just nodded, as expressionless as ever.

Vidar couldn't believe his ears.

"These swords you see about you," said B'rannit, "are yours." She leaned forward ever so slightly and her face was washed in the light from the braziers. It was more lovely than Vidar could have dreamed.

Her eyes flashed green fire as she spoke. "But first you must eat with us. The *dwarvin* do not travel on empty stomachs as our cousins aboveground do. No smith worth his mallet ever worked on an empty stomach."

XX

The *dwarvin* were few in Utgard, for Odin did not want them to honeycomb that world with tunnels as they had done in Svartheim. But that did not stop him from commanding them to construct a sailing ship. Not any sailing ship, mind you, but one that would weather even the fiercest storm. Some say that Odin wanted a ship that would not even touch the waves, but fly above them.

The under-elves accepted their task grudgingly. They complained of their working conditions. They did not like to work in daylight, on the beach, where the sun would burn their fair skin and the light dazzle their eyes. Give us something to do underground, they asked—a hammer, a sword, iron wheels for your chariot.

But Odin wanted a ship, and they could not refuse him. The *dwarvin* worked grimly for weeks, carving the wood of a nearby forest into masts and into timbers, which they bent into graceful curves with their clever machines.

Finally, the vessel was finished, and no one but the under-elves could have created it. It boasted proud sails bellied full of wind, a prow of grace and strong sides that would withstand any seas. It was not until Odin boarded the ship that he saw its flaw—it had no helm, no way to steer it. Why, he asked, did the ship have no steering mechanism? Would he not get himself lost in the oceans of Utgard without it?

The under-elves, painfully sunburned, said nothing. But their silence showed that what had seemed an oversight was full of purpose. They were not without a sense of humor, after all. And they did not like what they did not like.

Odin blasted them. There was nothing left, my lords. Nothing.

Sin Skolding
Samsey, 414 A.D.

XXI

Once washed in an underground stream, the *dwarvin* looked more like their cousins aboveground. They were handsome, fair-skinned people, with the same green eyes that characterized all elves. But where the *lyos* loved ornaments, the *dwarvin* were content to wear their simple, black tunics.

A long table was brought into B'rannit's brazier-lit chamber, and food appeared as if from nowhere. Vidar saw birds and fish and bread and vegetables, obtained mostly through trade with those above and, in part, from infrequent forays up to the surface. A few of the under-elves, in fact, had developed into pretty fair fishermen, Vidar was told, and never came back from aboveground without a net full of fish. Or so the fisherman, a jocular, green-eyed youth, had told him.

There was also mead of a sweet, caramel-flavored variety, which went down smoothly and warmed the insides. Once the fires were stopped—and contrary to Asgardian

rumor, the *dwarvin* did stop their work to sleep—it grew
cool in the caverns. The mead fed the inner fires, though,
and Vidar wondered that he had found such cheer here in
under-G'walin. In fact, these *dwarvin* acted more like the
elves of Alfheim than the elves of Svartheim—another Utgardian anomaly.

B'rannit did not eat with them, whatever her reasons.
Yet after the food was cleared, an elf told Vidar that he was
invited to join the lady in an alcove among the caverns, and
he offered to lead him there. Vidar followed him through
a chain of caverns and the walls turned from hard-packed
earth to chiseled rock. Tapestries were everywhere, it seemed,
and there were no bellows in these places.

They came to a narrow tunnel, and the elf signed for
Vidar to enter it, while he stayed at the entrance. Vidar followed the tunnel along its dark, wandering length, with
one hand running lightly against the stone for guidance. At its
end, he heard the sound of falling water, and he emerged into
a small, green grotto overgrown with lichen and with vines.

He found B'rannit there, and this time her face was not
veiled in shadows. It was illuminated by the light of small
torches set into the stone itself, as if the whole cave were
a candelabra—and she was beautiful, as all the elves were
beautiful, but with a touch of something else as well. There
was a vibrance, a freshness to her, that at once seemed alien
and agonizingly familiar. Until now, Freya had been the
most beautiful woman he'd ever seen—but Freya was dead,
and this queen of under-G'walin was exquisitely alive.

"Welcome," she said, smiling.

"Thank you, my lady," he replied. He found himself
staring and looked away, as if interested in something else.
Inside, he laughed at his own speechlessness. "You sum-
moned me, B'rannit?"

"I asked you to join me," she said. B'rannit wore a long
gown, dark as ebon, and its neckline insinuated itself deep
between her breasts. She was tall, almost as tall as Vidar

himself, and she was not quite as slender as he had first guessed. No, her body seemed strong to him, and her posture was breathtakingly erect.

Behind her, a small waterfall washed the stone, which had been stained green, orange, yellow and red by the minerals deposited on it over the many years. Baldur might have been the architect of this grotto, so clever was it in its pleasures.

Then, when she saw that he was not about to speak, she went on. "My lord, forgive my curiosity, but I know little of Midgard. Why did you retreat there after the Battle?"

Vidar sat on a ridge of lichen-covered stone to one side of her. B'rannit's eyes were greener than bright emeralds.

"I became tired," he said. "Tired of the killing, the faces that looked up to me with hope only to be dashed fighting Odin's wars. I grew tired of slaughter, the only life I had known. Since I was old enough to pick up a wooden practice-sword, I'd been tutored in the ways of war. Why should I have questioned it?

"Perhaps the doubts were there all along—but it was Ragnarok that opened my eyes. Watching Heimdall cut down at Loki's hands, seeing Frey die slowly, trying to keep his own insides from spilling out—it made me see how futile it had been, all the bloodshed that had gone before. If there was no Heimdall, no Frey, then there was no Asgard—nothing to live after—and what had been the point?"

Vidar found that his fists had clenched, and he relaxed them self-consciously. "Do you see what I mean, B'rannit?" he asked softly. "It was one thing to kill when I thought the killing had a purpose. I could even watch my retainers perish and chalk it up to glory. But it was another thing to see my brothers, my kinsmen, scattered like broken birds over the expanse of Vigrid. There was no one to reap the harvest of victory."

"Yet you won, my lord," said B'rannit.

"Yes," said Vidar, and he could not keep the bitterness

out of his voice. "We won. There wasn't a hrimthursar left standing. But our strategy had gone awry. We had hoped to catch them in a pincer movement, but there were more of them than we thought. They broke through our middle, dragging Hermod down with our banner and cutting off Odin's phalanx from Bragi's. And then the wolves—who expected to have to fight wolves?

"In the end, I still lived. I walked over the battlefield, the snow churned to mud underfoot. I was dazed, drained as much by my utter loneliness as by my wounds. As the sounds of battle fled on the wind and Loki's eldritch fires spent their black smoke on every side, I heard the cries of the Aesir—and they were mingled with the agony of the hrimthursar and the yelps of the wolves that Loki had brought down upon us. I saw that in pain and in death, there is no difference among us. That was the lesson of Ragnarok— that we are no different except as we choose to be."

B'rannit said nothing, only watching and listening, but she seemed to open the floodgates of memory with her silence.

"While I tended to the wounded, drawing out a little pain from each one that would live, I had time to think of how it had all started. How we had found the bodies of our women and their defenders strewn over the streets of As- gard, the mighty towers burning and the walls spattered with Aesir blood. Of course, we forgot the times we had raided Jotunheim while its warriors were away and worked the same evils on them. We blinded ourselves to the truth— that we were two edges of the same sword. So we carried the war back to them, and that was Ragnarok.

"I pondered all this, B'rannit, when it was too late. I heard Heimdall call to me, and he died in my arms. Heim- dall, who had taught me how to pick up a sword when I was barely bigger than the sword itself. I saw Bragi the poet, the eldest of my brothers, clutch at his stomach and try to keep his feet while death spread from the swordpoint in his guts to his knees and then his brain. There was death all about. The world was coming to an end."

"But it did not end," said B'rannit gently.

Vidar shook his head, his eyes glazed and staring. "No. For even on that plain of fury and storm, where Odin had perished in a burst of flame and even the youngest of the Aesir lay still—even there, I saw that it was not over. Vali the Avenger rode among the fallen, putting to death with his long spear any giant that still drew breath. Modi, newly bearded, smote corpses even as the tears rolled down his cheeks, as if that could bring Thor back to life.

"Of them all, only Magni, Thor's younger son, sat aloof. And when I looked at his handsome face, I saw the same disgust, the same weariness that I felt. But Magni had ever been a youth apart, an observer in the affairs of Asgard. If he had ambitions or ecstacies, he kept them to himself.

"As for me, I did my share, carrying the dead from Vigrid. My arms were covered with blood to the shoulders before we were done. We built a fire in the center of that iron plain. It took the better part of a foreboding day. The sky was slate, the sun nearly hidden, and red was the only color we saw.

"We said good-bye to our heroes—as we had said farewell to Baldur a short time before. Heimdall, Tyr, Frey, Hermod, Bragi and Thor—all lay shoulder to shoulder. They were horribly pale in the light of the blood-smoked sun, having died gloriously in the name of Odin's eternal enmity against the giants. But they were no less dead than the hrimthursar themselves, or Loki, who had led them to Asgard.

"There were no mothers and wives to weep for the fallen, so we wept for them. And we wept for ourselves as well, for what would life be without them? What would Asgard be without Odin?"

Vidar could see even now the faces of the dead, bloated by the heat of the consuming flames—and hear the impatient screams of the carrion birds. He drew a deep breath. B'rannit was silent and intent on his words, her eyes a balm for the pain he had unearthed.

"Then they were gone," he continued, "and Vali cried out that we must rebuild Asgard. Of all the survivors, only five of us were of Odin's blood—and neither Modi, Magni, Hoenir nor I challenged Vali's bid for the people's trust. He was like a wolf among sheep. The rest of us were demoralized, weary with fighting, mourning our kinsmen. But Vali rose from Ragnarok with vigor redoubled, as if he drew strength from the crisis. If he had not, there might have been no Asgard today. But he replenished its fires, slowly and surely.

"I had no heart for it, B'rannit. A few days later, I left. I said no farewells, nor did I take much with me. I left my sword behind, and by that I meant for Asaheim to know I would not be coming back. The mighty halls and the streets of gold had lost their luster for me."

B'rannit nodded her lovely head. "But why Midgard, my lord?"

"Because it had all but escaped the influence of the Aesir. At one time, Odin had trod a land now known as Europe, and recruited warriors for his battles with the hrimthursar. They hailed him as a god and he promised them eternal feasting if they should die fighting in his name—though, of course, he could never make good on his promise.

"Sometimes, I think there may have been something Odin wished to preserve there. After a while, he left Midgard alone. Oh, from time to time I or one of my brothers would explore it—but Midgard always seemed to escape our bolder intentions. I'm thankful it did. When I left Asgard, I wanted to find the farthest place I could from Vigrid and its ghosts, and Midgard fit the bill.

"At that time, Midgard was still shrouded in what has come to be called the Dark Ages. I could have made an appearance as Vidar the God, but I wished to forget all that came with that identity. I began my new life as a minstrel, a skald, and I traveled throughout the northern part of Europe and places now called Iceland and Greenland. My voice left much to be desired, but I had passable skill on the harp. After all, I'd had much time to learn it."

"You have not forgotten how to tell a tale," said B'rannit.

"Thank you," said Vidar. "But it would be difficult to forget this one."

"Was it a hard life, my lord?"

Vidar shrugged. "Not especially. It taught me humility, for my next meal depended on how well I sang, and what feudal lord I might please with my song. And I could not make any friends, for they would age and pass away, and I would not. But that suited me then—I had lost enough friends for a lifetime.

"Ironically, tales of the Aesir and their enemies were my stock in trade. It was all my hosts wanted to hear. In time, I found that others of my ilk also sang of the Aesir, but it was far from accurate. Time had twisted it or gilded it. I sang the truth, more or less, and after a while I—or Sin Skolding, as I was known—had some influence on the other skalds. First, only I would sing of Ragnarok. Then, everyone sang of it. Although it was not my intention, the spread of news about Ragnarok made it easier for a group of priests called Christians to convert the people of northern Europe to their own beliefs. Once the people of Midgard heard that the Aesir were dead, they began to clutch at new idols."

"Then what?" asked B'rannit, and she was childlike in her fascination. "Tell me more, Leathershod."

Vidar stared at her. "What did you call me?"

Her eyes opened wide, startled at his change in demeanor. Then she laughed. "Leathershod, my lord. I forgot—it's supposed to be a secret, isn't it?"

Vidar shook his head. "Yes. I thought it died with Baldur. B'rannit," he said with some urgency, "how do you know that name?" He felt naked, strangely, before that knowledge.

"You need not be concerned, my lord," she answered. "I am the only one who knows it, having learned it from my mother on her deathbed. As she learned it from her mother, and so on."

"But Baldur was the only one who knew . . ." And even as his voice trailed off, he realized what seemed so familiar in her face. It was elvish in its finely made features, its slightly slanted eyes, and its childlike softness—but now Vidar knew that the tales of how Baldur spent his youth in Svartheim had some truth to them. Baldur had long been fascinated by the *dwarvin*'s skill, with which they had fashioned an entire subterranean world. It was only natural for one studying to be *gaut* to take such an interest. But there had later been rumors that his visits to the caves and the smithies were camouflage for his trysts with an elvish female—something Baldur had neither confirmed or denied, taking it as lightly as he took everything else.

Was that how these *dwarvin* had come to Utgard, after Odin destroyed the first group? Through Baldur, who wished to keep his lover close while he put the finishing touches on the world Odin had made?

Vidar looked into B'rannit's eyes. "You have Baldur's blood," he said.

"Do not look so astonished," she answered, taking his hand in hers. It was only now, with her face so near, that he noticed the fine line of gold that ran through her hair from the temples.

But that realization was quickly swept away by the smell of her, honey and musk and poppy's breath, and the softness of her hands and the green depths of her eyes. Before he knew it, he had taken B'rannit in his arms.

She did not move to stop him. In fact, she gradually returned his embrace with more fervor than he might have thought her capable of. Her lips were firm and warm beneath his and he reveled in her—in the feel of her body beneath her thin, dark gown, in the hardness of her hips and the fullness of her breasts.

When he raised his face from hers, still light-headed with her perfume, B'rannit's eyes were open and looking into his. "Does this mean you do not wish to tell me more of Midgard?" she asked and half suppressed an impish smile.

"Yes," he said. "Some other time."

And as the night passed, Vidar found that there were more pleasures in the grotto than he might have guessed.

XXII

Vidar woke to find himself alone. Half of the torches had burned out, leaving a lazy, artificial dawn light in the grotto. B'rannit was gone, but someone had laid out a loaf of dark-crusted bread, some fish meat and a jug of cool water on a mossy shelf. Next to that was a black tunic. The yellow one he'd been given in Skatalund had disappeared, though his leather jerkin, his trousers, his boots and his cloak remained.

Vidar could not help but smile as he ate the breakfast B'rannit had left him. She thinks of everything, that girl, he mused, and he could not help but think of her as a young woman—although the elves lived much longer than men, if not nearly as long as the Aesir. When he was finished, he dressed. The elvish fabric felt silken and airy against his skin, putting to shame his woolen garment. The little waterfall in the grotto gurgled its approval.

Then, as if it had been known when he would eat and dress, a *dwarvin* male came in, and the look on his face—

not to mention the sword at his belt—gave him a very businesslike appearance. He introduced himself as M'rann. Vidar did not miss the family resemblance and he said so.

"B'rannit is my sister," he said. It gave rise to a warm feeling in Vidar to know that so much of Baldur had survived in his descendants. Here in little under-G'walin, he had found an unexpected branch of the family tree.

M'rann sat down. "We must chart a route to Indilthrar, my lord."

"To Indilthrar?" For a night, at least, he had forgotten about that. "Good. And thank you, M'rann. I guess I'd better round up Eric and Stim and get going, then."

"They await you," said M'rann, "with the other warriors."

"Other warriors? M'rann, I think you're a couple of steps ahead of me. What other warriors? I don't need an army to get to Indilthrar."

M'rann smiled, a glint of humor in his eyes. "Not an army, my lord. But enough of a company to see you safely through the tunnels to your destination."

"The tunnels?" echoed Vidar. "We can't reach Indilthrar through the tunnels—can we?" M'rann nodded. "How far can we get that way?"

The elf shrugged. "How far would you go? To the priests' own kitchens?"

Vidar laughed, and the grotto rang with it. "Where did these tunnels come from? When?"

"We of under-G'walin," said M'rann, "are not without foresight. We live so near to that city, after all. And there is not enough forgework to occupy all of us all of the time."

"Love that foresight," said Vidar.

"But I must warn you," said the elf, "that before we can reach the passages we made, there is a river to be navigated. An under-earth current, and not without its dangers."

"Such as?" Vidar asked.

"There is a riptide at one point. And rocks. Perhaps serpents, for we have seen them there."

Vidar nodded. "It still sounds less dangerous than aboveground, with Vali's armies all over the place, and no sure way to get inside the city." He pulled his cloak on over one shoulder. "Let's try it your way, M'rann."

"It will be my pleasure," said the elf. M'rann led him through the narrow, twisting tunnel he had followed the night before to the grotto. Then there were a series of caverns, some large and some small, and another tunnel. Finally, they emerged into the largest cavern he had seen yet, and Vidar found himself standing on the sandy shore of an underground lake. The water reflected light from a crack in the ceiling, and the play of sunbeams on the shadowy depths was mystical, almost entrancing. There was much beauty in Utgard, even below its crust.

A fleet of six slim, dark vessels awaited, moored to wooden posts at the shoreline. The *dwarvin* that would man them stood ready and armed, their black tunics reflected in the lake. Stim and Eric were among them, and Eric, too, wore the black tunic. Stim had either disdained it or they had been unable to find one big enough to fit him.

Eric grinned. The concern in his face when he had first learned of Vidar's travel plans was gone. In its place there was an eagerness. It seemed that under-G'walin had raised his spirits, too. Vidar was glad to see it.

B'rannit was there, also, with a number of elvish maidens. Seeing her again struck a chord in Vidar. She smiled. "Good morn," she said, her eyes dancing.

"Good morning, my lady," he returned. Then he strode over to her and took her hands. "If I ever get out of Indilthrar in one piece, I'm coming back for you, B'rannit," he said in a low voice. "How do you feel about that?"

"I shall look forward to your return, my lord," she said. But her eyes said much more.

Then he let go of her hands, reluctantly, and went down to the boats. He looked at M'rann and nodded, and the elf directed their company to board. Vidar himself stepped inside one of the wooden shells, where he found a couple of paddles and a pair of torches smeared with some kind of resin. There was also a flint with which to get the torches going.

M'rann got in after Vidar. "My lord," he said and held out a sword, hilt-first. "I thought you might need one of these." Vidar sighed and took it. After all, M'rann had said there might be serpents. And once he got to Indilthrar, how far could he get without it?

The elf turned around, drew his sword and cut the rope that held them. They drifted slowly out from the shore, and Vidar saw the other vessels drift out after them. Again and again, he heard the *thwack* that signaled freedom from the moorings. Narrow corridors of golden sunlight streamed down on them, an unexpected warmth in the chill of the cavern. When all the vessels had been released, M'rann took up his paddle and dipped it into the water. With one skillful stroke, he sent them skimming across the surface. Vidar dug his own paddle into the water and pushed a bit too hard. The skiff rocked perilously for a moment, then righted itself. He looked back at M'rann, and the elf was smiling beneath his dark brows.

"I'll get the hang of it," Vidar promised and tried it again with a little less enthusiasm. This time, he propelled the boat smoothly.

"There you go, my lord," said M'rann. Vidar turned to see if the elf was still smiling, but he wasn't even looking in Vidar's direction. M'rann was waving back at the shore, at B'rannit and the other *dwarvin*. Vidar waved, too, granting himself one more look at the elfqueen. He could not be sure, because the sunbeams slanted between them, but he thought she put her fingers to her lips.

He turned and dipped his paddle into the water again. Ahead lay Indilthrar.

The small fleet darted across the subterranean lagoon like slim, dark fish, and although the watery expanse was larger than it had first seemed, they reached the other side fairly quickly. As they approached a large tunnel on the far side, Vidar saw that the lake entered into it.

M'rann put aside his paddle and lit one of the torches with the flint. He pointed to the tunnel. "Aim for that," he said. Vidar nodded and guided the vessel into the opening, the light from M'rann's brand breaking up the darkness before them. They slipped into the tunnel quietly. But what had seemed like a large space quickly closed around them. After a few strokes, the roof was only a few feet above their heads, and they could have touched the wall on either side with their paddles. Vidar could not have stood up if he wanted to.

Water slushed about them and light danced off the slick, rock walls, as if it sought a way out of the tunnel's narrow confines. There was a sickly-sweet smell of rotting seaweed, or something similar, and the lower parts of the walls were covered with dark green slime.

His thoughts turned to Vali. Nearly four days had passed since his half brother left Skatalund. According to Eric's estimate, Vali would reach Indilthrar the following afternoon. What would he do once he got there? Normally, he would settle in for the night and bide his time. But this was no normal situation. Hod was a *stromrad*, an elemental— and that meant that time could work for both of them. While Vali let Indilthrar's food supply run down, the sky-serpent would be getting ever nearer.

Would Vali attack right away? Vidar hoped not. The longer he delayed, the more chance Vidar would have to talk them out of it.

The slimed walls past which they paddled began to blur as the current quickened, and Vidar's sight turned inward.

What would Baldur have said if he saw the conflict to come, and knew that Vali did it for his sake? If he could come back to life, even for a moment, he would know the words to soothe Vali's longing for revenge—and to cool Hod's lust for power.

Baldur. His name alone was like a balm. As brave in battle as any of Odin's sons, but only Baldur could be trusted with one's heartfelt secrets. He was everyone's confidante and no one's betrayer. Once, a thursar that Baldur had slain in Jotunheim whispered a message for his wife with stone-cold lips, and Baldur saw that message delivered. To this day, no one but Baldur and the giant's wife had heard his last words.

Maybe that was why he was loved so well—he carried a little part of everyone, the part they kept hidden from all others, perhaps even from themselves. But the last secret Baldur kept was the strangest.

It was after he had been placed on the pyre of his funeral ship, and his heavy-cloaked bearers had left. That was when Odin boarded and stood by Baldur's side. All the Aesir and the Vanir save Hod and Vali had come down to the quay at which the vessel was moored. And all could see the tear that hung on Odin's cheek and disappeared in his beard, signifying the first and last time Odin had been known to weep. The iron-gray sky groaned then, as if commiserating. Baldur's face was still beautiful in death, like ivory, but softer. Odin bent down, his great shoulders hunched like eagle's pinions, and whispered something into his son's ear. Then he folded Baldur's hands on his breast, turned from him and disembarked.

Last came Nanna's turn. Baldur's young wife was the gentlest of the Aesir, a fit match for him. She was not beautiful, but there was more virtue in her than in any of the others. And she lived for Baldur as no woman ever lived for man, taking her heat from his sun and her shade from his branches. He was everything to her.

When she boarded his funeral vessel, Vidar thought her heart would break. But she showed more strength than anyone thought she had. Yes, the tears ravaged her cheeks and her hair was in disarray, but she did not wail like a child. Instead, she embraced him, and sobbed, and her body rose and shuddered over his like the waves breaking on the shore. Nanna would have mourned so forever if her baby son, Forsete, had not finally called for her. She kissed Baldur's forehead and his lips, and she allowed Heimdall to help her back over the side.

The ship was fired and it caught quickly, turning into the current and the wind. The flames leaped off the golden armlets, the jewel-handled daggers, the iron-headed spears and the silver-bossed shields—the death gifts of the Aesir and the Vanir. The timbers creaked as if in agony, and there were cries of anguish from the women. From Baldur's brothers and his companions, there were whispers, hushed farewells. More secrets for him to keep, as if that were greater treasure than the iron and silver and gold with which he had been laden.

The ship fled east from Asgard, flames climbing high into the heavens, until their black smoke tinged the clouds and darkened them even more. The water in the ship's wake was the color of blood. The air about it shivered and rippled. After a while, the vessel was gone from sight.

Then Frigga turned to Odin, and there were tears in her wise, gray eyes. But Frigga could never be defined by one reason or one emotion, and even Baldur's burning was no exception to her rule. She looked up into Odin's frowning visage and asked in a low, steady voice, "Husband, what did you tell him?"

Odin met her gaze, and his eyes looked red-rimmed and wet. But he was still Odin, and Odin never gave ground to anyone. "I told him the truth," he said. "For once." And Vidar remembered how those words he'd overheard had chilled him, standing there on the quay, where the waters of Asaheim spread boundless to the horizon.

All this he recalled while he paddled mechanically. And the walls of the tunnel, which Vidar had only half seen, swept past them. The torch in M'rann's hand behind him imposed the shadow of his head and shoulders on the walls and the water up ahead, so that a black, wavering giant seemed to point the way for them.

The current seemed to be flowing faster now. "M'rann," he said, turning to peer at the elf, "is this where it starts?"

M'rann nodded. "Yes, I believe so. Should the torch go out, my lord, use your paddle to feel for the walls. If we get too close to one or the other, fend us off." The elf was no longer smiling, but looking ahead intently.

"I'll do that," said Vidar, wondering if the slender paddle would survive much of that kind of treatment. If the skiff should overturn, here in the darkness beneath the earth, what were the odds against surviving the riptide and the rocks?

There was no question that they were skipping ahead faster now. The water swirled about the prow. Vidar found that he was using his paddle more to steer than to propel them, and he actually felt an icy breeze ruffle his hair. Far off, there was a sound—a dull, constant thrumming that reminded Vidar somehow of a Spanish guitar. As they swept forward, the sound deepened, became a drumming. Vidar's shadow danced wildly as the torch flickered in the heavier air currents. The passage no longer smelled of decay, cleansed by the rushing water and the wind.

The skiff began to rise and fall abruptly. To one side, the passage widened and the river boiled up in a fountain of froth—the first sign of a rock jutting up through the dark surface. The drumming became thunder, and there was another sound beneath it—hissing like a pit full of snakes. The boat plunged ahead suddenly, and Vidar felt it drop out from beneath them as they skipped over unseen falls. The water churned and flung them against the wall on their right. Vidar wedged his paddle between the skiff and the rock and pushed them back on course, but the current smashed them against the wall again.

Then Vidar saw his adversary—a long cascade of water that fell from some height he could not see and pounded the river with trip-hammer force. He drove his paddle against the rock face again and fended it off, the muscles of his shoulders and back straining. Yet again they were slammed into the wall, and Vidar heard the gunwhale splinter. He fought to keep from being catapulted out of the boat. Regaining his balance, he drove the paddle into the wall with all his strength—and it snapped.

Suddenly without resistance, the river spun them around. Vidar fell backward, one arm plunging into the current to the shoulder. The torch was doused. Spray shot up before them. Behind, M'rann shouted something he could not make out. There was a *thud* and a terrible creaking sound as the skiff caught on a rock. Vidar could feel its timbers strain, until the tension gripped his whole body. Then they broke, and he was hurled into the flood. He tried to rise for air, but a dark weight of water drove him under further, until he thought he would be crushed against the rock of the riverbed. The pressure took him deeper and deeper still, until his lungs screamed for air.

Then, suddenly, he was free of it. Lights flashed wildly before his eyes as he clawed desperately for the surface. Just when he could hold his breath no longer, thunder filled his ears and he knew he had found air again. His lungs filled painfully while his arms and legs flailed against the freezing-cold current. Water found its way into his nose and throat, and he coughed it up. With a jolt, he came up against something hard, and he grasped at it, clinging, fighting the fury of the waterfall. It was a finger of rock, just slender

enough to get his arms around. For a time, he kicked against
the water that threatened to dislodge him, and then it won.
He was torn loose, and the water flipped him over, so that
once again he had to battle for a mouthful of air.

Something else banged against him, and he clutched at
it instinctively. Something sharp—a fragment of the skiff.
He threw an arm over its belly and kicked himself up onto
it until he lay half in and half out of the roiling water. His
cheek rested against the wood, and he coughed out more
of the water he had swallowed. Then he concentrated on
just hanging on.

It seemed that he fought forever until his head cleared
enough for Vidar to realize that he was past the full force
of the waterfall. He let his face fall back against the ruined
skiff. Breath came fire-harsh in his throat. Again he coughed.
The water was ice-cold, but he had no strength left to pull
the rest of his body onto this life raft.

M'rann must have perished. It was only through sheer
luck that he himself had survived.

The river passage was pitch-black. Vidar could feel the
current carry him farther down into the earth. It was as if
he were riding on the back of some huge, black mole,
tunneling down through the rock into the center of the world.
But there was something that would not let him let go of
consciousness altogether, something M'rann had said
about—serpents? Serpents.

Panic rose in him, but he fought it down. Quiet. He must
be quiet. When he had gotten himself under control, he
thought of the river—fluid, churning, never still, patiently
carving the rock for all time. Patient. He filled his mind
with it.

Slowly, he reached out, carefully, as a fisherman reaches
with his net to snare salmon in the day-bright stream. He
was a *lifling*, less adept at this than the *baleygs*, the in-
fluencers, but still, he had some talent. As he drifted, he

dragged the river bottom with his inner net, searching for that which might be lurking down there. If he could get inside it, he might be able to do . . . something.

Then he found it, far below him, writhing in the current. Its great coils were unwinding. In a corner of its huge, cavernous, never-ending midnight of a mind, it knew that something edible passed overhead.

Vidar kept still, clinging to the shattered skiff, his eyes closed. Yes, it knew he was here. But it was in no great hurry. It luxuriated in the current as it stretched forth its great, scaled length, gleaming dully like treasure lost in the river-mud. It had fins, too, but these were small, and claws, but these were even smaller. They played little part in the great uncoiling. At least, the serpent seemed to think so.

Finally, it was stretched, and it wove its way up from the bottom, merging with the flow of the river, becoming a current unto itself. A living current, with massive jaws lined with small, savage teeth. But there was time for that. The morsel it had sniffed was not going anywhere very quickly.

Vidar took a broken piece of the boat's rib and snapped it off, without moving his legs enough to stir the water. It made a halfway decent weapon. Then he shut out the cold, the *shush* of the river, the pain in his bones, the weight of weariness. He slithered along with the serpent, riding in its mind, as it came closer to the meal it enjoyed all too seldom. Through its eyes, he could see the feet that dangled below the surface—but there must be more than that to the morsel.

The monster let itself rise, and then reared its head. It broke the surface of the river and its slitted eyes blinked away the water that streamed down its crown, over the ridges of its brow, and dripped from its beaklike mouth. The maw opened and the creature hissed. A forked tongue slithered and darted out like a pennant in the wind.

It considered the morsel. Too big for one gulp, it estimated. But it did not move, either, so there would be time to dismember and feed slowly. Patience. No need to hurry. Wriggle closer.

Suddenly, light, too much of it for eyes that were sensitive enough to discern one form of darkness from another. Then pain, pain and rage—for pain had been unknown. Hiss loudly, till the walls echoed with it. Turn and face the light, the pain. Arghh! More pain, and one eye suddenly sightless, the light gone in that place.

Dive, forget the morsel, dive and leave the light and the pain behind. But the pain would not be left there. It stayed, though there was thrashing and churning of the water and coils pounding the river-mud. Arghh, the pain, the shoots of agony that dragged red streaks of fire across the dull slate of consciousness. Pain that would not die . . .

"Vidar!" It was his name, he recalled numbly, and he rose from the river depths, leaving pain and darkness behind. "Vidar!" He relinquished his niche in the serpent's brain and opened his eyes. He was so weary that his vision blurred. But when things finally came into focus, it was Eric's face that loomed above him. Eric . . . he looked about him, craning his neck. He was on his back. In a boat. Stim, there, in the next boat—his bulk was unmistakable.

"How?" Vidar asked, and his voice came out like a whisper. Water streamed into his eyes, and he wiped it away with the back of his hand.

"We saw your skiff break on the rock," said Eric, "and then we lost you. But when we got past the whirlpool, we turned the corner, and there you were—with that thing about to descend on you. Thank the gods for Stim. He handled those shortswords as if they were throwing knives. I don't think the beast knew what hit it."

Vidar managed a smile. "Thanks," he said. "What about M'rann?" But he knew the answer even before their silence confirmed it.

He was B'rannit's brother, and he had been killed in

Vidar's service. Baldur's blood, no less. Another victim—
he was getting used to the idea. But did it have to be
B'rannit's brother?

"I'm sorry," he murmured. Then fatigue overtook him.
He slept, but it was not a restful sleep. Vidar dreamed of
red anguish on the river bottom, and a drowning elf, and
the look on B'rannit's face when she learned of her brother's
death. Each nightmare was more terrible than the one before
it.

XXIII

Eric woke him. They had come to another beach in another cavern, much like the one from which they had departed. But there were no slanting sunbeams here. The only light was the flickering of their torches. All above and around them was the nether-night.

They dragged the skiffs up onto the barren rock. No need to conceal them here. Vidar looked about him, tired and charley-horsed from his ordeal. The other five boats had all made the trip intact. Only M'rann had been lost. Why couldn't he have sat with someone else, someone who could negotiate the maelstrom better than he had? Vidar sighed. He had taken his toll of the *dwarvin,* as was expected of the Aesir. But that would be all the blood they would spill on his account.

"Lord Vidar," said one of the elves, who had walked over to join him.

"Yes?"

The elf pointed out a tunnel that led from the beach into

darkness. "That tunnel," he said, "will lead us to Indilthrar."

"Does it split off?" asked Vidar. "Is it possible to make a wrong turn?"

"Well, yes, my lord," said the elf, his green eyes gleaming in the torchlight. "Once we get to the vicinity of the city, there are many wrong turns to avoid. We do not want to turn up in the wrong place, you understand."

Vidar nodded. "What is your name?"

"N'arri," he said.

"Then you'll be our guide, N'arri. The rest of your people will go back the way we came, or some other way, if they wish. But I'll not be responsible for your lives once we get to Indilthrar. It's bad enough that I risk the lives of my two companions."

"But, my lord," said another of the *dwarvin*. He looked very young to Vidar, but all the elves of under-G'walin looked young to him. "We have come with you for a purpose. We knew the danger, and still we swore our swords to you. It is Midgard you seek to protect—have we not the right to help you?"

Vidar shook his head. How many times before had he heard words like those? The willingness to plunge into battle for a cause—it was a madness like any other. Maybe there were good reasons to fight, but there was no good reason to waste a life. Here and now, this elf's life would be forfeit for no good reason. It would not take an army to get him to Ygg's door—just stealth.

"No," he said. "Return to under-G'walin as I have asked."

The elf shook his head. "Do not send us home like children." The others echoed his words and the cavern echoed them once again.

"You do them a dishonor," said N'arri. "Is it M'rann? Do not grieve for him, my lord. He would not have wanted to turn and go home either. M'rann died the way he would have liked. We will sing of him in ages to come."

"Songs," said Vidar, "are not as good as breathing or

eating or loving a woman. Once you are dead, you're dead, and no song is loud enough for you to hear it. Go home." There was annoyance in his voice, something he had not meant to let show. But he had to put an end to the endless line of beings he would slay or lead to slaughter. He thought of the tents before Skatalund. "Go home. I command you to go home."

What else could they say? They had been shamed. But before they left, each one drew his sword and saluted Vidar. Brave people, he said to himself. Then he watched as the *dwarvin* boarded their vessels and, one by one, pushed off onto the underground lake. One boat was left there and the last boat had but one rider. Vidar watched their torches disappear.

"My lord," said N'arri next to him, "the way back is not without its own dangers. They cannot ride upstream, so they will have to take a side-channel, and another tunnel by foot. They will emerge aboveground in the path of Vali's armies."

"Unless they are already past," said Vidar. "And even if they are not, your companions can wait until they're gone. Either way, they stand a better chance than if they had come with us. I don't know if you have heard much about Ygg, N'arri, but he doesn't seem to take kindly to elves or men."

The green-eyed one shrugged, the torch in his hand held high. "Should I meet Ygg, I do not think I would take kindly to him, either—my lord."

Vidar managed a smile. "I guess I deserved that. But no more 'my lords' out of you, N'arri. My traveling companions call me Vidar." He looked in the direction of the tunnel, then back to N'arri. "Shall we go?"

The elf nodded and went ahead, his torch brightening the entrance as he approached. Vidar came up next, then Stim, stooping to avoid a dip in the ceiling, and Eric brought up the rear with another torch in hand. They had not been in the tunnel long before Vidar felt that he had spent his entire life in it.

"I wonder what time of day it is outside?" he said.

"Just before dark," said N'arri.

"How do you know?" Vidar asked.

"There are markings along the sides of the passage to tell me how far we are from Indilthrar. By them, I know how far we have come, and I know how long it should take to reach this point."

"How long, then, before we reach the city?" asked Eric.

"Another day and a half, by my reckoning," said N'arri.

"The river cut some time off our journey, then," said Vidar.

"Yes," said the elf. "That, and the fact that we can walk faster through the tunnels than Vali can push his armies through the mountains."

But before the sun set tomorrow, Vali would reach the walls of Indilthrar.

"You know," said Vidar, "I've about had my fill of tunnels. I feel like I'm in prison."

N'arri laughed. "I've heard our cousins in G'walin say something like that. As for me, I feel imprisoned when I'm up on the surface too long."

They walked for another couple of hours, bantering like that, until Vidar could walk no more. His near-drowning had taken more out of him than he had realized. At his suggestion, they stopped and laid out their provisions, for food had been prepared and stowed in under-G'walin before their departure. Each of them had carried a portion, along with the extra torches.

After they had eaten, they laid out their cloaks and prepared to sleep as best they could on the hard, cold rock. Hundreds of feet above them—perhaps thousands—night had descended on the world. Since there were no land-going beasts to fear belowground, they let the torches burn down and did not start new ones.

This time, Vidar slept soundly. The underworld was nothing if not peaceful.

When he woke, he felt rested. His Aesir constitution had driven out the last vestiges of fatigue. Groping in the dark for the torch and flint that lay between Stim and himself, he managed to get a flame going with a minimum of noise. In fact, he could see by the light of the torch that Eric and N'arri were still asleep. Only Stim had propped himself up on one elbow.

"Good morning," said Vidar.

"Aye," said the giant, his small, black eyes looking even smaller in the firelight.

"Sleep well?"

Stim shook his head slowly from side to side.

"Why not?" asked Vidar. "Indilthrar?"

"Yes," he rasped. "Indilthrar."

"Have you ever been there?" Vidar asked. "What can you tell me of it?"

"I have been there," said Stim, still groggy. "It is a city of fanatics. It was so even before Ygg—and the nomads—rose against us, and the thursar were split, and my kind were no longer welcome there. It is a place of altars and prayer benches. The priests of Indilthrar do not hunt or fish, nor do they farm, nor do they guard the possessions of others. They lived, before this war, by trading prayers for sustenance."

"Who did they pray to?"

"Anyone a thursar called his lord," said Stim. "To Vali, most often. Sometimes to Modi. Sometimes to you, Vidar."

"To me?" Vidar was more than a little surprised. "Why me?"

"You were one of the living Aesir," said the giant. "That was enough."

Vidar chuckled. "That's interesting." He tried to picture an assemblage of great, robed thursar sacrificing lambs in his name. It was almost funny, unless you were a lamb.

"Sometimes," Stim continued, "they offered forbidden prayers. These were not for payment. These were the gods

they themselves had chosen." Stim's voice lowered an oc-
tave. "The hrimthursar. Loki. Surtur, Fenris and Jormungand. Hrym and Burgemir. Eggthur and Byleist."

The names swarmed around Vidar's ears like ghostly
bees. The lords of the giants, the enemies of Asgard who
had ridden through the gates onto Vigrid, mounted on their
shaggy chargers to meet the challenge with blades as long
as men were tall. The hrimthursar, once used by Odin to
define all the evil in the world. Dead, all dead now, like
their foemen.

Vidar himself had slain Fenrir, Loki's eldest son, and
the wolves that prowled by his side on the battlefield. He
had killed him with a blow to the clavicle that sent his
lifeblood spurting over the white snow. But the giant's body
had torn his blade from his hands, and the wolves were
upon him before he could drag it free. So he had slain them
with his bare hands, tearing their jaws apart until their necks
snapped and they, too, bled into the snow. It was only after
the terrible, cold battle-fever had subsided that he realized
how the wolves had scored him with their teeth, and man-
gled his hands.

And so he had avenged Odin's death, although he did
not know his father was dead until later. Fenrir had brought
Odin down not by his prowess—or so they said—but because it happened to be his spear that caught the Lord of
the Ravens as he whirled on his war-horse. Then Loki had
dealt the killing blow, the fireflash that had left not even
ashes. Loki's magic was powerful that day.

"It was the worship of the hrimthursar that spurred the
priests to build walls around Indilthrar centuries ago," said
Stim. "No one—not the elves or men or even the thursar
nomads—would countenance such sacrilege. It was blasphemy. All who lived near the city took up weapons to
silence those prayers. But the priests built their fortifications. There was a siege, and in time the priests promised

to destroy the images of their forbidden gods. But it is said that they were merely concealed, not destroyed."

So in Indilthrar, at least, the hrimthursar had survived, though Odin had not. No one worshiped Odin anymore. But it made sense—a priesthood of giants, who could not help but see that they were not made in the likeness of the Aesir. The elves worshiped no one, really, but the thursar needed gods, and so they retrieved from legend the only gods they could feel at home with. The hrimthursar.

What would Odin have said if he knew that in the world he created from nothingness—*his* world—Surtur's name was remembered at the altar before his?

But no—that was not quite true anymore. Strange how it had not occurred to him. Ygg was Odin's battle guise, and Ygg was worshiped. In that sense, whoever wore his battle mask preserved Odin's worship on Utgard.

Vidar recalled Modi's description of Ygg's camp in the hills and the sacrifices, and he shivered involuntarily. The same slaughter-lord would by now have established himself in Indilthrar. What imaginative sacrifices might be going on in that city right now? He couldn't wait to find out.

Beyond Stim's hulking form, N'arri stirred. He lifted his head and peered at them. "Sleep well?" he asked. "We should leave soon. Morning wastes."

Eric murmured something and sat up, too. "Oh, these tunnels," he groaned softly. "I feel like an eighty-year-old man in this chill. My bones are creaking."

N'arri drank from a water bag. "It will be a long march today, my friends. But we will be underneath Indilthrar not long after nightfall."

Vidar nodded, got up and shook out his cloak. The chill of underground had seeped into his bones, as well. But he was a lot older than eighty, anyway.

The going was a little rougher that day. The passages were not as straight as they had been, for here the *dwarvin* had tapped into a series of natural catacombs. The floor of the tunnels rose and fell but gradually sloped upward— gently at first, but the climb became more and more rugged as they went on. In some places, they were able to climb steps that the elves had cut into great blocks of stone in their path; in other places, they had to resort to handholds and footholds.

At what N'arri judged to be midday, they rested and brought out some food and drink. But their respite was short-lived. So close now to his goal, Vidar felt the adrenaline flowing and pressed them to make better time. Perhaps it was more than anticipation. Perhaps he sensed that time was still a factor in his mission.

Long after their lunch, after they had clambered up a slope of loose stones and rubble, only to find another such slope yards ahead, Vidar came up beside N'arri. Of all of them, only the elf seemed undaunted by the increasing cold and the pace they kept.

"N'arri, I need a plan," he said. "What are my options when we get beneath the city? How many ways into it do you know?"

"There are three," said the elf, and the torch he held illuminated half his face, leaving the other half in shadow. "We can come up through the main temple itself, through the food storage cellars and the kitchens. We can come up through another passage, which will take us through the pens, where they keep the animals they intend to sacrifice. And then there is a third way."

"What's that?" Vidar asked him.

"Through a minor temple, my lord," said the elf, smiling. "But the sacrifices there are of a more amorous nature."

"A whorehouse?" asked Vidar.

"Just so," said N'arri, "although it's a strange word you use to describe it. The thursar consider it a temple of pleasure. Even priests feel inspired to worship at such altars."

Vidar pondered while they made their way up the next incline. "Where are we most likely not to be spotted?"

"I am no expert on the layout of Indilthrar," said N'arri. "But it seems to me that both the kitchens and the sacrificial pens would be more than busy at a time like this, with all those nomad mouths to feed and their god in their midst."

"Whereas . . ." said Vidar.

"Whereas that third place might be uncommonly empty. If I were a priest, I would be giving Ygg my full attention at this time. And the courtesans' temple cannot be too far from the other places of worship."

Vidar smiled grimly. "Sold. We enter Indilthrar through the brothel. Let's just hope that Ygg doesn't have any sudden urges himself."

The elf shrugged. "That might be lucky, after all. He is likely to be more reasonable then."

The rest of their climb was made in silence, except for a few words that passed now and then between Stim and Eric. They were talking about Indilthrar, and not with great eagerness, judging by the tone of their voices.

Once more, they stopped briefly to eat. But that, too, was in silence, each of them lost in his own thoughts. The gloom that surrounded their lone torch—for they were down to one, now—seemed to press closer and closer as they neared their destination. And the cold grew worse, until they shivered even with their cloaks wrapped tightly about them.

Then, perhaps a couple of hours after they had eaten, N'arri came to a place where he had to use the dying light of his brand to peer closely at the markings in the wall. He turned and faced the rest of them.

"This is the junction. We are underneath the city now. Up ahead," he said, holding the torch high so that they could see three tunnels branching off, "is the way out."

Vidar nodded. N'arri turned and led them into the tunnel

that wound off to the left. As they climbed, trying to discern small boulders in their way and jagged projections from the walls, Vidar could feel his heart pounding against his ribs. The torchlight diminished quickly.

This was it.

XXIV

The ascent was not all that difficult, although they had to accomplish it in the dark. They clambered up the nearly vertical passage using niches that the *dwarvin* had chipped out of the rock for purchase.

At the top, the tunnel narrowed, so that Vidar's back brushed against the surface opposite the one he had been scaling. Stim had some trouble working his bulk up through the narrowing space, but he managed. After a while, N'arri called for silence and seemed to be working his fingers into the surface above them, searching for something. Vidar could hear the faint scrape of fingernail against rock. Then something moved aside and a faint light was revealed to them.

N'arri gestured and climbed through the opening. Vidar went next, then Stim, and finally Eric. The room they emerged into was dark save for the moonlight that fell upon them from an unshuttered window. There were low-slung couches and pillows scattered over the floor, a cistern in

the center of the room that was half-full of stagnant water,
rugs beneath their feet and the sickly-sweet smell of sweat
and wine and perfume. Vidar marked that none of these
smells were of recent vintage. It was a brothel indeed, but
a deserted one. Vidar was not surprised to find it altarless.
Among a population of priests, there was no need for the
pretense or the trappings of religion here.

A murmur from the next room—Vidar heard it and froze.
A voice, words spoken. Another voice, coming closer. Vidar
glanced around—no exit except for the one that led into
the room with the voices. Laughter, deep-throated, the mirth
of thursar females. Then another laugh, rumbling—a male.
Almost upon them.

Suddenly, Stim bent down, came up and tossed something at Vidar. It was a red courtesan's robe. There was no
time to think of anything else, so he put it on. The hood
fell over half of his face, though it did not quite conceal
his beard.

Eric and N'arri donned their cowls just as the shadows
that went with the voices crossed the threshold. Vidar tucked
his chin into his chest, hoping that his face would not be
seen—at least until it was too late to sound an alarm.

It was a thursar priest, but one who hung a sword from
his broad, leather belt, and two uncowled thursar courtesans—one under each arm. When he entered the room and
saw Stim with three more red-robed figures, he stopped
dead in his tracks.

"Ho, what have we here?" he boomed, with a voice like
gravel grating underfoot. Though he was clearly drunk, as
the empty horn in one hand evidenced, his face was expressionless. It was the curse of the thursar—that their faces
were as cold and unchanging as the icy slopes of Jotunheim.
The females, too, had the small, black eyes and the craggy
cheekbones of their race—though, in their own way, they
had a rough kind of beauty about them. At least, some of
the Aesir and the Vanir had thought so, Frey among them.

"Greetings, brother," Stim roared, doing a poor imitation of a drunken swagger. Vidar had all he could do to keep from howling out loud.

"Are you keeping all of those lovelies for yourself, then?" the priest asked. "Can you not be more generous and share some of this flesh?" One of the females by his side laughed brazenly and shook out her locks of raven hair.

"Are you still randy?" she asked in mock disbelief. "We have been at it all evening, Narfi." So much, thought Vidar, for the thursar reputation of lustlessness.

"Aye," said Narfi, "but I see some tidbits here I've not yet tasted, and my blood boils for them. Come, friend, share with me. You can only have them one at a time, anyway. Or do you nomads do it differently in the hills?"

Before Stim could stop him, Narfi lurched in Vidar's direction, and caught him by the waist. Narfi towered over him, cutting off the starlight. Vidar averted his face, smelling the giant's mead-soaked breath.

"Oh, a shy one," said Narfi. "I'll teach you better than to be coy with me." And he swept Vidar up in his arms. But as he did so, the hood fell back and revealed just what he had in his arms. Had Narfi's face had the capacity for expression, it would no doubt have been priceless. As it was, he just grunted.

The true courtesans shrieked as Vidar snapped his fist backhand across Narfi's nose. The giant staggered and dropped him, then toppled backward over a couch. Stim was on him in a moment, and all Vidar saw was the flash of his elvish blade in the light from the window. Eric and N'arri drew their own weapons and blocked the doorway before the courtesans could make their escape.

Vidar got to his feet and flung the red robe from him. He slid his sword free. "Now, ladies," he said, "I'm looking for Ygg. Can you tell me where he is?"

Fear blossomed in their faces like deadly-pale flowers, though their features did not move. They kept their silence.

"I don't have all night for you," he said. "If you can't give me the information I want, I'll have to cut your throats like old Narfi's and seek it elsewhere."

One of the courtesans snarled—there was no other word for it—and spat on the floor. "All right, I'll tell." The other one looked at her reproachfully, but said nothing. "He sits just across this courtyard," she said, gesturing past the doorway with one giant hand, her long nails gleaming red as her sleeve fell away. "But he is well-guarded, as you'll find out. And he is a god, not to be tampered with by a thursar traitor and a few child-sized thieves."

Vidar almost corrected her, but let his ego surge pass. It would be better for them if their identities were not known. "Tear up your robes," he said to his companions, "and bind them. Put your thickest strips between their teeth or they'll wake the dead with their cries."

"Aye," said Stim, who had no doubt had some experience with it. While Vidar held the courtesans at swordpoint, the others shredded the red robes—both those they had worn and the others they found lying about. It was left to Stim to truss them up—only he stood tall enough to gag them.

"Now," said Vidar, after he had thrust his sword back into his belt, "let's see if their directions were accurate or not," And, served well by the black tunics of under-G'walin, save for Stim, whose garb also blended well with the night, they slipped through another chamber, then an antechamber and out into an open courtyard.

It was empty, uninhabited, though by this time Ygg must have brought thousands of nomads within the city's walls. But then, this was a sacred precinct, probably reserved for the priests. All around them stood windowless stone buildings, and beyond those loomed great, snow-covered peaks. But it was the spectacle in the center of the courtyard that drew their attention and held it captive.

Under the full light of the moon, they surveyed what looked like some gargantuan chessboard of alternating red and white tiles—and the Aesir were the pieces. Tall, blue-gray marble statues reared up against the cloudless, ebon sky in the likenesses of Ragnarok's survivors. Eric whistled his admiration softly, and Vidar acknowledged it with a nod.

Vali was the first on their right. He held Odin's spear, Gungnir, in his right hand, with its butt end against the ground and its point piercing the heavens. In his left hand he cradled an arrow—the one with which Hod had slain Baldur, presumably. This was the work of no raw talent, such as that Eric had brought to bear on his statuette. This was the product of the finest skills, shaped by the moonlight, which favored one cheek but not the other at this point in its passage. Vidar marveled at Vali's features, cold and deadly on the moonlit side, but mournful and lost-in-shadow on the other. He looked as if he were about to speak.

At the feet of Vali's likeness, there was a stone, carved with large, intricate runes. It named him in many ways—Spearslayer, Avenger, King of Asgard, He-Who-Never-Tires, Lord of the Wolves.

The statue that faced Vali's was Vidar's. It was Vidar as he had been, warlike, hair braided in a warrior's braid, horned helmet on his head, a great sword balanced in his hands. His mouth was set in determined silence. Yet as Vidar gazed at the statue, he thought he saw something of Midgard, not Asgard, in the shadow-side eyes. There was doubt there, perhaps reluctance. Even conscience. Had he been that way before he left Asgard? The runestone named him Jawbreaker, the Silent One, Odin's Revenge, Wolf-slayer. It did not mention Leathershod.

They stalked between the statues of Vali and Vidar. The courtyard was silent but for the shuffle of their feet against the flagstones. The wind sighed, soft about them, cool on their faces. Modi and Magni, Thor's sons, rose up next. Modi, of course, held Mjollnir across his chest. His beard was full, his hair long and wild. The sculptor had carved fierce arrogance into this visage—but the half of Modi's face that stood in shadow was boyish, compassionate, almost gentle. His runestone proclaimed him Thunderer, Hammer of Heaven, the Hurler—all names which had once belonged to Thor.

Magni held a bow of elvish manufacture. That had always been his favorite weapon, for sport as well as for war. His hair was combed back over his shoulders. In the moonlight, he looked like his mother, Sif—wise, self-possessed, graceful in his bearing. In darkness, it was the face of a dreamer—no, more—of a madman, hopelessly mired in his private fantasies. The runestone called him Elfking, Windrider, Thor's son, Huntlord.

"Strange, isn't it?" Eric whispered at his side. "No sacrifices. No smell of lamb's blood, no flowers, no sheaves of grain spread before them. It has been a long time since the priests tended to these gods."

"Ygg," said Stim. "Perhaps his influence was felt here long before he became known to us in Skatalund."

Eric nodded. They moved on, crossing the empty courtyard, beneath the statue of Hoenir that loomed on their right. Odin's brother had been wrought long-legged and stately, his cloak draped jauntily over one shoulder. In his left hand, he held a mead horn, for even among his worshipers his love of strong drink would be known. But his right hand, half-concealed by the cloak, rested on the pommel of a dagger tucked into his belt.

And his face? A wide-open, congenial nature by moonlight—and in shadow, an envious, ugly sort, dangerous when crossed. Only in Hoenir had the sculptor failed, Vidar thought. For there was more to his unholy uncle than bitterness. He was Odin's brother, after all. And while he did not have Odin's power or Odin's guile, he had walked the naked worlds with him before any of the others—save Lodur—had been born. He knew more than he would ever let on—and knowledge was a distinct kind of power in itself, especially when there were no scruples to temper it. At Hoenir's feet, the runestone did not do him justice: Eldergod, Lord of Laughter, Odin's brother, Next-Highest.

No one stood opposite Hoenir. Hod would have had a place here if he had not slain Baldur—but while Vali was Lord of Asgard, there would be no worship of Hod. At least, not out in the open.

Then the courtyard ended. But beyond the red-and-white-patterned stones, there was a greenlawn covered with a light snow. Beyond the lawn, there rose a stone tower. If the courtesans had not lied, it was there that Ygg slept and organized his defense. There was an entrance to it that faced the god-court, with no sentries posted. Why post sentries to protect a god from his worshipers?

N'arri tapped Vidar on the shoulder and pointed upward. Vidar looked. At the top of the tower, a window showed candlelight. Ygg's chambers?

They stalked silently across the snowy field. The wind caressed them, strangely benevolent. The night air was cool and crisp, redolent with the fragrances of some mountain grove.

Vidar reached the entranceway first. It was blocked by a massive, wooden door, bound in iron and set into the stone on great hinges. There was no clasp or knob by which one might open it from the outside. Vidar tried it once with his shoulder, and heard the rattle of a bolt behind it. Locked. A sign, perhaps, that Ygg did not quite trust all of his fanatical priests? Backing off a few steps, Vidar said, "This might be noisy. Once we're inside, move quickly and quietly. We're going to gamble that Ygg is in that uppermost chamber."

Then he threw all his weight against the door, and it shattered inward with a groan of wood and a scream of bursting metal. Just as Vidar fell into the entrance after it, he heard a flock of cries go up like frantic birds at the far end of the courtyard. Someone must have come across the courtesans.

He scrambled to his feet and ran down a gray, stone hallway, with no light to see by except for the moonlight that had spilled in with him. A corner—and there, at the end of another short passage, some kind of illumination threw back the darkness. Vidar raced toward it, his blood pounding in his ears. The others were right behind him.

He turned right and almost ran past a flight of narrow steps. Skidding to a stop, he caught Eric as he hurtled by, and shoved him up the stairway ahead of him. They ascended into a blackness relieved only by the light from narrow window-slits and came to a landing, where the choice was either right or left. The four paused for a moment, gasping for breath. Vidar chose the right-side passage again—and chose wrong. At the end of the hall, a couple of thursar nomads—blades drawn—charged at them.

Vidar slipped his own blade free. He took the lead warrior's sword on his own, then lunged and stuck him in the throat. The giant collapsed, but the other one leaped over him and hacked at Vidar's head. This time, the son of Odin only managed to deflect the blow and it caught his right shoulder. There was sudden spasm of agony, and then his entire sword arm went numb. He fell back against the wall, still grimly clutching his weapon. Switching hands, he warded off the next downstroke, then came in under the thursar's guard and plunged his sword in between two ribs.

"The other way," he said, withdrawing his blade as the giant fell to his knees. He followed Eric in the opposite direction, back down the passage. As he passed the stairway, Vidar heard shouts of pursuit. "Let's go," he cried. "Keep going. We've got to get to him before they get to us!" Pain was starting to sink its fangs into his shoulder again.

They followed the narrow passage to its end, where they encountered another door, this one slightly ajar. Stim threw it open and bounded past, N'arri after him, then Eric. There was light beyond the doorway. By the time Vidar plunged through, too, it was too late to turn back.

For a long, terribly long moment, there was hushed silence. Ygg, masked, sat in his seat at the head of the table, with a crowd of nomad clan-chiefs and robed holy men seated or standing about. All along the torchlit walls, in lots of two or three, there were giant swordsmen or spear-carriers, probably there to support their separate chieftains. When Vidar and his companions charged into the room, they all turned and gaped.

But not for long. Vidar winced at the rasping, leathery sound of a couple of dozen blades drawn at once. Finally, they had found Ygg.

Vidar heard shouts from the hallway behind him and slammed the door to the chamber shut. Quickly, he bolted it. That was one quarter, at least, that they would not have to worry about. The thursars advanced, swordpoints dancing like fireflies, circling around them. Eric, N'arri and even Stim collapsed into a tight knot around Vidar.

There was a blood-chilling yell, and a thursar brought his blade whistling down at Stim's head. But the giant took a step to the side and battered it away. Another thrust at N'arri, but the elf took his attacker's sword and thrust beneath it, slashing the nomad's side and backing him off.

But they were closing in now. The clamor at the door behind him indicated that there would soon be enough bodies back there to break it down, bolt or no bolt. One of the nomads feinted at Vidar, but he held his ground. The only thing that had saved them until this point was the fact that, knotted together as they were, only three or four of the giants could reach them at once.

"Ygg," Vidar said, and his breath came hard. "I've come a long way to talk with you. Is this how you treat your guests?"

The figure who wore Odin's mask said nothing but rose

slowly from his seat at the table. A nomad hacked at Eric, who barely turned his blade aside. Another one thrust at N'arri, but the attack fell short as the elf retreated. The thursar were shouldering past one another to get a crack at the intruders, rumbling and cursing.

"Lord Vidar," said Ygg, and this gave the giants pause in their brawling. Some of them turned to watch Ygg, while others, especially the priests, who had hung back, peered at the Aesir swordsman. Ygg walked around the corner of the table toward them. He was bigger and broader than a man, but not as tall as a thursar. Vidar remembered the strength he had encountered in the tent that night, and believed that this physique could command it.

Ygg approached them, and the nomads parted to let him pass among them. But they did not sheathe their swords. The masked figure stopped before Vidar. His own sword hung from his belt, though he was within striking distance of Vidar's weapon. Ygg took no notice of Stim, N'arri and Eric. He stood face to face with Vidar, mere inches separating them now, but Vidar could not see the eyes that fixed on him through narrow slits in the savage mask. They were concealed in shadow.

"You are Vidar," he said simply. "At last. It has been a long time."

Vidar searched for something familiar behind the mask. The voice he heard was calm but bristling with power. And he did not recognize it. So much for talking Hod out of his grab for power. This was not Hod.

"Who are you?" Vidar asked. "Who dares upset the peace of Utgard?" he added, hoping it would sound convincing—if not to Ygg, at least to his followers. But he knew as soon as he had spoken the words that they weren't buying that line.

Ygg just laughed. A dry, hollow laugh. Then he turned and walked back to his seat at the table. No one moved. Even the torches seemed not to flicker. Then, when he was seated, he said, "Begone. Take those three with you. But leave the Aesirman with me. Go."

"No," said Vidar. "They stay with me."

Ygg shrugged. "Take them," he said.

Then the flurry of blades and the clanging of iron on iron began in earnest. Vidar didn't remember much of it afterward—his right arm hanging useless, he had taken blow after blow and turned them away. The others had not been so lucky. Eric went down under the press almost immediately. N'arri cried out once, but kept fighting, until he, too, was brought down. After a few minutes, all Vidar could see out of the corner of his eye was Stim—great, valiant Stim, who had pledged his sword to him in another world—hacking and cutting at his attackers. He was spattered with thursar blood before a single blade found its mark in his belly. But when it did, he slid to his knees, and Vidar was fighting alone.

It was sheer weariness that did him in. His arm tired and it seemed he no longer had any room to maneuver. A couple of times, his sword bit deep—but most of the time, he had all he could do just to protect himself. Finally, a point found his wounded shoulder, and he cried out with the pain. Somehow, he found the strength to recover and beat back the other blades that darted at him like serpents' tongues. Then they began to find their marks. Little by little, he lost what strength was left to him. Exhausted and slumped against the wall, he saw a length of iron arcing down at him that he had no power to parry. There was a resounding clang, and then darkness, welcome darkness.

XXV

A bird tittered. A ray of sunlight streamed in through a window, warming his naked chest. Then, as he watched in stupid fascination, it faded. The air was mountain air, fresh and uncluttered. Vidar started to smile. Then he smelled something else on the air—something harsh. Something evil—there was no other word for it.

His eyes focused and he saw his surroundings. It wasn't Woodstock after all. He was in a small room, lying on a low bed. The only other furniture was a table and two chairs. In the corner of the room, there was what looked like a wooden manhole cover, apparently so that he could relieve himself.

Vidar swung his legs around to stand up, but a stalk of red agony shot up his right arm to the shoulder. He whistled. At least he still had an arm. He slowly took his weight off that side of his body and leaned the other way. It hurt to sit up at all. It seemed that every little motion revealed another wound. Standing was a hardship. Nonetheless, he managed.

The breeze from the open window was cold on his face. He approached the rectangle of blue sky slowly. Damn, he said to himself. He felt like a cripple. Then he leaned against the wall with his left hand, which felt like rubber, and looked outside.

The view was something like what Eggthur—the hrim-thursar watchman—must have seen from his tower when the armies of Asaheim came to avenge themselves on Hlymgard in Jotunheim. Could he have known that he was looking at Ragnarok—at the extinction of his race?

He squinted at the light. The tableau was spread out before him like eggs on a plate. Below, within the walls of Indilthrar, the nomads were so densely packed that they barely had room to move. Some of them were on horseback, most on foot, but each saw to his own separate preparation for war. There were also the females and the young ones, carting food or weapons from place to place, or cooking out in the shadow of the ramparts. It was chaos, punctuated by the presence of the thursar priests, who seemed to be the only element of order down there. They shouted to the nomads on the walls, or tried to clear away a cooking fire in the midst of a busy supply line. Mainly, however, the nomads did as they pleased.

But beyond the walls, and beyond the mountains that encircled Indilthrar, there was a thin thread of color working its way up through the highlands. It was still too far away to discern the emblem on the banner that rose before the column like the rearing head of a snake—but Vidar did not have to see it clearly to know it was Vali's blazon, a black wolf rampant on a field of gold.

He was too distracted by pain and weariness to figure out how he could have beaten Vali to Indilthrar. Vidar chuckled at his own lack of curiosity.

When Eggthur had seen the banner that led the Aesir and the Vanir, it had been a black raven's wing on a field of silver—Odin's colors. Then it had signaled Ragnarok. This banner of Vali would begin another kind of ending—a Rag-narok for Utgard. And it seemed that only Vidar, in his tower prison, could see that clearly. No matter who won this battle, a race would be wiped out. If Ygg survived the siege, then the race of men on Utgard would be hunted down to the last. And the elves after that. If Vali broke through Ygg's defenses, all the nomad tribes would be slain, though he would be sure to call it a "cleansing." Either way, half of Utgard would be served up to the carrion birds.

There was the sound of footsteps outside his door, and Vidar turned, painfully, to face whomever it might be. A bolt was released. The door opened easily. Ygg came in, still masked and still armed, and closed the door behind him.

"I thought you would enjoy the view," he said.

"Lovely accommodations," Vidar snorted. "What have you done with the three I came in here with?"

For a moment, Ygg said nothing. It was as if he were puzzled. "Oh, yes. The thursar, and the boy and the elf. They have been taken care of. Let's sit." He pulled up one of the chairs, easing his bulk into it.

"I don't like the sound of that," said Vidar. "What happened to them?"

"I asked you to sit down," Ygg repeated, and there was an undercurrent of something ugly in his voice. Vidar gauged the distance between the two of them, decided it was worth a try, and lunged for Ygg's sword. Ygg's fist came down on the side of his head and he hit the floor. Hard. That was all he had the strength for. Ygg knelt over him.

"I thought you had more sense than that. Come on," he said and lifted Vidar like a rag doll. He put him down on the bed. "Such ingratitude, my lord, after I've taken the trouble to share the pain with you..."

Share the pain? Vidar peered at his captor, his senses still reeling from the blow.

"Who are you, damn it?" he breathed.

Ygg laughed like leaves rustling. He sounded like F'lar, the old elf in G'walin.

"Who do you think I am?"

"Don't play games with me," Vidar said. Ygg laughed again. But this time he brought his hands up, on either side of the gray battle visage, and took the mask from his face.

At first, Vidar did not recognize the face, so horribly was it scarred. The flesh of one entire side had been fused and twisted by fire, so that the cheekbone was sheathed only in a thin, livid membrane, and ruin had worked its way across the mouth and chin of the other side as well. Then it hit him—and he could not believe what he saw. After all, he had seen him die.

"Odin," he said, and the name-saying somehow jarred him more than the realization. "I don't believe it. You can't be alive."

"You're right," said the scarred face, his mouth writhing horribly as he spoke, and on one side what was left of his lips pulled back in a wolfish smile. "Odin is dead. But Ygg lives."

"You've lost me," said Vidar. "I don't get it." His mind was still dulled, as if, along with his pain, this monster had drained away his will to think.

The piercing blue eyes danced with their old power. "I was Odin. I led the charge on Vigrid, the Iron Plain. I slew Hrym and Byleist, and I shredded Loki's wolves like so much cloth. You saw me take the wound from Fenrir, didn't you? Yet still I lived, and I would have avenged that wound if Loki had not seen me so beset. I couldn't raise a hand to stop him when he hurled his fire against me." He laughed, more a hissing than anything else. "I was burning like a torch. My face was cooking inside my mask. But I was able to make a gate, even while the flame was consuming me— I opened a gate and vanished through it. And escaped."

Ygg shook his head, slowly, from side to side. "Odin died then. He could not stand the horror, the ugliness. He had always had whatever woman he desired—even your mother, Lord Vidar—and when he rolled over to see himself in the mist-shrouded stream, he could see even through the mists how ugly he had become. No female would come willingly to his bed, not anymore.

"But Ygg had survived, my lord. Ygg, who stands over you now, ready to crush Asgard before it even knows who slays it. Ygg survived while weak, vain Odin perished— in Niflheim, where the fog fills the world with such sorrow it cannot be borne. It breeds, Vidar," he said, and he lowered his face toward him. "It breeds . . . insanity." Then he laughed again, reeds in a dry riverbed, brittle and whispering.

Odin was right. He was mad and he knew it. Vidar surveyed the fire-ravaged terrain of Ygg's face, which had once inspired songs of manly beauty. All that had been left untouched was the quadrant that encompassed his left cheek and forehead. Even his silver-white mane had been cropped close to his head. The effect was frightening, even to Vidar. Especially to Vidar. This monster was his father.

"Why?" Vidar asked. "Utgard was your creation. Why tear it down?"

Odin—Ygg—shook his head. "No. It was my greatest act of foolishness. Of all of them, Vidar, you should know that, you who abandoned Asgard when you realized how empty it was."

"It was the killing, the wars that were empty," Vidar said, propping himself up on his good arm. "Not Asgard itself."

Ygg stared at him, fixing his eyes on him as a hawk transfixes a mouse. "You've only learned half the lesson then. I thought . . . but no. Only Magni has had the wisdom to see it all. Nothing matters, nothing—not here, not in Asgard nor Midgard nor Alfheim. I once knew that, long ago, before even Bragi was born. When Lodur and Hoenir and I were young and created the gates, so that we could see what the rest of the cosmos was like.

"And with every gate we made, we found a new world— Jotunheim, where we found enemies, beings who would not submit to us. Alfheim, where we found sometime-allies. And Midgard, where we found worshipers and foot soldiers for our armies.

"When you are building and exploring and conquering, it is easy to blind yourself to the facts. That's what we did, my brothers and I. We blinded ourselves and constructed a great, glorious Cause—the war with Jotunheim. It gave it all meaning. And we built up Asgard from a mean, little pile of stones, because such a Cause deserved a palace to house it.

"And then I peopled the Cause with princes to carry its banner—first Bragi, my poet and chronicler. Soon after, Heimdall and Thor and the others. We found the Vanir in Vanaheim. We warred and we made peace with them, and Niord and Frey pledged their swords to our Cause, sealing the alliance by sending Freya to live in Asgard, with her brother.

"Suddenly, or so it seemed, I could look out from my tower in Asgard and see Something where there had been Nothing. Where there had been deathly cold, there was warmth. Where there had been purposelessness, there was purpose. But it was self-delusion."

Vidar remembered how he had wound Gjallarhorn and how he had touched the deathly cold and the purposelessness—the Chaos. Odin and his brothers had wrested Order from that.

Vidar sat up. "Why delusion? It was the greatest challenge of all time, to bind a universe together. Just the Cause was wrong, the war with the hrimthursar."

Ygg hawked and spat. "It was wrong, all wrong. I learned that in Niflheim. You've never been there, have you? No, of course not. You should go. It would complete your education." Again, Ygg laughed, but this time there was irony in his voice. "The first time I journeyed there, I was with

Lodur and Hoenir. It was a place of numbing cold and mists, and we thought it was unpopulated. It turned out otherwise. We destroyed the gate as soon as we had withdrawn, because we sensed the danger there—the peril to our Cause. We did not fit words to it, for that also would have been dangerous. Words would have given the meaninglessness substance. But we sensed it, each of us, and we sealed it off. That was the first time, Vidar.

"But in my haste to escape Loki's fire, I reopened the gate to Niflheim, if only for a moment. This time, I was Ygg, and I was stronger. I didn't flee from the truth—I embraced it. And that is what enabled me to survive."

Ygg turned suddenly and brought his fist down on the table. The wood splintered and the legs creaked. "Do you see the irony, Jawbreaker? I took the truth of purposelessness and hammered it into the greatest purpose of all!" His voice trembled and hissed. "To tear down what we had wrongly built up. Starting with Utgard, the greatest blasphemy of all. Even the Nidhoggii were able to appreciate the humor in that."

"The Nidhoggii?" asked Vidar.

"Yes," said Ygg. "My doctors in Niflheim. They healed me, as best they could—or cared to. It was they who taught me—or reminded me—of meaninglessness. And I was an apt pupil."

"No," said Vidar. "A madman."

Ygg grinned his wolfish grin. "I said as much. Or haven't you been listening?"

Vidar let the air whistle out between his teeth. "Do you want irony? I'll give you irony. I risked my endless life to reach you here, to talk you out of this rampage. I thought you had a simple motive, like hatred perhaps, or a lust for power. Then I find out that you're not Hod or some crazed nomad—you're Odin, the creator of Utgard. And you're bent on destroying the only thing you ever built that really did have meaning."

"What do you mean, my lord?" Ygg was still grinning like a death's-head. "That there is something noble here that I might have overlooked?"

"Have you bothered to examine Utgard? It's a beautiful world. And a strange one. Before you arrived, men and elves and thursar all lived together—and in peace, most of the time. Can you imagine that? Thursar and humans living side by side in Skatalund? That's the truth, father—not a Cause, you're right about that—but the simple truth. And maudlin as it sounds, the meaning of Utgard lies in the bonds of brotherhood that bind thursar and man in Skatalund."

Ygg snorted. "Princely words. I'm touched. But you sound like a hen with diarrhea. There's only one truth, and it's annihilation."

Vidar ran his fingers through his hair. "I should know better than to argue with you. You never listened even when you were sane."

"Don't worry, my lord. You'll see things as I do. Eventually. But for now, I'll give you time to think about it."

As Ygg rose and turned to leave, Vidar tried to stand up. He managed, barely, then lunged for the table when he felt his left leg giving way. Holding onto it for support, he yelled after his captor. "Father!"

Ygg stopped and glanced at him over his shoulder.

"What happened to my companions?"

Ygg was silent for a moment. Then he asked, "Do you really care?"

"Yes, I do," said Vidar.

Ygg shook his head. "You certainly have changed, boy. They live. For now." The next sound Vidar heard was that of the door closing.

He hobbled over to the window again. The wind had grown cold. A storm front had blotted out the sun, throwing a premature dusk over the mountains. Each side would probably take it for some sort of omen.

Hunger gnawed at his belly. But more than that, he found

that he was tired. Very, very tired. And if Odin hadn't split the pain with him—preserved him for his own reasons—he'd have been more than tired. He would more than likely be dead.

XXVI

Each of Odin's sons was born with a talent. Odin's blood was power and mystery and it took many forms.

So it was that when the lord Vidar came of age, the lady Frigga took him for a walk in the forest near Odin's hall in Asgard. She was not his mother, for his true mother had died in childbirth—but he was Odin's son, and she loved the lordling as though he were her own.

As the sun reached its zenith, the cool shadows retreated before its warmth, Frigga came upon what she had been looking for. It was a small sparrow, fallen from its mother's nest. When Frigga picked it up in her cupped hands, it fluttered one wing, but not the other.

"Its wing is broken, mother," said Vidar.

"Would you like to heal it?" asked the lady.

"Yes," said the lordling. "Let's bring it to Heimdall."

"But Heimdall must guard the gate to Asaland, lest the hrimthursar catch us unawares," said Frigga.

"Then we'll take it to Thor."

"But Thor went off with your uncle, Lodur, to pick himself a house for his birthday."

"Then we'll take it to my father himself," said Vidar.

"But your father is off hunting with Hoenir."

"Then the sparrow will die," said Vidar, sadness creeping into his voice.

Frigga smiled "Would you like to try healing the bird?"

Vidar looked up at her with his wide, child's eyes. "I have not been taught to be a *lifling*, mother," he said. "What can I do?"

"Try," she said, the sunlight touching fire to her hair. "Here, hold the bird in your hands."

He took it from her and he could feel its tiny heart beating beneath the down of its new feathers. Heal it? He did not know how. He looked into its little black eyes, though, and he thought he saw pain there. The more he looked into the sparrow's eyes, the more he saw of that pain.

And then, there was a twinge in his right arm, and he almost dropped the sparrow. His arm hurt. Oh, it was a small hurt for a big-boned young lad's arm, but for a small bird it had been agony. He flinched as the pain in his arm throbbed up to his shoulder.

Then it was gone. His arm still hurt a little. But the sparrow, suddenly—with a squawk of delight and wonderment—flung up its wings and took off through the interwoven branches above them. Vidar watched it go. The fingers of his left hand absentmindedly grasped his other arm and felt the heat that had taken hold there. It was as if a fever had wrapped itself about the bone.

He looked up at Frigga again, and she was gazing

at him with what he would know later to be pride. "You are *lifling*," she said, her gray eyes made golden by the afternoon. "You have split the pain with another—and this time, the pain was so small that you could take it all."

"*Lifling*," said Vidar. "Like Heimdall and Thor."

"Yes, my lord. You have the same gift."

But Vidar's brows knit and he said, "If I am *lifling*, I cannot be *baleyg*, like you, mother, or *stromrad*, like Bragi. Or *gaut*, like my father and my uncles."

"That is true, Vidar," said Frigga. "You cannot mold the world as Odin does, or muster the elements like Bragi, or change someone's mind as I might. But there are things you can do that they can't. You can save their lives if they fall on the battlefield, because you are a healer. You will always be welcome, at any hearth you visit, for there is much pain in the world. And anyone who can relieve some of that pain is a welcome sight. But you must also be careful, my son."

"Why?" asked the lordling.

"Because you will lose a little part of your life every time you draw the pain out of someone else and into you. Do not fear, Vidar—it is a very small thing you will lose. But the more you use your gift, the more you will age, and at the end of your life you will pay the price for your good deeds. It is the way of the world, my son. Every gift has its price."

"Do you pay a price when you change someone's mind, mother?" asked Vidar.

"Of course, my child," said the lady.

Vidar pondered a moment. His arm still felt warm. "Then I will pay it, too, if I have to," he said.

Frigga knelt and hugged him, something she rarely did with any of Odin's sons, once they were old enough to walk.

"And there is more to being *lifling*," she said as she

took his hand and started back toward Odin's hall.
"But there is time for you to learn about that."

Sin Skolding
Hlesey, 438 A.D.

XXVII

The next morning, Vidar stood at his window again, watching the construction of a catapult below, when Ygg entered unannounced. This time, he did not remove the battle mask.

"Have you thought about it?" he asked.

"Yes, I have," said Vidar. "And it still stinks."

"Keep thinking," Ygg said. "I've been in contact with Hoenir."

"Oh?" Vidar's pulse quickened, but he tried not to show any great interest.

"Yes. And I've presented my arguments to him, as one brother to another. As one who has recalled the truth to one who has forgotten."

"And?"

"He seems . . . of two minds. For now, at least. But I think he will see the truth of Niflheim as he saw it once before. If anyone should see it, it would be him."

"Great. Why are you telling me all this, anyway? What difference does it make?"

Ygg seemed to chew that over for a while. "Because," he said, and his voice was empty of all emotion, "you are my son. Should you go to your death ignorant of the truth?"

"Then you plan to murder me?"

Ygg laughed, wind wheezing through a hollow log. "I plan to murder all of us, if that's what you mean. But it would help matters considerably—make it easier—if I had some help, Vidar. From you. From Hoenir. Perhaps even from Vali and Modi, after they have been crushed."

"Vali will never submit—not even to you."

"Probably true," said Ygg. "But he is intelligent. I hold out some hope, even for him."

"Look, maybe I'm being a little naive," said Vidar, "but why don't you just tear Utgard apart the same way you put it together? Can't you do things like that anymore?"

Ygg shook his head. "What makes you think that destruction should take less time than creation? It cost me thousands of years to beat Utgard into existence. I cannot wait that long to submerge it."

"What's your hurry?"

Vidar could almost see the scarred skin working itself into a semblance of a smile behind the mask. "My earlier foolishness gnaws at me, Vidar, like a vile little beast. I look around at my handiwork, and it disgusts me."

"What about Baldur's handiwork? Does that annoy you, too?" Ygg stiffened, as if Fenrir had impaled him a second time. Vidar knew that he had struck a chord.

"Aye," said Ygg, "that irks me most of all." His voice was low and dangerous. "Speak not to me of Baldur."

"Why?" said Vidar. "Because it's harder to deny the worth of his creations than yours?"

"I said, speak not to me of Baldur!" Ygg raged. His gauntleted hands balled into fists. "He, at least, had the good sense to die before Ragnarok, the ultimate farcical act in the Cause. More sense than you or I, Vidar."

"But could you have destroyed him as you propose to destroy us?" asked Vidar. "Could you have slain Baldur?"

"Gladly," Ygg hissed, but there was no conviction in it. There was at least one chink in his armor, then.

"Oh," said Vidar diffidently. "I see."

"I do not think so," said Ygg. "But think on it, and you will. With time. I am confident of it." Then he left.

Later in the day, a thursar priest came to bring him wheat cakes and a queer-tasting kind of tea. "Siege-food?" he asked. But the priest said nothing, just left the tray and locked the door once he was outside.

His wounds were still painful, but they had healed a bit since the day before. He could feel the drain on his energies as the same forces that enabled him to heal others went to work on his own body. The worst of his wounds was a rather ugly-looking gash in his shoulder. He also bore cuts of various lengths and depths on his thighs, on his biceps and on his upper chest. There was a particularly troublesome gouge in his calf, which kept him hobbled.

But then, he also felt a weakness that his wounds could not account for. Certainly, the healing process sapped some of his strength—but he still had the feeling that Ygg had somehow dulled his mind and drained his will. Bile began to rise in his throat as he wondered. Had Ygg drawn out his vitality along with his suffering? He who had been the All-father was capable of it, surely. And a docile prisoner was preferable to a hostile force within one's own walls. The more he thought about it, the more he believed it.

But it seemed that even thinking wore him out. The warm tea had made him drowsy. He sprawled on the bed and slept.

When he woke, it was late in the day. It was raining outside, and his room was dark as a result. He got up and stretched, then limped over to his one diversion. He still felt lousy.

He leaned against the windowsill. Vali seemed to have pushed his armies into the mountains. Another day and he would be at Ygg's doorstep. Vidar chuckled to himself. "What would you say, Vali, if I told you that you're up against our dear old dad? You might not be so eager to climb into the mountains, then, would you?"

Then again, it might not matter. Vali had a way of rationalizing his acts of violence. Once he had started on Ygg's trail, he would see it through—and find ways to explain it as he went. But still—Vidar would have given much to see the look on Vali's face when Odin took off his mask.

The rain was turning to snow. It was a wonder that it had not done so before, considering that even the lower land around G'walin had been blanketed in unbroken expanses of white. There must have been something unusual about Indilthrar's place in the mountains that protected it from cold air or exposed it to warm currents. Or maybe it was just Ygg playing with the weather.

Vidar watched Vali's distant banner. It was time to take sides. The stakes were higher than he had realized. Maybe Vali had been right—maybe his perceptions had grown dull in Midgard. In any case, Ygg must be stopped, and at any cost to any one world. So, once again, Asaheim was his team.

He watched the nomads building a second catapult, and a third. They looked a little more organized than they had before—Ygg's doing, no doubt. Vidar wondered how long they would remain so zealous in their adoration that they would be content within Indilthrar's narrow confines. These were, after all, tribesmen, accustomed to the open steppes and hills and the canopy of the stars. If the siege lasted, even Ygg might be hard-pressed to control them.

And what about the priests? Stim had called them fanatics. But they might not be fanatically loyal to Ygg—not all of them, at least. Many of them had worshiped Loki and Surtur in secret, apparently. Some still might. And if they could worship the hrimthursar in secret, might not some of them still offer sacrifices to Vali and the Aesir in secret? These priests all carried swords. If there were a sect still loyal to Vali—or even to Vidar himself—then there might be a pawn that Ygg had overlooked.

Vidar shivered and retreated from the window. Ygg— he did overlook some things, after all. He must have been shocked when he heard the wail of Gjallarhorn sweeping through his encampment like a tortured angel of death. Yet he did not mention Gjallarhorn when he had tried to convince Vidar of the rightness of his mission. By now, he must have discovered or deduced that Vali had the horn, but he did not mention that either.

Nor had he asked Vidar how he'd gotten into the city. A breach of his security should have been of utmost interest to him—but it seemed to be much more important to Ygg to talk philosophy than practical matters. In the old days, Odin would have seized on these loopholes in his information and closed them as quickly and efficiently as possible.

But Odin was insane now, wasn't he? Unless—and Vidar's brain reeled as he realized how he had underestimated his captor—unless he was using Eric and Stim and N'arri to obtain his information, and saving Vidar for some higher purpose. Vidar pounded his fist against the wall. His friends were being tortured, and he had no power to stop it.

The bolt slammed open suddenly and his thursar waiter brought the evening meal. Vidar could not tell if it was the same one who had brought his first meal.

But when the giant set the food down on the table, Vidar put a gentle hand on his wrist. There was no sense in antagonizing his one potential source of information, and he did not think he could have restrained the priest if he had really wanted to. "Tell me," he said, taking a sidewise route, "how do the priests of Indilthrar feel about these wild, godless nomads within their walls? If it were me, I would not like to see my temples defiled with their cook fires."

The giant stared at him from beneath his cowl, dark, shiny eyes meeting his. "I cannot speak to you," he rumbled. "It is not permitted." But he did anyway. "The nomads are our brethren. They do not defile our temples."

"What about my comrade, Stim, and the other thursar who ride under Vali's banner? Are they not your brethren—and civilized, like yourselves?"

"Yes," the giant conceded. "But they do not follow Ygg, as we do. Therefore, they must be our enemies."

"But have you seen my comrade? Is he not flesh of your flesh, blood of your blood? How can Ygg deny that? Is he thursar himself?"

The giant removed his hand from Vidar's grasp. "Your comrade is dead. I must go."

But even after the bolt slammed to once more, the priest's words resounded. Stim was dead. Vidar ran the fisted knuckle of his forefinger slowly over the tautness of his lips. Ygg had killed him. Stim was dead. Another victim, Vidar mused, and he could not defend against a pathetic replay of the giant's last battle in Ygg's council chamber. Yes, he had gone down. But had he died of his wounds, uncared for? Or had Ygg tortured him to death? Something within Vidar knew with a surety that it had been the latter.

He had a debt to settle now with his father—or the disfigured husk that had been his father. For Stim's life, Ygg's.

Now where was a sword, when he needed one? Vidar hobbled across his tiny prison in a parody of a man pacing. And he wondered about Eric and N'arri, hoping with all his power to hope that they, at least, still lived.

XXVIII

His dreams were troubled that night, filled with vague and half-seen shapes, ghosts of warriors he had led into death's maw and those he had slain himself. Or so he surmised when he woke to a gray dawn, with the snow turned to sleet. His wounds ached and his bones seemed to creak as he rose, wiping sleep from his eyes with the back of his hand. The floor was cold on his bare feet. He drew his boots on stiffly.

Once at the window, he could see Vali's banner clearly. His half brother had completed his journey. He sat before the walls of Indilthrar, an imposing figure even in the hellish weather, a golden helm with wings of gold on his head. The horn hung at his side, protected from the elements with a swaddling of animal skins. Behind him, his armies—Asgardian and Utgardian—made preparations to set up their camp. Only his captains sat horsed behind the Lord of Heaven—about a dozen of them. Modi sat at his right hand, cradling the hammer in his arms. Hoenir, graybearded and cloaked in blue, sat on Vali's left. Eric's father was there, and a couple of other humans. There was one captain that Vidar recognized mainly by the color of his hair—Irbor. So he had managed to catch up with the main siege force.

Vidar wondered how Irbor had explained to Vali that he'd allowed his brother to escape Skatalund—and what Vali's reaction had been. Not too severe, apparently, for here was Irbor, still in a place of prominence. A political decision, no doubt, and more than likely, the redbeard's family was influential among the Vanir in Asgard. Now was no time to alienate a faction of Asgard's strength-at-arms. Even from a distance, Vidar could see that a large number of the Asgardians Vali had brought with him were marked by the red hair of the Vanir. So Irbor was made a captain.

You've covered all the angles, brother, but you've still got some surprises coming, Vidar mused.

And just as he thought that, the first of those surprises materialized. With a roar from the thursar below, one of the catapults let loose a load of stones with deadly velocity. Vali saw it coming, but too late, of course. His steed reared. Another fell, unhorsing one of Vali's captains. The others retreated in a hurry. Meanwhile, some of those who had been erecting the foremost tents lay dead or sorely wounded on the muddy ground.

Vali rode among his men, forcing them back out of range of the stones. When the second flurry came, as he knew it would, all those who could withdraw had done so. There were no more casualties. But Ygg had scored first and Vali knew it. The catapult volley had not been meant to kill, primarily, or Ygg would have let loose all three of his catapults at once. It had been a reminder of whose turf they fought on now.

Vali must have been lavishing Hod with curses a hrim-thursar would have blushed at, never knowing that Hod had nothing to do with it. So many surprises, Vali. But since he was rooting for Asgard, he decided to spring the lot of them immediately.

"Vali," he called, reaching out with his mind.

There was a moment's pause. "Vidar? Where are you? How did you beat me here?"

"One question at a time. I'm up here, in a tower. I can see you from my window. As for how I got here—I'd rather not say. Didn't you expect catapults?"

"Oh, shut up. I've been mountain-climbing for days in this cursed weather, and these damned nomad guerrilla bands ready to descend on me every time I turn a bend. The mountains are full of them."

That explained what had taken him so long. Nomad sneak attacks and this weather, which must have followed Vali all the way through the mountain passes.

"Now you sound like the Vali I knew and loved."

Vali regained some of his composure. "So you've thrown in with Hod."

"Not exactly. I'm a prisoner here." Vidar cautiously left out the part about his wounds.

"Certainly, Jawbreaker. And I'm a rutting hrimthursar. How did you get here before me? I thought there was but one route through the mountains."

"There is," said Vidar, "as far as I know. But that's not important now. What is important is for you to know what you're up against. Ygg is not Hod. Brace yourself. It's Odin. He survived Loki's blast by creating a makeshift gate and escaping to Niflheim. That's where he's been all this time. And he's mad, Vali. He wants to destroy everything. Asgard, Utgard, the works."

Vali seemed to weigh the information. He was looking straight at Vidar's tower now, probably wondering what Vidar had to gain by deceiving him.

"Odin, you say? Come on now, Vidar. You can do better than that. Why not Loki, or Hrym? They, at least, had a motive."

"You're not listening, brother. I said that he's mad. The fire scarred him terribly, and Niflheim had centuries to work on his mind. None of us knows what that place is like. He doesn't even think of himself as Odin anymore. And there's more—he's been in contact with Hoenir, and recently."

"I'm disappointed in you, Vidar—though I'll give you points for imagination. That's Hod behind the mask—why else would you try to convince me otherwise? And you won't divide us by making me suspect Hoenir of treachery. Nor will you scare me off by telling me that it's Odin we're up against. Tell Hod you've failed. I've got the horn now and neither you nor anyone else can protect him." If there was any doubt in Vali's mind, he didn't let on.

"False bravado, Vali. You can't have attuned to the horn so quickly. Even a *lifling* would have needed more time." Vidar stopped himself. How could he convince him? "I wish you could see him, Vali. There's . . ." But his thought went unfinished. Suddenly, there was static on the line. Ygg was blocking their conversation, as only Odin could.

But he had given Vali the facts. Now, if he would only see past his need for vengeance and heed them. Vali turned from gazing at Vidar's tower and saw to setting up the tents. But from time to time, he would look back over his shoulder. Perhaps he had gotten through to him, after all, pig-headed avenger and all.

Then he had to rest. The meeting of minds had drained him. Soon, he slept, and his sleep was deep and free of dreams. He woke when the priest brought his meal.

"How goes it?" Vidar asked.

The priest was silent. Then, "I cannot talk to you. I have been given orders."

"Pardon me, but are you the same priest who has been bringing my food all along?"

"No," said the giant, glancing over his shoulder. "You will not see him again."

"Did Ygg kill him for talking to me?" Vidar said, rising, anger tearing away the gossamer of sleep.

The priest said no more. At the threshold, he paused, as if he would, but he did not. The bolt slid into place resoundingly.

He did not see Ygg all that day, nor the next. The old boy doubtless had his hands too full for discussions of philosophy. Vidar found a spider, though, in the corner above his bed. It was strange that he had not noticed it before. He watched it for hours as it walked the strands of its web, waiting for an incautious fly to come along. When none appeared, it began to spin new strands.

"Say, spider," Vidar said, his voice sounding a little strange in his ears after hearing no other voices for a couple of days. "Don't you know that it's all for naught? What Cause are you laboring for?" Then Vidar smiled, still watching it. "Look at me. I'm talking to spiders."

He went over to the window, where the sleet still pelted the wall outside his room. Vali's camp had been put together. He could not see his brother's pavilion, however. It must have been erected beyond a shoulder of mountain that concealed all but the uppermost part of the encampment. Vali's forces must have laid down stakes for more than a mile back down the mountain pass, so narrow was the space between the sheer, rock cliff walls. And if the nomads were still hiding about them, the siege-layers would find that where their ranks were too thin they had become the besieged.

Directly below, the thursar were loading stones into the catapults again. Every now and then, they sent a volley over the walls, just to refresh Vali's memory of the first one. The field outside of Indilthrar was littered with their barrages.

Everything—the tents, the catapults, the mountains and the sky, had a gray cast to it. The wind whipped savagely and the sleet fell.

Days and nights passed slowly. The weather grew even grimmer, and Vidar realized that Vali truly was besieged—not only by the nomads that raided along his camp and his supply lines, but by the bone-chilling cold and the endless sleet. The heavens seemed to groan, purpling like bruised flesh, as Ygg forced them to pour out their lifeblood. There must have been depression and misery among Vali's tents, frustration and rising tempers, the teeth-grating harshness of close confinement.

In Indilthrar, however, tensions were mounting also. Vidar could see it in the number of flare-ups between the priests and the nomads.

It could not go on like this much longer. One commander or the other would tire of waiting and attack. After all, the longer Ygg waited, the more time Vali would have to attune to the horn. But it was also a matter of time before Ygg could call up the sky-serpent.

Odin came to him once more, with his rhetoric, leaving in the darkness after sunset, which Vidar knew only by the failing of the dim light at his window. He found himself thinking a lot about Asgard, of Baldur and of Odin. With only the sound of the sleet and the dreary square of sky for company, once the spider had departed for parts unknown, Vidar recalled faces he had not seen in many years. Halfar, the kindly lord of Rogaland, and his son, Hjalmar, somewhat less kindly. Lars the Minstrel, first a friend and then an enemy.

And before he could stop himself, he thought of a woman in a fishertown. It had been a long time since he had allowed himself to think of her, but his weakness and captivity, and Odin's insane argument, and the never-ending deluge from the swollen sky had torn down his mind's defenses.

He had been a fisherman, then. It appealed to him at the time. That was how it had started. Then he had met a fisherman's daughter. She worked as a clerk in a millinery store. But she was beautiful, in a strong, simple way, and he was searching for something, casting his lonely nets out to sea in the early morning. It was the hour before dawn when they met, she coming back from her father's boat, her heels clattering on the cobblestoned streets, a basket in her hand. They spoke, good day or something, a pleasantry. But after they had passed one another politely, Vidar looked back over his shoulder and saw her doing the same thing. Then she laughed, and it was a bright, lovely laugh in the straining darkness.

He saw her much after that, as often as he could. Her father disapproved of their public displays of affection, but approved of Vidar himself. He was a good fisherman, after all, and had the brains to be prosperous if he set himself to it. Then there was a morning when she went out to sea with him, and the sun came up on their passion, and no fishing was done that day.

It was not much later that she learned she was pregnant. Vidar had to remember that this was not Asgard, where a prince could sire a bastard and no more would be said of it. He himself had been Odin's bastard and yet Frigga had not been unkind to him. The woman did not ask that he marry her, but he could see it in her eyes. And he loved her. So they wed, and the entire village rejoiced with them, and they spent that night in his boat, feeling the sea undulate with their rising, falling bodies. For once, he was happy.

The child was a girl, and she was mortal. Vidar knew it as soon as she was born. Mortal, but beautiful like her mother. And he loved her, perhaps even more than he loved her mother, for she was the only child he had ever called his own. Even down the long corridors of the centuries, he had never sired a child before.

Vidar's wife had suffered during the birth. There would be no other children. He named her Ingrid, after her mother.

The tide ebbed and flowed and Vidar did not notice, in his happiness, that as the years spun away his wife grew older. Her face, once so soft and flawless, took on a harder look. There were lines, small ones and not easily noticed, around her eyes and in the corners of her mouth. And her hair, reddish gold like his beard, showed a few strands of silver.

He did not prosper, as Ingrid's father had hoped, for what was small-town ambition to one who had trod the streets of Asgard? But they ate well enough, and his daughter grew into a vision of young womanhood. Her mother's figure seemed to soften, as the years took their toll. She did not lose her beauty entirely, but it changed, mellowed here and toughened there.

Vidar himself did not change. For perhaps twenty years, it went unmarked by the villagers. His beard was long and his hair was long, and his face was made rough by the harsh weather. There was no telling his age. He could have been twenty-five or forty-five. If Ingrid, his wife, noticed, she did not speak of it.

One day his daughter met a man, a carpenter. The village was growing, for moneyed people had found their cove a pleasant place to live. There were more carpenters than fishermen, it seemed. Vidar saw the same look in the young ones' eyes that he had seen in his wife's eyes many years ago, and an emotion rose up in him which he could not name. It was only after he had worn himself out fishing one day, and started home, that he realized what it was.

He was jealous. Not of the young people's happiness, as might perhaps be expected—but jealous of his daughter's affections. She was young, she was beautiful—she was her mother twenty years ago. And she was his, had always been his. This was a father's reaction, he told himself. No man wants to give his daughter away.

But there was more than that, he knew. Suddenly, he realized that there was a longing in his loins, and he named it. Incest. He could not, he would never—but how could he stop himself? Loneliness is much worse for an immortal, and here he had been given a second chance.

Vidar found that he was trembling. She was so beautiful. He shook his head, the wind spraying salt in his eyes. No, he could not allow it. But how could he prevent it? They lived in the same house. He kissed her good night. He steeled himself for the answer, the only answer—he must leave. Say good-bye to his wife and . . . no. That was not the way. It must be done without good-byes.

The next morning, mercifully, there was a storm brewing. He kissed his sleeping daughter on the forehead as she slept. She smiled, but she did not waken.

His wife asked him where he was going in this kind of weather, and he told her there was not enough food in the cupboard to take a vacation. Then he took her in his arms, his beloved Ingrid, who had shared the best twenty years of his life with him. He told her so, and for a moment she looked frightened. Then, it seemed, she knew. And she understood. Perhaps she had suspected all along. Or perhaps it was just a trick of the wan light. He kissed her deeply and left for the wharf.

The storm took him that day, or at least all there was of him that the village knew. They didn't even find his boat. But six months later, his little family received a letter from a lawyer in New York. Vidar's uncle had died and left them a fortune in his will. It was guilt-money—but at least the cupboard would never be empty.

Afterward, there were years of emptiness. Painful, terrible years, soaked in hard liquor and dusted with cocaine— anything to help him forget, if just for a little while. There were women, armies of them, faceless, with white arms or dark arms or arms that would not let go. There was everything but peace.

He fell asleep, and in his dreams, Baldur's eyes—those beautiful, horrible, piercing eyes—accused him of something he could not remember. Or did not want to.

In the morning, he woke with a start. There was a by-now familiar sound at his door—the priest with his morning meal. He gazed a moment at the blue-black clouds, like the storm he had sailed into that day, and put the memory aside.

The thursar placed his meal down on the table, his huge, bony hands effecting a parody of daintiness. Vidar turned and walked to the window, listening without interest to the clatter of eating utensils.

A hand came down on his shoulder, urging him to one side. He turned and looked into the graven face of the priest. The giant was holding his cup of tea.

"What?" he asked. "Do you want to feed me now? I'm not so weak that..." And then, as he allowed the giant to move him away from the window, the priest extended his hand out into the sleet. Then he turned the cup upside down, and the liquid poured out. The thursar looked down at Vidar for a moment as he left his hand out there. Then he brought it back in, and the cup was full of ice and water.

Vidar cursed himself for not thinking of it sooner. Something in his drink, to keep him weak as a kitten... mad as he was, Ygg was no fool.

"Thank you," said Vidar. The giant just turned from him and left. The bolt shot to.

But Vidar managed a smile. There was a pawn, as he had suspected, that might not have been provided for in Ygg's strategy. And even a pawn could knock off a king.

XXIX

Vali's siege engine was a beauty. Vidar saw it in its final stages of construction, after four ranks of thursar and Aesirmen had dragged it up through the valley and it had been left in full view of the nomads on the ramparts. Somewhere, Ygg must also have taken note of it. It was fifty feet high, constructed of whole trees that Vali's men had cut from the canyon walls around them. There was no telling how many troops Vali commanded, because his tents appeared to stretch well back into the mountains. But they were numerous. And with so many hands at his disposal, the work had gone quickly.

Up on top of the engine, there was a platform with room for twenty archers in two files. Below that, there was another platform with space for twenty more. At the base of the machine, however, a huge log hung suspended from a series of crossbeams. This was the battering ram, and it protruded like a great, ridiculous phallus. But it looked the measure of Indilthrar's walls, given enough time to buffet them.

Vidar tried to contact Vali again. Just static, this time. Then he called out mentally for Ygg. There was a half-distracted response.

"I haven't seen you in three days," said Vidar. "And the weather seems to be improving. I was worried about you."

"Doubtless," said Ygg, and Vidar could tell that half his mind was preoccupied. "Did you enjoy your tête-à-tête with Vali?"

"Immensely. Did you enjoy torturing Stim?"

There was a pause. Then Ygg said, "It was necessary. I had to learn all I could of Vali's forces. The giant was an officer in Skatalund. And then there was the little matter of how you had gotten into Indilthrar."

"I would have told you that myself. Why didn't you ask me?"

"Why torture a potential ally?"

"I'm not talking about torture. Odin would have known enough to just ask me. He would have known that I'd have told him in order to save my comrades. You know what I think? It just rankled with you. You didn't want to let on that you'd been fooled into thinking you were secure here."

"Perhaps," said Ygg.

"Just as you were surprised when I showed up with the horn at Skatalund."

"Yes," said Ygg. "I was surprised, Vidar. But I won't be surprised this time. I know that Vali has the horn—and I know that he values his own wretched life too much to use it until he attunes to it. And I know that it will take him more time to do that than he has left. Is this all you had to say to me?"

"Stim was my friend."

"And he died for his Cause."

"I warn you," said Vidar. "If you kill the others as you killed him, I'll make Loki's fire seem like a fond memory."

Ygg laughed hideously. "You're scarcely in a position to make threats."

"I'm Odin's son," said Vidar. "I threaten whomever I please."

"A waste of time. I thought you had more sense than to bother with revenge—but I see that I was wrong. You would let one dead thursar stand in the way of enlightenment. You're as dense as your brother Vali. A pity, Vidar, a real pity. It would have made it so much easier to have you at my side."

"Sorry to disappoint you, old man." But Ygg did not reply. He had already turned to some other business.

Vidar smiled, flexed his wrists. He felt better. All the aches had gone away except the one in his shoulder, and even that had diminished. But more importantly, he could feel his strength returning.

There was a commotion and a clamor in the city below. Vidar focused on the siege engine. Sure enough, it was lumbering forward on eight round wheels, Vali riding alongside. A path had already been cleared through the foremost encampment. Perhaps a hundred Aesirmen and thursar pulled it and pushed it through the mud, until, finally, it loomed just outside the range of the catapults. A few yards before it, the field was littered with stones that the giants in Indilthrar had sent whistling over the walls—treacherous going for such a large and clumsy vehicle.

The sleet had all but disappeared. Though there was no break in the grim, sunless sky, the day seemed cheerful in comparison to those that had preceded it. And Vali had seized upon this unexpected lull to make his move.

Thursar spearmen took their places along Indilthrar's ramparts. The city of the thursar priests did not boast the double barriers of Skatalund, but the single wall they did have was thicker and seemed sturdier than the ones Eric's ancestors had built.

The nomads were not much for archery, so they would have to wait until the engine was fairly close before they could go to work with their javelins—and in that, Vali had

an advantage. Nomad females and children scurried about
with more stones, to pile them into the cups of the catapults.
What priests there were did not dirty their hands with such
work, nor did they clamber up onto the ramparts with the
nomads. But they shouted their fair share of commands.
Under their guidance, wagons full of stones for the catapults
were trundled out from unknown storehouses.

Then Ygg himself ascended to the ledge on which the
spearmen stood. He held a heavy thursar spear as if it were
a toothpick and watched the siege engine lurch toward them.
When it stopped, he waved his arm and barked orders to
those below. And waited.

Modi led a second contingent out of the mountains. These
were the Aesir and the Vanir, half-blooded descendants of
the immortals Vidar had fought beside long ago, before
Ragnarok. They carried long ladders for scaling. Vidar
counted them—ten ladders, which would be planted at in-
tervals along the walls. When Modi reached Vali's side, he
wheeled his horse around and dismounted. The ladders were
placed on the ground.

Then the men that Eric's father had recruited from Skatalund and the surrounding countryside clambered up onto
the archers' platforms, and they wore no mail to protect
them. Vali must have promised them a place at his feast
table in Heaven. But they had slung bows over their shoulders, and quivers full of arrows hung at their backs. Forty
archers took their places. Another hundred or so amassed
on either side of the engine, and these wore mail and helmets.

Below the wheeled tower, the thursar of Skatalund gathered—more than a hundred in all. The nomads jeered at
them, waving their spears in mockery. The city-thursar bore
it silently.

Meanwhile, Ygg was directing the nomads on the ground,
who swung the bases of the catapults around a few degrees.
Then he turned his attention to the giants on the wall, shout-

ing commands even Vidar could almost hear. All the catapults were now trained on a point perhaps fifty feet from the wall. Ygg meant to bring Vali's tower down.

The Asgardians, under the leadership of Modi and now Irbor, picked up their ladders and their thick, iron-bound shields, tucked their swords and their hand-axes into their belts. Vidar shivered, though with the lessened sleet had come a less savage wind. Vali had the Gjallarhorn at his disposal, and Modi hefted Mjollnir. But Ygg had been Odin, and Odin had never lost a battle, much less a war. Even his last battle on Vigrid had been a victory of sorts.

The siege engine rumbled forward, and the first line of the thursar soldiery that moved it raised its shields high to protect those behind them. The archers notched their shafts, bows at the ready. On the ramparts of Indilthrar, the hooting of the nomads grew louder. The women and the young ones drew back into the safety of the city streets, among the priestly buildings, and the space inside the walls filled with a seething mass of warriors, all armed with spears as long as a man is tall.

Vali and Hoenir hung back with four of the captains, including Olof, and another human. Behind them, a knot of cavalry that must have been the head of a terribly long snake coiled ready to strike should the walls once be breached.

Then there was a signal, a horn—but not Gjallarhorn, mercifully—and the Aesirmen rushed forward on foot with their ladders. They raced across the field of mud between Vali and the battlements, avoiding the stones and boulders—but there was no barrage from the catapults. As they neared the wall, a hail of spears fell, and a few found their marks—even plunging through the thick, reinforced shields. Warriors cried out and fell, but all ten of the ladders took root at the base of the wall. The siege tower struggled forward.

Then the walls of Indilthrar, the mighty walls of stone, shook like leaves in a heavy wind. A flash of blue lightning jumped out from the place where one of the ladders had gone up. It was the sign of Mjollnir in Modi's hand. Had the weather been drier, the barrier might have cracked and exploded in flames. As it was, it smoked in that spot.

The engine had come close enough now for the archers up on top to reach the battlements with their shafts. Vidar saw one of the nomads topple from his perch on the wall, then another. The spears they threw in retaliation fell short of the siege tower—all but one. Ygg hurled it, and it buried itself in one of the bowmen, carrying him clear off the tower. There was some confusion after that, but the archers closed ranks and fired anew.

Ygg took one of the ladders half-full of Aesirmen and flung it from the walls. Another ladder, where Asaheim's warriors streamed up like a clinging vine, he cleared with a down-flung spear. An arrow glanced off the side of his helm, but he seemed not to feel it. And still the engine drew closer.

Finally, the moment had come. Vidar tried calling to Vali or Modi, but Ygg still maintained the mental barrier. He turned his masked face to the city and raised his arm so that they could see him below. He brought it down suddenly. The catapults flew forward, seconds apart, and a huge swarm of rocks darkened the sky. For a moment, it seemed to hang there, imminent. Then even Vidar could hear the bone-snapping impact as the stones fell on the archers and the thursar beneath them. Men were crushed. Others fell to their deaths. The cries of the wounded rose as high as the gray-domed sky.

The siege engine came to a halt. Too many of the thursar that bore it had been crushed for them to bear it any further. And even if they could, there were too few archers left alive to offer them cover. Some of the supports had even been shattered, so that the top deck looked none too steady.

But the thursar did not have a vantage point from which to survey the damage, so they struggled grimly to get the tower moving again. Ygg grabbed a spear and skewered one of them, then another. Only nine or ten of the archers were still firing.

Ygg moved along the wall, shouting through the din. He tipped another ladder with his foot just as an invader was poking his head over the battlements. Then he grabbed a spear and disemboweled a Vanirman who had clambered over the top.

Modi hammered again at the barrier, and again the blue lightning flashed. Vidar could not see Thor's son from this angle, but he could see the top of the ladder that he held steady. Again and again, the nomads had pushed the ladders away, though each time the Asgardians had planted them anew. This time, the ladder that Modi guarded held fast, and a red-haired warrior poured over the wall. He was met by a thursar, who went down before his sword. The next thursar in line spitted him on his spear, but in the meantime two more invaders had made it up the ladder, and more came up behind them.

This time, the flash of rampant electricity and the thunder of Mjollnir were felt higher up the wall. It meant that Modi was taking his turn at scaling.

Ygg finally turned his attention that way. Vidar cursed. Jostling his own warriors, the monster plucked up a new spear and flung it at one of the Aesirmen. It went right through him and imbedded itself in the warrior behind him. The light of Mjollnir flared insistently, and the wall shivered. Ygg stumbled backward, groping for balance as the stones beneath his feet righted themselves. Not far from where the ladder leaned against the wall, a crack appeared, and some stones fell free.

Two more Asgardians vaulted over the wall. One slashed at Ygg, and he who had been the Lord of Asgard had to scramble backward to escape the blow. In his haste, he pushed a couple of the nomads off of the wall. Then Ygg's hand found a spear in the hand of one who had been slain, and he caught his opponent's blade on its thick shaft. He

stabbed at the warrior, who might have been his grandson
by Heimdall twenty times removed, and impaled him just
below the collarbone. Blood bubbled from the man's mouth
and he fell forward. Ygg whipped the spear free and jabbed
at the next Asgardian before him. After a moment's
weaponplay, he drove his spear into his stomach, then tossed
the corpse aside to get at the next Aesirman.

But Modi was the next Aesirman. Ygg seemed to hesitate
for a moment, either taken aback by the appearance of
Thor's firstborn—or licking his lips in anticipation of his
enemy's death. Modi, on the other hand, had worked himself
into a berserker rage. He pounded on the wall as an ape
beats his chest, and little shards of stone flew about them.
Where he had struck, another crack opened. Both Ygg and
Modi crouched for balance, lest they slip off the battlements.
Then they faced each other, but so intent was Thor's son
on destruction that he did not seem to realize it was Ygg
who stood before him, in Odin's terrible battle helm.

Modi lunged and brought his hammer around toward
Ygg's head—but the masked spearman leaped backward
out of harm's way. Modi whirled and struck again, but Ygg
stumbled back again, barely avoiding the head of Mjollnir.
The hammer crashed instead against the lip of the wall,
crumbling it. Lightning sizzled and a cloud of mortar dust
rose up.

Other ladders had sprouted successfully in the meantime,
and Asgardians leaped up all along the wall, met by the
hulking nomads. It looked to Vidar like a thousand raids
on Jotunheim—nothing new, after all. Except that Thor's
hammer and Odin fought on different sides this time around.

Modi swung at Ygg again, and Ygg backed off once
more, cat-quick—but this time he poked at the arm that
wielded the hammer and drew blood at the wrist. The Thunderer hardly noticed it, pressing him again, blind to all but
his prey. He brought Mjollnir well back behind his shoulder
and then leaped forward. But there was no retreat this time,

because Ygg already stood back-to-back with one of the thursar on the wall. So instead, Ygg came forward and closed with Modi corps-a-corps, spear held like a quarter-staff above him to catch Mjollnir where the head met the haft.

Lightning crackled and danced about them. If he had not already thought of it, Modi must have wondered now at his opponent's strength. Who had ever held Thor's mallet in check with a mere wooden shaft? Or survived such proximity to Mjollnir's raw, surging energy? For long moments they struggled, an island of power in the currents of war, legs bent and spread wide apart, each striving for an advantage. Modi's face crimsoned with his exertion. Vidar felt that if either of them moved, the other would explode with force unbridled. The gray sky stood mute witness to their contest, and the wild, blue glare of Mjollnir, and the clamor of cursing, clashing warriors all about them.

Ygg finally won, managing to slide his spear down and strike Modi with the butt end in the groin. Modi grimaced and nearly doubled over, and Ygg tried to run him through. But Thor's son was too quick. He twisted his body away from Ygg's point, but as he did, the tortured edge of the wall he had struck earlier gave way beneath his feet and he toppled out of Vidar's sight. Ygg flung his spear after him, but Vidar could not see the result.

It was the turning point of the battle. Having disposed of Modi's assault, Ygg was free to range over the battlements and rally his thursar. One ladder was tipped over, then another, until they had all been dislodged. More and more of the nomads clambered up onto the wall, their shouts of victory raising a din like that of a mountainslide. With their reinforcements cut off, the handful of invaders still slashing away on the wall were brought down quickly. A couple leaped down to the ground, but it was a long drop.

Then the catapults let loose again, just for good measure. Whatever archers were still standing on the tower were buried in that rain of rubble. Most of the thursar that could still walk had abandoned the siege engine, however. The hail of stones was more a gesture of triumph than anything else.

Vali had pulled back his forces, once he had seen that there was nothing more to be gained with scaling ladders. Ygg stood on the wall, steeped in blood, a grim figure against the dull, iron sheen of the heavens. He egged his nomads on, his spear waving in Vali's direction. The thursar shrieked like birds. Nor was the display lost on the Lord of Asgard, though he appeared to sit his horse calmly beneath his banner of black and gold. Ygg had won again— but the game was not yet over.

Then Vidar saw Modi being carried back to the tents. He was stretched out on a litter, apparently conscious and clutching Mjollnir to him, but sorely hurt. He might have broken bones in his fall, Vidar mused, if not damaged some internal organs. But he was alive, and Vidar found that he was thankful for that.

All in all, there was not much else to be thankful for.

XXX

The days passed, and Vali played a waiting game. He relied on three things. First, that Indilthrar's food supply was limited enough to force rationing and, ultimately, starvation. This was a logical assumption, since the city's storage capacity had been designed to fill the needs of the priests alone, and not the nomad hordes that had crowded in with them.

Second, Vali knew that the nomads were not trained and civilized soldiers, used to defending a garrison. In close quarters, penned like cattle behind the walls of Indilthrar, they were bound to get unruly. If Vali waited long enough, they might start fighting among themselves. Then, Ygg would be forced to leave the safety of the city and attack, and Vali could bring his cavalry to bear.

Third, Vali was gambling that he could master Gjallarhorn before Ygg could summon the sky-serpent. Since there was no telling how long the latter might take, Vali must have made significant progress in the former. Perhaps with

Modi's knowledge of *lifling* lore, he was getting close to complete attunement.

Vidar hoped that Vali would win before he might consider winding Gjallarhorn—for selfish reasons as well as altruistic ones. If Vali did resort to the horn and its power, Indilthrar would be wiped out. The priests, the nomads, the threat of Ygg—but also Vidar himself.

Meanwhile, it was taking Ygg longer to marshal the elements here at Indilthrar than it had at Skatalund. Hoenir must have something to do with that, Vidar thought. But he was not able to stop him altogether. The jet-black thunderclouds that gathered in the east threatened to make the sky-serpent over Skatalund look like a garden snake. He had seen Odin create a world, this world, with such fury. And so had Vali. Perhaps now he was beginning to believe Vidar, and to acknowledge whom he faced.

How long could Hoenir keep the storm at bay? Odin had always been the stronger brother. It seemed, as time passed slowly for Vidar in his tower prison, that the black thunderheads trundled inexorably closer with each passing moment.

So the waiting became a double-edged sword. The longer Vali held back, the shorter the food supplies, and the more time for attunement. But the closer the storm.

Only Vidar really benefited from the stalemate. Each day, he grew stronger, his Aesir-born vitality healing his hurts, his confidence growing. The robed giant that brought him his meals began to give him information, if a precious little at a time.

Vali's gamble was working better than he knew. The nomads seethed in their city-prison, itching for action. Fights had broken out among them. There was dissension in their ranks, though it was submerged by a healthy fear of their masked warrior-god. But the nomads' brawling had recently spilled over into the holy precincts, and some of the shrines of the old gods—the Aesir—had been defiled. Bad enough. Then some of the nomads had stumbled upon the altars of the forbidden gods—the hrimthursar—in one of their drunken forays. Accidentally, said the priest . . . behind a stout door and down a long, winding tunnel, until they came upon the images that Indilthrar had shunned long ago—or so it was claimed. Apparently, the worship of the hrimthursar was not so dead as Indilthrar would have the rest of the world believe.

Loki's likeness had been smeared with excrement. The statue of Jormungand they had urinated on, and, having run out of offerings to bestow upon the remaining idols, they had chipped away at them with their iron spearpoints until the stone faces were unrecognizable.

This had made the sect that still clung most closely to the hrimthursar quite angry. As it happened, this was also the most violent of the priestly factions in the city. The morning after the desecration, a number of those who had taken part in it were found around their family fires with their throats cut. This, in turn, had stimulated a certain degree of hostility between the nomads and their robed hosts, and the rift was widening. In fact, the priests had, for the first time in centuries, decided to ignore their petty jealousies to unite and protect themselves.

When Vidar saw his visitor leave on the eighth day after the battle, he went to the door and tested the bolt. He applied perhaps half his strength, and it held—but it screeched and sang, on the verge of bending. Given a few more days, he ought to be able to break it.

Vidar slept peacefully that night. He dreamed one dream, of Baldur's Beach, and the way back to Midgard. In his dream, there was no war, no Ygg, no Vali. He was going home. It was a dream of freedom.

But the first sight that greeted him the next morning was Ygg's bearlike presence in his doorway. He was careful not to swing his legs over the side of the bed too quickly, lest his captor see that he'd gotten his health back.

"You don't have to play the sickly prince with me, Vidar,"

said Ygg. "I know you've recovered. Did you think you could conceal that from me?"

"Silly of me," said Vidar. "You know everything that goes on in Indilthrar, don't you?"

"Yes," said Ygg, striding into the room. "I even know how you got in, now. Your other friends were more... pliable... than the thursar was." He seemed to walk with something of a limp after the battle.

"What can I do for you?"

Ygg looked at him, and Vidar sensed that the grotesque features were shifting behind the mask. "Kind of you to offer," said Ygg. "I do have need of you, my lord. I suppose you know that there is trouble in the city—between my priests and my nomads. I can't have that. I require both their loyalties if I am to defeat Vali." His voice sounded tired, reedy. "I need a sacrifice."

"So?" said Vidar. "Kill a couple of lambs. Why tell me?"

"Because," said Ygg, "you're the sacrifice. You are the thursars' devil, now, the villain who drove their brothers mad unto death on the field before Skatalund. That word has gotten out, you know. Until now, only a few of the priests knew you were imprisoned up here—the ones that used to hold you up as their god. If the nomads had known, they would have torn you to pieces. Even I might not have been able to stop them."

Vidar nodded. "It's a diversion, then."

"Of course. The nomads will be reminded of whom they came here to fight—the Aesir, with their cruel and arbitrary ways. And if their priests are the ones that actually execute you, the nomads will forget their distrust. Hostilities will be forgotten, at least for a while."

"That's terrific. But do you think it will really make any difference? Will it make them brothers for more than a day or two? And then what?"

"A day or two is all I need," said Ygg. "Hoenir is weakening. His will is not as strong as mine—never was. It's too bad I could not have won him to my side, or I would have washed Vali out of the mountains long ago. But no matter—I've got more than magic to work on Vali."

"And what's that?"

Behind the mask, there was a sound like chortling or coughing, Vidar could not tell which. But whatever expression Ygg wore, the mask concealed it. Just as well.

"Vali thinks that he has seen the strength of my nomads in the hills. But while a few have clawed and pecked at his camps in the night, the latecomers—the thursar from the far steppes of Hlivheim and Orrilland—have gathered above them in the hundreds. Do you know how many warriors Vali brought against me? Two thousand warriors, perhaps a few more than that. And me here, with a paltry eight hundred. But I've got another eight hundred on the slopes now, and more arriving every day.

"Their leaders," he wheezed, and there was that sound again of his restless features rustling behind the mask, "believe that they receive divine inspiration, and that they have been called here by their redeemer-god. Of course." Ygg paused. "Which brings us back to the fact that all I must buy is a little time, not much. Just enough for my raiding parties to nip at Vali's back and flanks, cut off his supply lines and throw his forces into disorder. Then the sky-serpent. And following that, your brother's head on my spear."

"And you would slay me to buy that time?"

Ygg nodded. "I just thought you would like to know. It could have been otherwise, Vidar, but you just didn't have the perception to see the truth." He drew his blade from his belt and pointed it at Vidar's breast. "A precaution, my lord. Just in case you don't take kindly to the shackles." Then he snarled for someone outside the room, and four of the hide-covered nomads maneuvered their bulks through the doorway. One carried a pair of thick, iron manacles—*dwarvin*-made, by the look of them. And strong.

The thursar with the manacles leaned over to snap them onto Vidar's wrists, and he took the only chance he had. He grabbed the giant by the front of his dirty tunic, stood and launched him in Ygg's direction. Then he drove his fist into another's belly and kicked the legs out from under a third. One more to go, but this one had had time to get his sword out. Vidar caught his wrist as it brought the blade down, twisted and heard the bone snap. The giant screamed as Vidar bolted for the door.

But there were other blades there, and they stopped him cold, just short of plunging into them. A fist came down on his shoulder, and he fought for consciousness as he fell to his knees. Vidar felt something sharp in the small of his back and heard Ygg's ragged voice. "What does it matter, Vidar? You've lived much too long anyway, haven't you?" The manacles came out again, and this time he suffered them to be put on.

"Where now?" Vidar breathed. "Have you dungeons in your city of priests?"

Ygg laughed his hideous laugh and said nothing.

They took him to the court of the Aesir gods, and they chained him to the foot of his own statue. First they had removed the manacles, which had been so effective a symbol as they paraded him across the square from his tower to the holy precincts. The nomads had rejoiced to see Vidar Death-winder—a new nickname—in their midst. But when they reached the courtyard, still an oasis of space and silence in a city of spears and squabbling, the manacles had been removed and replaced with new bonds—thicker and even stronger than the first. They pulled his arms back around the statue's shin, ran a chain through the rings on his shackles, and locked it behind the statue's colossal calf.

It was there he saw Eric and N'arri, bound as he was, each to one of Vali's massive legs. Ygg had not been kind to them. There was a patch of dried blood on Eric's forehead, and his bare arms and legs were badly lacerated. N'arri's chin was covered with blood, some of it still wet and glistening in the little light left them by the bulging storm front. His black tunic had been torn half away, and he bore what looked to be savage burns on his chest.

Yet they still stood. Stim had not been so fortunate, his garb marking him so obviously as an officer of Skatalund. It had been a fair-starred moment for Eric when he had donned that elvish tunic. Ygg must have tortured him and the elf to make Stim talk, never knowing that he held the heir to Skatalund's throne in his hands. Once Stim was dead, however, he had taken to tormenting the other two, and one of them had given him an answer he liked.

Ygg had placed guards all around the perimeter of the courtyard, on the edge of the green lawn, nomads armed with curved scimitars. But there was nothing to stop the captives from talking to one another.

"How badly are you hurt?" Vidar called across the expanse of red and white stones.

"I'm fine," said Eric, although his voice was hoarse. "But I'm afraid that you'll not get an answer from N'arri."

Vidar looked into the elf's eyes, and realized then what the fresh blood on his chin meant. They had cut out his tongue.

"I'm sorry," Vidar sighed. Then louder. "I'm sorry. Forgive me. This was not your battle."

The elf's expression did not change. But his palms, drawn tight against the stone, turned upward, and he shrugged.

"He forgives you, Vidar," called Eric. "Though there is no need for it."

"Bravely said, Eric. But do you know what plans they have for us here?"

Eric shook his head. N'arri's brow furrowed. Vidar cursed and strained at his fetters. Damn it all! Even his death would have more victims trailing after it. And he would have to be the one to tell them.

"We're to be executed," he said and watched the realization cross their faces. "That's how Ygg hopes to rally his forces."

There was silence for a second, in the pall of the Aesir survivors.

"Vidar," Eric called. "Did he say how?"

Why hide anything now? "Ygg called it a 'sacrifice.'" Vidar looked meaningfully at the stone altar in front of Eric.

The boy nodded, slowly. N'arri just let his head drop onto his chest.

The ebon thunderclouds in the east had grown menacingly close, but it made little difference to the three of them.

XXXI

They stood chained to the gods of Indilthrar for the rest of that day and into the night. At dusk, priests brought them something to eat. Barley-cakes this time, and they had to be eaten off the plates that the priests held up to their mouths. "My compliments to the chef," Vidar called as they retreated, with a bravado he did not feel. No one laughed.

The night was chill and long. In the far west, there were faint stars, and Vidar kept looking that way, to his left. If he just kept his head turned that way and did not look at the wall of darkness that blotted out the stars in the east, he could imagine that there was no war on Utgard, no siege engine bogged down in the mud just short of the city gates and no bloodthirsty demon out of Niflheim raging over the walls. As he had dreamed. By concentrating on those pinpoints of light, he could imagine that there was hope— where there was none.

Vidar found it difficult to believe in death. As a youth, he had risked his life time and again in the raids on Jotunheim. He had left his blood in the snow on the slopes. But he had never really believed he would die. None of them had. And in nearly two thousand years on earth, death had been the farthest thing from his mind. He was immortal, or close to it. Still a youth, compared to Odin or Hoenir.

So even with the reality of death so close, he could not quite take it seriously. It was only in the faces of Eric and N'arri that Death showed its own face to him. Looking to the west could not change that—but it made it seem distant for a time.

The night passed slowly. A numbness slithered into Vidar's bones, and he shivered. But he did not sleep. Exhausted, N'arri slumped in his chains but woke with a start. And then slumped again. Eric dozed fitfully, mercilessly caught between sleep and waking. When he slept, he moaned. After all, he was just a boy. Otherwise, the courtyard was empty of sound, and even their guards did not break that silence.

It must come tomorrow, perhaps at dawn. Or the time of dawn, anyway, because the sun could not be seen behind the sky-serpent's nest. Ygg could not chance waiting much longer—the hostility between priest and nomad had been obvious even when their food was brought to them. Offhand remarks by the guards, stealthy looks from one cowled face to another. Yes, it would have to be tomorrow.

Halfway through the night, the guards changed. The stars in the west vanished one by one as a light, natural cloud cover passed over them. The ponderous black sky, meanwhile, came ever closer. It seemed almost upon them.

Dawn came as a slight lessening of the dark. With the muted sunrise, Ygg appeared in the courtyard. He gave the orders to a couple of the nomads, then watched them depart. Did the grim battle mask conceal any regrets? Vidar had always gotten along well with Odin, where many—even his sons by Frigga—did not. In any case, it was too late for such things.

First came the thursar priests, solemn and decorous. They

took their places beside the altars and placed the lambs they had brought on the cold stone. Their robes were belted and from the belts hung short, ceremonial swords for the sacrifice.

Then the nomads poured into the courtyard—the warriors, the aged, even the hairless, bawling infants. It was just a fraction of the tribal population that Ygg had gathered under his grim banner—maybe a couple of hundred—but it would do. They would return to their people and the word would catch like wildfire, until all the forces of Ygg had heard it. So that they might forget their enmity, reminded of the common enemy—man and his Aesir gods.

Ygg walked to the center of the courtyard, and when he raised his hand, the raucous noise of the crowd died down. There was a long roll of distant thunder from the east. Then Ygg spoke.

"Hear me, my children," he said, and his voice echoed among the stone statues. "Hear me. Not long ago, when I came among you, I promised you the lands that men took from you and the freedom to hunt and trek as you pleased. I vowed an end to men's dominion on this world. A new age for the thursar, long past due. And you followed me, your god, here to Indilthrar."

Vidar marveled at the monster's stentorian oration. Ygg modulated his voice so as to disguise its harsh, dust-dry quality and made use of tone and pitch to sound as guttural as the thursar themselves. Truly, the voice of the people.

"This is not the place for you, who make your homes in the expanses of the wide fields, in the lap of the hills. But this is where you will win the freedom you seek. Long after Vali has fallen and the land has been restored to the thursar, your children's children will sing of your deeds here. And Indilthrar will be known as a shrine to your deeds.

"Here are the priests of Indilthrar. They will keep the shrine, as they have ever kept Indilthrar a holy place. In these priests—your own people—resides your immortality.

Yours is the spear that frees the thursar—but theirs is the hand that inscribes it in runes. Brothers, all of you. A nation of thursar."

Ygg had them mesmerized. Again, a rumble of thunder, perhaps closer now. A bit more of the sky was crowded out.

"Lies!" Vidar cried over the din in the sky. "He leads you to your deaths! Lambs to the sacrifice, no different from those you see on the altars. Why trust him? Who is this god? Have him take off his mask, and you will see . . ."

Ygg strode toward him, and Vidar noted the controlled fury in his gait. "What kind of god hides behind a mask?" he continued. "A fearful god! A dissembler, who will throw you away as soon as you've served your—"

Ygg's mailed fist came down across his mouth. For a moment, blackness engulfed him—then he fought it off. There was blood in his mouth. He spat it out. But he heard a murmur thread through the assemblage, a guttural undercurrent of doubt.

"I could make it painful, Vidar," Ygg whispered. "You've never felt such pain."

"There'll be no freedom!" Vidar yelled. "Just death, death for your families—"

Ygg struck him twice, back and forth across his face. Then he turned savagely. "Here is the god of men, the vaunted hero!" Ygg picked Vidar's head up by his hair. "See how helpless he is before your god, the lord of triumphs! This is how we'll humble those who wait outside our walls." The crowd fell silent again.

Ygg signed to the priests. "We sacrifice on the altars of the old gods, the dead gods," he said. "But the sacrifice is Ygg's!"

In unison, six priests cut the throats of six bawling lambs. They kicked to free themselves even as their blood ran out onto the cold stone altars. Then three of the priests, with sacrificial blades drawn, took their places by Vidar, Eric and N'arri.

The sky droned. The storm was close now, moving faster than Vidar had expected. Lightning lit the underbelly of the black, roiling clouds. The air stretched taut with a faint smell of ozone. Ygg paused, allowing the din of the storm to come to a long, crashing end before he spoke again.

"See the heavens, my children," he said, and he pointed a finger into the sky. "With this, I'll sweep the forces of men from these mountains! With the fury of the sky itself!"

The throng of hide-clad nomads cheered and threshed the air with their iron-tipped spears, rivaling the noise in the heavens. Beneath it, Ygg said, "It seems Hoenir will weaken sooner than I had thought. We could have avoided this if I knew that the storm would be so soon at hand."

"It's not too late," said Vidar, blood running from his mouth.

"Not too late?" Ygg said. "Of course it is. For all of us." It was dark now, almost night. Only in the west was there even a sliver of light. The nomads' roar grew louder, feeding on the growing darkness.

Suddenly, there was a voice within the thunder of Ygg's followers, a voice inside his head.

"Vidar! Where are you?"

It was Vali.

"In the holy precinct, somewhere in the center of the city." Vidar eyed Ygg, who stood but a few feet from him, studying the heavens. A priest stood next to him, awaiting instructions. "About to be sacrificed to Ygg."

"Really?" said Vali. "Right now? How much time do you think you have?"

"A minute. Maybe."

"Too bad," said Vali. "I'll need more time than that. Stall him and your death won't go for nothing."

That was all. Meanwhile, the tide of thursar voices had

crested and broke, and Ygg was turning once more toward
Vidar. He held out his hand meaningfully, and the cowled
giant at his side placed the hilt of the ceremonial knife in
his hand.

Stall him? "How about a last request?"

Ygg grunted. "Quiet. I'm trying to decide whether to
disembowel you slowly or just cut your throat and be done
with it."

"Tell me one thing, father," he pleaded. "One thing, and
I'll suffer any torture you devise."

Ygg considered. He gestured and the priest backed off
a dozen paces. "Swear allegiance to me before you die.
Proclaim my truth, and I'll answer your question."

"First the question," said Vidar.

"Vow by your mother that you'll cry out your allegiance
once I've answered."

"I swear," said Vidar, wincing as some blood from a cut
on his temple ran into his eye.

"And the question?"

"What was it," Vidar asked, "that you whispered to Baldur
on his pyre?"

Ygg did not answer, but placed the point of the blade
against Vidar's left breast. Vidar strained against his chains,
to no avail. The skin broke, and the blood trickled forth.
Then Ygg sliced diagonally down, slowly, and stopped at
Vidar's hip. The blood flowed freely.

He had failed. Ygg had rejected his proposition and decided to go ahead with the sacrifice.

Once again, Ygg punctured the skin, this time just below
Vidar's left nipple, and drew the razor-edged blade straight
across. On the other side of the courtyard, Eric grimaced.
The thursar mob hooted as Ygg cut, but Vidar did not cry
out. There was worse to come, he knew. Another slice,
beneath the first. Then another. His chest felt as if it were
on fire.

But so intent was Ygg on his ministrations that he did

not see the sudden build-up of gray clouds against the black sky—the towering, impossible height of the storm column as it grew—the ugly, rearing head of the sky-serpent as it writhed and spat tongues of lightning.

When the wind came, it was sudden and furious. Ygg was about to press the red-running point into Vidar's flesh once more when he felt that wind and looked up. Thunder trundled mercilessly across the heavens, and Vidar felt a cold drop of rain on his shoulder.

"No," Ygg whispered savagely. "It's too soon." A rain-drop glanced off the hideous battle mask.

Then, through the haze of his pain, Vidar heard a tumult at the spot where the nomads had entered the courtyard. Ygg turned to listen to the guttural shouts. Then he cursed and flung the sacrificial knife down on the flagstones. Drawing his own stout broadsword, he made his way through the mass of thursar and disappeared in their midst. Above, lightning danced and thunder bellowed, splitting the sky. The nomads piled out of the courtyard after their god, leaving the priests to guard the captives.

"Vali?" Vidar called in his mind.

"Not now," said his half brother. "We're almost through." It grew dark, impossibly dark, as the sky-serpent loomed over them. He could barely discern the statues to which Eric and N'arri were bound. Suddenly, the courtyard was white-hot with the glare of day. There was a deafening clap. The ground shook. Then the darkness closed down again and the rains came, pelting the courtyard and the statues so hard it sounded like a herd of wild horses.

The priests that had stayed behind ran for cover now. Winds screamed and drove the rain in sheets that hissed against the stones. It stabbed Vidar's bare skin like needles and traced lines of agony in his fresh wounds. He found himself gasping for air, drowning in the torrents that flooded his face. A flash of searing white light made his eyes burn. Then there was the thunder, all around him, crushing his eardrums. And then a tremendous crash. Vidar tried to see through the water that ran into his eyes.

It was one of the statues, struck by lightning and smashed against the flagstones. Its legs still stood, the rest of the body severed at the knees.

The lightning walked again. Thunder filled his brain. There was no letup. Lightning, then thunder, lightning, then thunder, and the world went blind and roared, mourning its blindness. The rain battered him nearly senseless. He felt his legs slipping out from under him, but the shackles kept him from falling. His arms hurt as if they would tear loose from their sockets.

Vidar breathed in water, gagged and coughed it up. He managed to plant his feet and slowly stood up to relieve the tension in his shoulders. Then there was a hand on his arm, and another at his wrist. Ygg's priests, come back to finish the job? He felt rather than heard the crunch of iron against iron, and again, and then he was free of the chains—though he still wore the iron manacles. He hunched over against the pummeling rain. Someone slipped a cloak over his shoulders.

"A sword," he gasped, breathing deeply in the shelter of the cloak. "I want a sword!" And that, too, was given him. He looked up through the streaming downpour into the face of his benefactor. It was pale and dark-haired beneath a black hood. A *dwarvin* face.

Then he looked around and saw more of them stalking the courtyard like ebon ghosts, tall elves with their rune-swords drawn. They had freed Eric and N'arri as well.

Ygg. Vidar started off against the force of the wind toward the opening in the courtyard through which the no-mads had vanished. On the other side, he came upon a narrow street—and at the end of that street, he saw the blurred edge of the battle moving past him. He ran in that direction, cloak flying behind him.

A startled thursar whirled and saw him, but before he

could react, Vidar had buried his blade in the giant's belly. He twisted and it pulled free. A second thursar hurled his spear at Vidar and missed, then ran.

Lightning turned the world into an inferno, throwing the bodies of the combatants into stark relief. Vidar fell upon another of the nomads, burying his edge in the giant's collarbone. He wiped water from his eyes with the back of his free hand, unable to keep from surveying his handiwork. But there was no time now to mull over the morality of his deeds. Later. At his side, an elf's sword whistled and a thursar doubled over.

Then there was a rush of females and children, and Vidar nearly struck the foremost before he could tell what they were. Once they passed, the street was empty. Vidar followed its length to the cross street and found a handful of thursar backed against the wall by a larger group of yellow-haired swordsmen.

The rain fell in sheets, and the darkness was relieved only when the lightning flashed. Sometimes Vidar could see where he was going, and sometimes not. Mud lapped at his feet.

He moved into another street and found himself near a square. A knot of dark-clad elves caught up to him and gathered around. He peered at their faces, half-hidden by their cloaks. It was the same group that had freed him. Very well, then—if they were so eager to follow him, he would lead.

In the square ahead, there was the clatter of weapons, but Vidar couldn't see through the curtains of driving rain. He waited until lightning stabbed Indilthrar and he could make out the nature of the struggle. At the far side of the open place, giants fought against giants. Vidar stumbled and nearly fell as his foot caught on a priest's body lying face down against the mud. Then he barked his challenge at the nearest nomad.

The giant turned, catlike, and slashed at him with the

point of his spear. With one stroke, Vidar cut the shaft in two and opened the nomad's throat. An elf fell in Vidar's path, impaled. He plucked the spear out and hurled it over the clot of battle, as he had vouchsafed his victims to Odin's glory in days long past. But this dedication was for a meaner lord—the one that raged in him now, demanding blood as the sacrifice for Ygg's defeat.

Another giant launched himself at Vidar, a priest, with curved scimitar raised high above his head. Vidar slashed upward, disemboweling him. The thursar's bulk fell on top of him, shutting out the roar of the rain for a ghostly moment. He rolled out from under the corpse quickly, leaping into a crouch. But there was no one waiting to spear him as he got up.

Another giant came at him, and another, and he dispatched them. The battle droned on for an eternity, a dull haze over the scene of death, penetrated by his own pain and sudden sights frozen into the memory: a headless thursar female, whose living child still clutched at her breast; a Vanirman whose mouth had filled with rainwater like a birdbath; two priests pinned together like lovers by a single spear. All he could remember afterward was cut, parry and stroke, the cold business of killing. He lost most of his elvish companions somewhere along the line. Only two stayed with him as he plodded through the muck and the puddles churned red with blood.

Vidar's head felt like bursting. He had shrugged off his cloak, drenched through as it was, and now stalked the streets of Indilthrar naked from the waist up. He passed narrow alleys, empty of all but corpses, and heard the cries of mourning in the dying wake of the thunder. The storm was diminishing. It must have been hours since he had been liberated. Water and blood ran like rivers over the cobblestones, where there were cobblestones, clutching at his ankles.

Yet there were still sounds of conflict, and he hurried

toward them. As he turned a corner, an Aesir horseman galloped past, within a sword's breadth of trampling him—two nomads fleeing before his rush, rainwater spattering with each hoofbeat. Here the battle still raged full-blown, Vali's riders whirling and cutting desperately in quarters too close for cavalry. Vidar spied one face that he knew—Hoenir's—and just as he spotted him, Hoenir was dragged down from his steed. Vidar vaulted in that direction.

A thursar rose up in his path, grinning, his spear dripping with Aesir blood. Vidar decapitated first the spear, then the giant himself. Two more charged at him, and he battered at their weapons, circling to his left, keeping them both before him. A third saw the unequal odds and came up on his left flank, forcing him to back off, wary of their spears.

They came at him together, all three. One shaft he shattered. Another, he managed to turn aside with his bare hand. But the point of the third one slashed his forehead, and blood fell into his eyes, blinding him. Vidar backpedaled, blinking, trying to stay out of range of their thrusts until his vision cleared.

Then a horseman cut between them, and Vidar heard the thud of an axe falling—once, twice. The third nomad flung his spear and retreated. Vidar looked up to see who his rescuer might be and saw the face of one of Irbor's brothers. Their eyes met. Again the axe lifted, and Vidar wiped the blood from his eyes, bracing for the Vanirman's attack. But it never came.

"Some other time," he said, "Lord Vidar." He reined his horse about, sought out a mass of thursar and was absorbed into the ebb and flow of the battle.

Vidar breathed deeply, then remembered Hoenir. His uncle had gone down—where? There, more or less. He made for the spot, still blinking at the blood in his eyes. The blow had sent his senses spinning. But he held his sword high with both hands on its rune-carved hilt and ran forward. A thursar fell under the fury of his charge. Another poked him in the thigh, but was cut down by a mounted Aesirman before he could try again.

Gradually, Vidar won to the place where he had seen Hoenir fall. But he was not the only one who had come to Hoenir's aid. Vali, too, had lost his horse. He stood astride Hoenir's inert form, thrusting and cutting at the hulking, hide-skinned giants, bleeding from a dozen wounds. Vidar could not help but admire Vali's courage—and his swordplay—as the battle parted for a moment. Vali's blade was like a thing alive. Then there rose a cry, and a fresh wave of nomad warriors came pouring out of one of the streets behind them.

At their head, his helm unmistakable, was Ygg. His arms were dipped in blood up to his shoulders, and blood ran down the front of his mail. In one hand, he held an iron-tipped spear. In the other, he dangled an elf's head by its long, black hair. Some of those he led also lifted heads on their spears, and the rain had cleansed the white, gaping faces of enough blood to make them recognizable to their comrades.

Ygg reared back and threw the elf's head over the battle. It spun wildly and hit the side of a building. Then he charged, a solid wedge of spears in his wake. An Aesir horseman bore down on him, hoping to cut off the head of the snake before the coils could contract. But Ygg caught the warrior on his spear, and the Aesirman's own momentum lifted him high off his horse and into the air. For a moment he hung there, writhing. Then the spear snapped, and he fell. Ygg picked up the warrior's axe, almost without breaking stride, and brandished it at the cavalry that had forced its way in through the gates.

Ygg had the advantage here. With the fighting going on shoulder to shoulder, there was no room for Vali's mounted troops to gain any momentum. The riders were dragged from their horses now as soon as they slowed down. Vidar again wiped away the blood that oozed from his temple.

Dizzy now, he fought off nausea, reaching into himself for an inner reserve of strength—the strength that only Odin and his sons possessed. It manifested itself in each prince of Asgard in a different way, but the strength of the *lifling* and the strength of the *stromrad* were essentially the same. It seemed that the battle slowed as he drew on that inner well.

The sound of iron on iron and weapon cleaving bone drifted away. Vidar saw clearly, as if there were no rain and no cloud-begotten darkness. Inside him, the candle of his soul burned quickly. It would cost him, someday, this nova-flame of pure, bright vitality—cost him months, perhaps years of life. And there was nothing the Aesir feared more than to lose precious pieces of their immortality. But the payment was far off.

Vidar warded off a spear strike—effortlessly, it seemed. Another thursar blocked his way, and he cut the giant down at the knees. Three more bodies between him and Ygg. Hack, parry, thrust, parry again and cut, and another fell. A well-placed point and only one was left. The final barrier was swept aside almost too easily.

Ygg must have seen the cast of his eyes, for he took a step backward before Vidar's onslaught. And with that step he, too, must have plumbed his inner depths for twofold strength. Perhaps more—for was there any limit to the power Odin had commanded?

But this was not Odin, not entirely. What might Niflheim have done to quench the fires of Asaland's king?

The battle faded away all around them. They slipped into another stream, where time passed more slowly. Two of them, all alone in the universe, dancing to the thunderous doom-beat of the blood in their veins.

Ygg struck first, his axe falling as if from a distant peak. Vidar stepped back—and the axe fell short of its mark. Ygg circled to his left. Vidar feinted, but Ygg saw it for a feint. A second time he feinted, and this time Ygg reacted, shifting his weight to his right to avoid the stroke that never came. Instead, Vidar lunged to Ygg's right, and his point bit deep into the monster's side.

The axe came down, and Vidar twisted the sword free. He beat the axe blade aside just before it would have crushed his skull. Ygg staggered back, his free hand going to the wound that Vidar had dealt him.

The son advanced and the father stood his ground. Ygg bled between his fingers. With any luck, thought Vidar, his next blow would be the death stroke. He shuffled to his right, looking for an opening.

Then there was a terrific impact on the back of his head. Mud and water filled his mouth. Vidar turned his head, spat and propped himself up on one elbow. Ygg had disappeared into the melee.

Someone knelt by his side. It was Eric, his face smeared with blood.

"Vidar," he said. "Are you all right?" Vidar nodded. "It's almost over. We've won."

"Ygg," Vidar muttered. The nova-change was wearing off.

"Don't know. They're still hunting down the last of the thursar." Then Vidar saw the *dwarvin* faces that hung behind Eric's. One of them belonged to N'arri.

"Glad you made it," said Vidar. Suddenly, he was too exhausted to stand. "Give me a hand, will you?" Eric pulled Vidar's arm over his shoulders and with some help from the elves, lifted him to his feet. The rain had slowed to an insistent, gray drizzle.

One of the *dwarvin* picked up Vidar's sword, still wet with Ygg's blood. Vidar held his hand up, palm forward. "Let it lie there," he said. "Or keep it."

But even after the elf had tucked the blade into his belt— for the *dwarvin* did not just throw away the swords they labored over—even then, the elf stared at Vidar's chest.

He pointed, and the other *dwarvin* crowded in to see for themselves.

"What is it?" Vidar asked. They seemed to be pointing to his chest. He looked down. All he could see there were the shallow cuts Ygg had dealt him in the courtyard. He had been lucky.

"Rune-work," said one of the elves, looking up. His green eyes danced. "Intricate work, at that."

Ygg's work. "What does it signify?" Vidar asked again.

"It is difficult to read with all the blood and the other cuts you bear," the elf said. "But it seems to say—'Odin is to blame. He dreamed too high, he loved too much.'"

And then, suddenly, Vidar thought he understood.

"What does that mean, Vidar?" asked Eric. His brows were knit in puzzlement.

"It was Ygg's answer to my question, Eric. I was trying to delay him, because Vali had called to me and asked me to do that. I asked Ygg for one thing—to know what Odin had whispered to Baldur on his funeral pyre. This is what he must have whispered."

"That Odin was to blame for Baldur's death?"

"Yes."

"But how could Ygg have told you what only Odin could have known?" asked one of the *dwarvin*. "It was the greatest of secrets."

Vidar looked about them as Vali's forces gathered the surviving nomads into small groups, ringed about with swords and horses. The sky was still blue-black, battered and swollen, but in the east now he could see a slender ribbon of fairer weather.

The battle was over—but not the danger. Would Utgard ever be at peace again if Ygg could prove he was Odin returned? If he could somehow remove his mask and remind them of their ancient duty to the All-father? Then he might find himself with more followers than just the thursar. There might be human lords behind him, then, Olof's counterparts in other regions.

For who could fail to worship his Creator? And could Vali execute him, then? Vidar hoped that Ygg had been slain before he could try to reveal himself to someone else. But until the monster was discovered, dead or alive, Vidar would stifle the rumor that might fan the flames of Ygg's power anew. His identity must be kept a secret.

Emerald-green eyes waited expectantly. "Swear to me," said Vidar, "that you will never repeat what I am about to tell you. As you love your world, swear to me."

They swore, all five of the elves that had gathered tightly about him and Eric as well. And he told them.

"Oh, god," said Eric. "Oh, my god."

XXXII

Vali pounded his fist into his other hand. "Damn! I should have guessed that he'd have an escape route. Our father is still as crafty as ever, Vidar. He'll not be easy to find now."

Vidar considered the hellhole that opened at his feet. He could feel the energies that pulsed about it, marking it as a gate of Odin's making—heretofore unknown, though it must have been here since the creation of Utgard itself, long before Indilthrar was built above it. No doubt, the priests who had founded the city had been awed by it and so chose this spot for their mountain fastness.

Hoenir stroked his short, gray beard. He was still a handsome fellow, and he had not aged much at all since Vidar saw him last. Thanks to Vidar's *lifling* abilities, he had recovered from a concussion he had suffered during the battle.

"He never fails to amaze me," said Hoenir. "First, turning up when we all thought him dead. And then, slipping in a gate where even I, who had a hand in shaping these mountains, didn't know one existed."

"But where does it lead?" asked Modi. He winced as he spoke, making it plain that he had still not completely healed after his fall, despite his protestations to the contrary. "You mentioned Niflheim, Jawbreaker—could this be a gate to Niflheim?"

Vidar shook his head. "I don't think so. He never had an affinity for that place until he fled there from Loki's fire. And this gate was made before Ragnarok."

Hoenir smiled. "Not an easy place to develop an affinity for, my lords. When we stumbled on it the first time, Odin and Lodur and I . . . well, it was like dipping your soul in ice water. Even Jotunheim looked a lot cheerier after Niflheim."

"Ygg did say one thing," Vidar remarked. "He mentioned Magni."

"What?" Modi glared at him. "What about him?"

"Ygg said that only Magni understood what he was doing. He implied that Magni was allied with him, carrying out his plans in Alfheim."

"You're lying," said Modi.

Vidar shook his head. "What for?"

"Then this hole might lead to Alfheim," said Vali. "Or it might not. Even if what you say is true, Vidar, Odin could not have had these circumstances in mind when he created the gate here. He took the only route he had, and it might still lead anywhere."

"Aye," said Hoenir, his smile turning subtly grim. "There are the worlds we know—Asaheim, Alfheim, Midgard, Utgard, ruined Vanaheim, Jotunheim and now Muspelheim. There are Svartheim, Nidavellir and Niflheim, which we can perhaps rule out. But what worlds might exist that we don't know of—worlds Odin may have come upon alone and kept to himself?"

Hoenir's eyes flicked from Vali to Vidar to Modi, and

then back to Vali. "There are others. I can tell you that. In many cases, we just didn't have the skill to bridge the gap between one of our worlds and those others. At least, I didn't, nor did Lodur. But Odin—he was always our master at that." Hoenir laughed. "At most things. Who would have thought that even he could have escaped Gjallarhorn? My brother has abilities even I never knew existed."

There was silence for a moment, as they gazed into the strangely dense, black depths of the hellhole.

"Well, Vidar?" Vali asked. "In Skatalund, you said that we three should be more than a match for Ygg. What do you think now?"

Vidar frowned, rubbing his wrists, from which the iron manacles had been removed only minutes before. "I think that I underestimated the danger. As you yourself did, when you heard that Hod's emblem flew over the dead at Dundafrost. We assumed that it was only our brother we would have to deal with—at worst. And I was wrong, I'll grant you that. But I still don't like your methods, Vali."

"Of course not," said Vali. "That's why you're standing there with the blood running off your sword—because you don't believe in war."

Vidar glared at him. "There are wars and there are wars. Ygg is a madman and it falls to us to stop him. But there's a difference between an enemy that is real and one you seek out to give your warriors something to dull their swords on."

"You're blinding yourself to the truth, Vidar. It is only a matter of time before each of these worlds we speak of becomes a threat to Asaheim. Why not anticipate—seek them out before they come seeking us?"

"That's your mistake, Vali. You think everyone is like you—thirsty for dominion. Maybe these other worlds just want to be left alone."

Modi spat. "And while we debate, uncles, Ygg is on one of these worlds raising another army."

"Modi's right," said Hoenir gently—too gently. "Let's not fight among ourselves, shall we?" He laughed ironically. "It's good that we have an enemy, isn't it, to unite us under one banner? Why resist it, Vidar? I mean, as long as all our purposes coincide?"

Vidar suppressed his anger. Hoenir had a way of calming people that had not grown dull with the years. "All right, then," he said. "I pledge my sword to Ygg's demise."

"And then?" asked Vali.

"And then, we shall see, brother."

"But for now," said Hoenir, pausing meaningfully, "we must go after him."

They stared down into the darkness. "Yes," said Vali. "But what if he already has a following at the other end? I've never seen a better tactician than Odin, and a good tactician always plants more than one crop—in case the first should fail."

"You mean that he may have an army ready-in-waiting?" said Modi. "An interesting possibility." He grunted. "We may be leaping into a trap."

"And there may be no easy way back here, or to one of the other worlds we know," said Vidar. "This is a one-way proposition, isn't it?"

Hoenir nodded. "It would seem so. I have never seen a gate that led straight down, as this one does. All the others are more-or-less level passages."

"Then we can't get back?" asked Modi.

"Precisely," said Hoenir. "Nor can we send a reconnaissance mission, because there is no way for them to return, either."

"Then we'll take an army," said Vali. "I would hate to enter some unknown territory without sufficient strength to hunt him down. We can't call on more troops if we find that we're shorthanded, can we?"

Vidar nodded. "That will take some time—getting your

forces in order and all. Why don't we get some rest until Indilthrar is secure?"

"Aye," said Modi. "Let the captains organize the troops. I could use something to eat."

Vali and Hoenir nodded their assent. They made their way up out of the underground chamber wherein the hole had been discovered and emerged into the smoky light of day. The weather was improving swiftly. A patch of cornflower-blue sky had opened up in the east, and the air had grown colder.

Eric had waited for Vidar outside the temple of Vali— once the temple of Odin, it seemed. It struck Vidar that the boy had grown older since they left Skatalund, but that might have been the effect of the blood and the grime that still clung to his cheeks and forehead.

"What news, Vidar?" he asked.

"Ygg has escaped to another place," said Vidar. "Another world—though we do not know which one. We're going to follow him." The boy nodded.

"You don't have to go, you know," said Vidar. "There's no telling where we may end up. You still have a duty here, Eric. It will take a lot of hard work to fashion a peace that men, elves and thursar alike can live with. And then to implement it, that's a whole other task, and..."

But it was no use. Eric's attempt at a grin was his answer. And Vidar had to admit to himself that he was pleased about it, after all. He had grown attached to Eric.

"I'm going," the boy said. "Incidentally, do you know whom we have to thank for our lives?"

Vidar nodded. "B'rannit. Vali told me the whole story. After we had been gone too long, in her sweet judgment, she sent a messenger to Vali. And once he learned that she knew a way into the city—had, in fact, gotten us in—he had to trust her. Of course, he had little to lose. It was the *dwarvin* that took all the risks, slipping inside to open the gates. And once the gates were open, Vali was able to bring his horsemen to bear."

"But," said Eric, "did you know that she was here?"

Vidar knew that he must have looked startled, for Eric smiled. "B'rannit? Here?" He felt the blood rush up into his face. "Quit smirking and talk, Eric."

"Of course," said the boy. "I heard it from one of my friends, who rode with Vali from Skatalund. The word was that she gathered an army of *dwarvin* from every tribe from here to the sea, trading on her influence and collecting on past debts. Half of her forces came in underground—the narrowness of the tunnel preventing more. B'rannit rode with the rest to join Vali and his chiefs. I daresay that she was the only female on the right side of the walls."

Vali smiled. "Will you excuse me for now, Eric? I've got some business to attend to. I'll meet you back here in about an hour. If any of my relatives ask after me, tell them ... tell them anything. And ... say, I forgot about your kinsmen. How did they fare?"

A glint of pain showed in Eric's face. "Most of them fared well. My father was wounded, but he will recover. Do you think an hour will be enough time to find him in all this mess?"

Vidar nodded. "Get going. And send this word, from me—to consider the nomads next time he walls off a hunting preserve. It wasn't all Ygg that fired their rebellion."

Eric said, "I will do that," and was gone. Vidar looked over the square full of milling soldiers. B'rannit, eh? He spotted an Aesir warrior on a brown gelding and walked up to him.

"Your pardon, lord," he said, "but would you give me a ride outside the gates?"

The rider peered down at him from under an iron helm. "You're Vidar, aren't you?"

"That I am. And I need a ride."

"Climb on up, my lord. I'm a healer, too, you know."
Vidar swung up behind him.

"What's your name?"

"Ullir."

"Well, then, Ullir, I've got another favor to ask of you.
After you drop me off, could you see to the lord of
Skatalund?"

"Aye. I only wish there were more of me to go around.
There are never enough of us on a day like today." Ullir
took his helm off, shaking his yellow hair free. "Pity the
enemy—not a healer among them. And it would have been
worse—much worse—if Vali could have unlocked the heart
of Gjallarhorn before the storm."

"He still can."

"Aye, and then what happened at G'walin would look
like a drop in the ocean."

"What happened there?" asked Vidar.

"Food," said Ullir, "no more, no less. One of our Aesirmen
tried to bargain for it with the *lyos*. It started out innocently
enough, it seems, but then words came to blows, and blows
to blades. An Aesirman does not like to be turned down
when he is offering a worthless belt buckle for a loaf of
good bread and a healthy hunk of cheese. It was not an
evenly matched fight, I'm afraid. What I meant by G'walin
and the drop in the ocean is that the *lyos* there weren't
opponents. They were victims, like anyone who has to listen
to the horn."

"You've got some strange sentiments for a warrior of
Asaheim, Ullir. A lot like my own."

The rider laughed. "Some part of any healer must be that
way, I suppose. At least, we mortal ones. Father Heimdall,
I understand, would have frowned on the way I talk. But
he was . . . well, Heimdall."

"Your ancestor?"

"Aye, my lord. There's a bit of Heimdall in me, and a

bit of Bragi, too, but mostly I'm just human—like the rest
of us."

"You come from good stock, Ullir."

"Is there anyone in Asgard who can't say the same?"

It was Vidar's turn to laugh. They passed through the
gates of Indilthrar and out onto the hillside, where they saw
the great, hulking war engine still mired in the mud. The
slope was covered with warriors walking their horses. Here
and there, healers tended to the wounded, who had been
brought out from Indilthrar on litters. With so little of Odin's
blood in them, however, they could not help much. Chieftains rallied their men to their grimy banners, trying to make
some order out of the chaos. The word had already gone
out—the war was not yet over.

The Asalanders might not be too surprised at that, having
already made the trip between worlds to get here. But how
might the simple, parochial humans, the thursar and the
elves react?

Vidar chanced to glance back at the walls of the city,
and his eyes were drawn to a great crack that ran from the
top of the barrier to the bottom. From his prison room, he
had not known all the damage Modi had done. But from
the outside, one could see that in scaling the wall, he had
taken great pieces out of it with Mjollnir. Given a few more
moments on the ramparts, he might have brought a whole
section down.

Ullir rode between the banners, among blood-spattered
warriors that had barely gotten used to the idea of victory.
There was a clearly discernible look on their faces—a mild
surprise that they still boasted all their arms and legs. Vidar
had seen it a thousand times before. It was much preferable
to that other look—the worming knowledge that one's fears
had been justified, as one looked for limbs one no longer
owned.

"Where are you going?" asked Ullir. "For whose banner
should I look?"

"No banner," said Vidar. "A *dwarvin* queen. She'll be ringed about with black tunics."

Ullir pulled his horse about suddenly to the left. "B'rannit? I know her camp. You can imagine that she caused quite a stir among us. Do you know her?"

"Yes," said Vidar.

"Lucky."

Ullir was true to his word. The *dwarvin* had made their camp just over the crest of a hill. Vidar could see the warriors carrying their wounded in to the circle of their own kind. They tended to their own, both those who had tasted iron and those who had gorged themselves on it.

She walked among them, tall and comely, her long black hair tossing this way and that in the wind. Here, above ground, she was even more beautiful than Vidar remembered.

When Ullir drew up, she glanced at him and knelt to speak with one of the wounded. B'rannit had not seen who it was that rode behind the Aesirman. When Vidar dismounted and clasped Ullir's arm, she did not look up to see who walked into her circle of elves. Even when he stood behind her, blocking the slanting rays of the sun and casting a shadow over her back, she did not seem to notice.

The elf she knelt over, whose brow she caressed, was struggling for breath. A trickle of blood traced a fine line from the corner of his mouth to his ear. Vidar saw that his tunic had been slashed open just above the groin. He was terribly pale, even for an elf. And as Vidar watched, he coughed up a spout of blood and died.

B'rannit's head fell to her breast. Vidar crouched behind her, encircling her slim arms with his hands. Slowly, she turned enough to see whose fingers held her so.

Then she spun about and Vidar saw the tears standing out in her eyes. Wordlessly, she let him pull her to her feet. He embraced her. And for a time, he held her while she sobbed into the small of his shoulder.

Horns sounded, and she raised her eyes to meet his. In daylight, they were the pale green of river shallows. She managed a semblance of a smile.

"You live, Leathershod," she said. "I'm glad."

He searched her face for resentment. "M'rann," he said.

She nodded. "I know."

"It was my fault."

"Yes," she said. "And the fault of the whirlpool. And the fault of his boatmaker, and the fault of our mother for bearing him. Don't be a fool, Vidar Leathershod. M'rann died bravely. We've lost many others since. They all knew the danger. Did you think my warriors would go home and forget you when you told them to?" She looked into his eyes. "Did you think I would forget you?" Her gaze was frank, unflinching.

"Come," he said. "Let me take you away from here, just for a few moments." He took her hand and she walked with him out from the circle of her kind. Before she left, she said a few words to one of her captains.

All the level places were occupied, so they climbed a steep hill that rose almost as high as Indilthrar's walls. On the far side of that hill, they had some privacy.

"I see that you were not treated kindly," she said, glancing at Vidar's wrists. His arms, too, were scored with shallow cuts, and his chest burned beneath the folds of his cloak.

"More kindly than the others," he said.

"It's not over, is it?" she asked. "You did not find Ygg."

"No," he said. "He had a gate to another world ready, just in case he lost here."

"What will you do?"

"The word is going out now. Whoever can ride or march, I'd say, will be asked to follow us."

"Through the gate?"

"Yes."

"To follow *us*, Leathershod? Are you counting yourself among Vali's captains now?"

Vidar sighed. "A good question, B'rannit." She put her hand to his cheek and wiped off some of the dirt and the blood. "When I returned to Utgard, I thought I had changed. I wanted no more of swords and war. Now, as you can see"—he patted the hilt at his hip—"I've changed my tune. It makes me wonder if Vali's way is not the only way—if one can avoid war just by closing one's eyes. Is war the price of peace? Is it worth it?" He closed his eyes. "Don't mind me. I'm just a little tired."

She brushed her lips against his and made a clucking sound with her tongue. "My lord seems confused. Is that not the prelude to wisdom?"

Vidar looked at her. "What do you mean?"

"When you came to under-G'walin, you were certain that the lord Vali's way was wrong. Now, you find that you must ally yourself with him to fight a greater wrong. Does that make Vali's way right? I think not, my lord Leathershod. We *dwarvin* hammer swords into the world, because there will always be a need for swords. Some will use them in need. Others will use them when something else might prevail. Is it not wisdom to know one from the other?"

Vidar looked from B'rannit to the mountains, where the sky had deepened to a robust blue. Only tattered clouds still lingered. "In other words, I might have been less than wise to leave Asgard without a fight—to let Vali work his empire-building without some opposition." When he looked back to her, there were tears in her eyes again. He kissed her, and pulled her gently into the circle of his war-weary arms.

"Back somewhere, I wondered what you would look like aboveground. Whether you would fit." He smelled the near fragrance of her hair, warmed by the sun.

"Do I?" she asked, her face buried against his neck.

"I think so," he said. "I'm not sure."

For a time, there was no war, no Ygg, no Vali and no thought of the future. There was only the golden present, brief, too brief.

As he held B'rannit, some of the fatigue and the horror drained from him. It was as if she, too, were *lifling*, healing his mind again as she had in under-G'walin. He wished that the wars were over as he had never wished before—for the true peace-lovers are those who have something to lose. Stroking the elfqueen's hair, Vidar rejoiced in that thought—after all these years, he again had something to lose.

Then B'rannit raised her head. "I must get back. There are the wounded. And some of my warriors will want to go with the lord Vali."

Vidar nodded. He helped her up the hill, and they crested it together. The sweep of land before Indilthrar had changed in their absence. Where before there had been single warriors and pairs wandering about their own business, the stamp of discipline had been brought to bear. Once again, the armies of Asaheim and Utgard were ready to follow Vali into hell.

The *dwarvin* had done what might be done with their wounded, of which there were many. N'arri was among them. When he caught sight of Vidar and B'rannit, he stood and walked out to meet them.

There was a new fire in N'arri's eyes, a colder fire than Vidar was accustomed to seeing in an elf. It was not unlike the glint he had seen in Or'in's eyes outside G'walin.

N'arri slid his sword out from its sheath and, kneeling, laid it at Vidar's feet. No tongue in him, thought Vidar, as the elf looked up into his face. But eloquent as all hell.

Vidar looked to B'rannit. "I think he speaks for all of them, Leathershod," she said. "I cannot lead them. You would do them a great honor."

"They could do better," said Vidar.

"They could do worse," said B'rannit. "And so could you."

Vidar smiled. "You've got all the answers," he said. When he placed his right hand on N'arri's shoulder, a fierce

cry went up among the *dwarvin*. "Those who are whole—
or close enough— follow me," he said, and they rose to
gather on the slope below him.

He turned to B'rannit again. "I'll be back," he said.
"We'll be back." He gazed at her intently, striving to record
her features in his mind, for one never knew. Her raven
hair, her light green eyes—these things he would not forget
easily. Vidar kissed her lightly on the lips.

"Fare thee well, Leathershod," she whispered.

Then he looked away and led the *dwarvin* down to the
gates of Indilthrar. He came upon Eric there, but the boy
seemed lost in his thoughts.

Even after he looked up and recognized Vidar, he seemed
perplexed. "Vidar," he said. "I'm . . . a chieftain."

"Your father?" Vidar asked carefully.

"No, he's not dead," said Eric. "One of the Aesirmen is
healing him now. But he's too badly wounded to follow
Vali. It falls to me to lead the troops that came from
Skatalund."

Vidar grinned. "There couldn't be a better leader here,"
he said, clasping the boy's shoulder. "Just beware—your
lords will all want their due. You'll have to watch what's
going on behind you as well as before." Valland's face
loomed in Vidar's memory. "You'll have to be careful,
Eric."

The boy laughed. "You sound different, Vidar. That's
the first time I've ever heard you talk about politics."

Vidar winked. "I'm running for president." When Eric
frowned to show his lack of understanding, Vidar laughed
also. "Nothing, Eric, nothing. Just another one of those
Midgardian mysteries."

But a shadow fell suddenly over Eric's face. "Oh. One
other thing, Vidar. I saw Stim's body. Ygg made quite a
mess of him." Eric swallowed hard.

Vidar nodded. "You knew Stim better than I, but I think

we'll both be looking for Ygg to settle that score. Stim was a brave one, wasn't he?"

"Yes," said Eric. "Well, I'll go get the troops together now. And I'll look for you on the . . . other side, I guess."

Eric shrugged self-consciously and made his way to the spot where the banner of Skatalund flapped against the breeze.

It was time.

XXXIII

Vali was the first to spur his horse into the well through which Ygg had escaped. For a terrible moment, Vidar thought that they had been wrong, for horse and rider fell like a shot. But after they had disappeared into the pit, and there was no sound for a tense minute or so, it became apparent that the hellhole was what they had thought: a vertical gate.

There was deathly silence in his wake. At this moment, only Vali knew where the rest of them were going. Only he saw what was at the other end.

"You're courageous, brother, I'll give you that," said Vidar to himself. "But it seems that you were right to fear me. Even I didn't know how right you were when you imprisoned me in Skatalund. But you've got a rival now in Asgard."

Hoenir was next. Before he urged his steed into the bottomless hole, he seemed, for a moment, noble once again. Or was it just Vidar's naive, childhood memories that painted Hoenir as a gentle, laughing soul—before Vidar grew up and came to see his scheming and his lechery? No matter. The years had not stripped him of his power. If he had not suddenly refrained from stalling the sky-serpent and instead added to its momentum—thereby throwing Ygg off-balance—they might still be fighting for possession of Indilthrar.

Then Hoenir, too, plummeted into the unknown darkness, and it was Modi's turn. Modi, whose unshakable allegiance to Vali seemed to leave no room for personal gratitude. After all, he would likely have died back there in the gorge except for Vidar's intervention. Modi was like his father in that respect—Asgard came first, and nothing came second. Modi yelled and his horse leaped. The pit claimed them both.

After them came the rest of the Aesir, all forcing their rearing steeds to step off into the hole. Each waited a minute, as agreed, to allow the one before him to get out of his way on the other side. They reminded Vidar of nothing so much as lemmings leaping to their deaths across some precipiced expanse of black night. It was almost comical.

Irbor and his two surviving brothers led the Vanirmen. Vidar had managed to avoid them throughout the aftermath of their siege, but he knew that he would keep an eye on them. They had a blood debt to settle. And, beyond that, they were Vali's henchmen.

The armies of Skatalund followed the Vanir, and who at their head but Eric? He plunged into the hellhole without so much as flinching—and his armies, both human and city-bred thursar, came after him with the same abandon. Eric's was the largest contingent among Vali's forces, and it took the longest to depart.

Then all that remained was Vidar's *dwarvin* and the human army that had been left behind with Eric's father to disperse the nomads. Perhaps after all this was over, Eric might be able to introduce some reforms into his father's system. Perhaps in Asaheim, too, there might be some reforms.

But first, the hunting of Ygg—and on his ground. Vidar glanced behind him at the ranks of tall, black-suited warriors, all on foot. Their green eyes were bright even here, below the earth—no, *especially* here below the earth. They looked eager to test the darkness.

Vidar was on foot, too. Unbecoming for a son of Odin, but quite appropriate for one who led the *dwarvin* into battle. He stepped forward and sprang a little with that last step, in order to clear the stone lip of the pit. He fell and his heart pounded while he waited for some floor—something—to rush up beneath his feet. But there was no floor, just a bottomless void without light, without sound. He fell like a stone and it seemed that he would go on falling forever. Silence roared in his ears, a swarm of silence that beat at him like a thousand tiny bees.

Finally, he felt a wind come up around him, cold and harsh, but welcome. It smelled of salt and seaweed, and it washed away the droning bees. Vidar found himself laughing as it stung his eyes and buffeted his ears. He could hear nothing now but the shriek of that wind, not even his own laughter.

Then his feet met with the solidity of earth, though a bit more rudely than he would have liked. It was still dark, but there was a light nearby, as the sky wedged itself into a cave mouth. All about him, there was howling and confusion, and he barely remembered to get out of the way lest the *dwarvin* behind him pelt him like black boulders.

"Broken leg here!" someone cried. The healer in him attracted Vidar to the voice. Then there was another cry, this time one of intense pain, and another.

"Vidar," said a familiar voice. It was Hoenir. "Good. I was hoping that you, at least, would come through."

"What do you mean?" Vidar asked, and there was a

premonition of something deadly wrong climbing the rungs of his spine.

"I mean that the others are gone," said Hoenir. His face was strained. "Or somewhere else. Vali, Modi, most of the Aesir—they're not here."

It took a moment for the information to sink in. When it did, Vidar realized that Ygg had been smarter than all of them.

"It was a split gate," said Hoenir, confirming what Vidar had already guessed. "We used to talk about the possibility of turning a gate in two separate directions, but I never thought that he could do it. A split gate, Vidar—and now we're only half of what we started out with." Hoenir shook his head, smiling grimly. "Damn him!"

"But which route did Ygg take?" Vidar asked. "What world is this, anyway?"

Hoenir looked at him, their eyes level. "It has been a long time for you, Vidar, hasn't it? Look outside."

Vidar threaded his way carefully among the lame and those who had suffered worse injuries in their fall from the hellhole, until he stood at the cave mouth. Even after more than a thousand years, he couldn't mistake the city that sprawled below him, jutting out into a glittering, blue sea.

"Asgard," he said, and its very name was an incantation.

"Yes, Asgard," said Hoenir, standing behind him. "And we were fortunate enough to be the half of Vali's armies that followed my brother through the gate."

"How do you know?" asked Vidar, turning away from Odin's city. Hoenir smiled and held up a battered iron mask. It was Ygg's mask, the mask called Ygg.

"It was found here, by the cave mouth," said Hoenir. "Discarded."

Vidar turned again toward the city by the sea. "You mean that Ygg fled to Asgard?"

"Yes. The last place we would have expected him to have a stronghold."

Vidar breathed the cold, fresh air. "Then there may be traitors," he said. "Besides myself, of course."

Over the chaos within the cavern, Hoenir's voice was strangely calm, but it sounded like Gjallarhorn in Vidar's ears.

"Odin has returned."

About the Author

Michael Jan Friedman traces his passion for science fiction back to his sixth summer and a House of Mystery comic book. Soon after, he discovered Edgar Rice Burroughs and used his allowance to compile a paperback collection of the *Tarzan, Carter of Mars* and *Carson of Venus* tales. He still has that collection.

When he grew a little older, he was dazzled by Bradbury, awed by Tolkien and inspired by Roger Zelazny. It was their work that impelled him to become an author.

Mr. Friedman has a B.A. in English literature from the University of Pennsylvania, where a favorite professor once asked him, "What makes a kid from Queens want to write about leprechauns?" It was there that he learned to fence under the tutelage of Lajos Czisar—although he spent more time warming the bench and shouting, "*Alás*," than cutting and thrusting.

He received his M.S. in journalism from the Newhouse School at Syracuse University, where he met his wife, the former Joan Laxer. The Friedmans currently reside on Long Island.

Their commuting time to Manhattan is twenty-nine minutes.